Funny
Thing

R D McGregor

Gangway Publishing

ISBN: 978-1-8380793-0-7

R D McGregor

CONTENTS

R D McGregor

God bless all clowns.
>   Who star in the world with laughter,
>   Who ring the rafters with flying jest,
>   Who make the world spin merry on its way.
God bless all clowns.
>   So poor the world would be,
>   Lacking their piquant touch, hilarity,
>   The belly laughs, the ringing lovely.
God bless all clowns.
>   Give them a long good life,
>   Make bright their way – they're a race apart!
>   Alchemists most, who turn their hearts' pain,
>   Into a dazzling jest to lift the heart.
>   God bless all clowns.

Unknown

'Freddy, London, 1961'

R D McGregor

Prologue

It's a curious thing the weight of a head. When it sits on the neck and shoulders it really doesn't seem too heavy. When it's removed from this plinth it seems to take on a new mass. It's that awkwardness of shape. It's that fleshiness of cheeks with the boned dome of skull. It's the protuberance of ears and thick puckeredness of lips. It's the jut of the nose. It is never at any point in weighted symmetry. As I pick it up it rolls clumsily in my hands and falls towards its natural home, now bloodied and stumped; hacked and chopped through the spinal cord with a serrated edged bread knife. I've never been the squeamish sort but this really tested my mettle, so to speak. It was this messiness that made me search Norman's cupboards for a tool kit. I thought a jigsaw might be a handy little implement for removing the feet from the legs and the hands from the arms. I found one under the sink, close to an old soup pot with the lid sitting on top. It's where I put it when I tidied his flat. I had to do that as I was staying there more and more often since Janice's death and the steady progress of his debilitating disease. I cannot abide mess. I am a very ordered person, very neat in my habits. Fastidious, Norman would say, usually with the words 'little bastard' added. But I think we were both cut from the same cloth. I recognise now, though, that cloth was not quality material. I see more clearly that even the worst of the comics presenting the poorest of their work were better than Norman and Freddy presenting their best. We had a fatal flaw for anyone in show business: we hated our audience.

I dragged out the soup pot and dropped the head into it. There's something that I never said to my partner in all these years of such close physical contact: his breath was like honey, sweet and rich even when he'd

9

been drinking. O! how shall summer's honey breath hold out... [1] *Maybe in this black ink, dear friend? That must have been one of the reasons women loved him. There would be the golden-haired lover with nectar in those loving words that would carry each and every one of them to ecstasy. With this in my thoughts I pulled at his ear to get the face looking up; his dead lips lay on his marbled face like stranded fish. But now the honeyed breath had been stopped. Shut off forever. And no more, I thought, would the girls swoon as that breath caressed their flushed cheeks. Lid on, and then I had the first bury-able container.*

---

[1] Shakespeare's sonnet LXV. I first read Shakespeare's sonnets sitting up in bed in a Glasgow slum during the hot summer of that 366-day year of 1956. My mother had puffed up my pillows and left me in peace. While I read, I could hear the children's voices rise from the back courts. In my mind, I would forever hear those voices when I dipped into the Bard's verse. Halcyon days, I realise now...

1

R D McGregor

1

The meeting 1961
'…that third-rate decade…' Norman Tebbit

It was while cutting off my partner's head that I thought of our first meeting in the spring of 1961.[2] The wonderful Mister Dickie Valentine introduced us at a Brittle Bone Society Charity Dance. The weather was still cold after a bitter, snowy winter. The BBC weather had said a cold front was moving southwards from Scotland over the next few days. The mention of my ain country caused something of an unexpected pang. Not enough to bring a tear, but enough for a moment's thought about my grand adventure. It was the last time I would ever have a catch in my throat about bonnie Scotland. I was determined to move forward and carve out a successful future.[3] Part of that future would, I believed, have been assisted by the purchase of a good suit in preference to a sensible coat.[4] This I did, and as a result found myself furiously rubbing my freezing hands together, while sitting on

---

[2] I was 19 years old and was living in a seriously dingy flat in W10. Somehow the children sound in the street below my room made me think of my Glasgow life. The poverty was identical to what I'd left at the turn of the year. On that morning I caught the bus I saw a photographer take a lot of shots of the life in the street, the children, the young men and women. I got his name; it was Roger Mayne. I had thought about asking him to do some publicity shots of me to send around agents. I didn't, and what a fool I was. His pictures became part of a successful exhibition documenting the area. There was one of me walking behind some lads on the very day I met Norman. I believe the pictures are now in the Victoria and Albert Museum.
[3] When you're nothing there's always the chance of being something. But you must live a long time before you understand the dice are loaded for sure.
[4] Some blokes in Glasgow were still walking around in their demob suits. After the army, they had gone for a Burton and not entered a tailor's establishment since.

the upstairs upholstery of a number 57. Although it was cold, the sun had broken through and the sky was, for a few hours, cloudless. It was a beautiful late morning London. The energy and freshness to the day I put in part down to that unique capital sunshine: the other part was my youth, where we find every morning a wondrous experience.

I had taken a bus as the local train station had closed a few weeks before. Looking down, a newspaper headline caught my eye: MOSCOW RECRUITS RUISLIP COUPLE. The rest of the journey was taken up with me imagining I had been recruited by the Ruskies: it might have gotten me a nice semi-detached in Ruislip. This was a legitimate thought in my aspirations. Few at this point had dreams of mansions. It was the easy chair of middle-class Britain we craved; a garden, the papers and milk delivered, a modest car and maybe a caravan later, a few pints a few times a week. And the applause. Of course, the applause.

It wasn't a short journey, through Wimbledon and getting held up in the Saturday Chelsea traffic. Some supporters were singing songs about sheep as they walked along the road: this appeared to be directed at a small contingent of Cardiff support on the opposite side.[5]

The location of the charity dance was a scout hall in Tooting, south London. Not the most salubrious of venues to jump start a career, but I had wanted to approach Dickie with the hope of getting a very small slot in his all-star variety show

---

[5] As part of my research before leaving home I had studied the football teams of England and Wales. How this might help me in advancing my career I wasn't sure, but knowledge of any popular entertainment was, I felt, time well spent. Much later I would meet many sporting greats – not least of all George Best, who would sleep with any woman that asked, and never felt at a disadvantage in discussion. This was very much how I have been throughout my life. Later, when we travelled, I would research the countries, the customs and the practices. Knowledge is not an accident; it is gained through study. And all knowledge should be respected and sought.

at the Hackney Empire. A lot of entertainers were still raw. No doubt in part from the poverty from which they had sprung. There was a fear that everything was going to be taken away as quickly as it had been given.[6] And so a lot did these charity events to keep the face to the fore. Not that Dickie was one of those. On the contrary, he was a true gent and a real trouper. *One of the finest English voices to top the hit parade in the 1950s.* That was how he was described in the local rag that informed me he was making this appearance. I told him that I had come down from Glasgow in the hope of securing work in this great profession of ours.[7] He congratulated me on my English. I told him that I had studied elocution with Norah Cooper for two years. He nodded, obviously impressed by my single-minded dedication. You see, it is important to be focused 100 per cent on your goal if success is to be achieved.[8]

---

[6] This was not just in the world of comedy; it was a fear pervading the entertainment world in general. Entertainment was a road out of poverty. This was usually the prerogative of boxing or football, or perhaps even gangsterism. In the world of acting, Osborne and his kitchen sink were moving from the stage to Pinewood. What lovely actors would come to the fore over the next few years: Courtney, Finney, and even Caine and Connery. Forgive me; I am getting ahead of myself.

[7] And in the great metropolis. I, of course, didn't mention that my abode for the last few months had been Southam Street, Golborne. This was the W10 I have mentioned. When anyone enquired where I first stayed in London I would always reply W10, never Southam Street, Golborne. Well, you wouldn't, would you? It was as slumlike as the Glasgow I had left. But it was London. No doubt many thought like me, bedazzled by the history and myth. It took me many years to learn that people come to London who no longer wish to belong. They come to disappear, reinvent themselves as from blank canvas. Fame can help this. There are no mirrors involved; it is all smoke.

[8] Not long before I had travelled down to London from my Glasgow home. This was probably the scariest move I had ever made in my short life. As I slipped out the door with my mother still in bed. I remember leaving the radio on tuned to the Light Programme and Sing It Again! with Benny Lee

I commiserated with him over the lack of success of his show *Bresslaw and Friends* that month. Dickie told me that his was a guest appearance in Bernard Bresslaw's[9] show. I gently pointed out that it would have been a regular slot had the show not been cancelled after one outing. Throughout, I was aware of someone hanging about in the background.

'Mr. Valentine?' He had managed to jump in during one of those awkward pauses that people often have at the start of close friendships. I usually have a backup of *fillers* for such occasions. I was ready to mention that the recent deaths of both Dashiell Hammett and Sir Thomas Beecham saddened me.

'Yes, I am,' said the ever-polite Dickie, taking Norman's arm and pulling him towards me.

'I'm a comedian. My name's Norman Riddell.'

'A comedian,' said Dickie. 'Tell us a joke.' Dickie had a sterling sense of humour and was no mean impersonator of other balladeers. So, when he followed it up with, 'I like a good laugh,' there was nothing patronising or indeed mocking in his tone. Norman, God bless the old sod even now, even headless, came up with a line that invited me into a partnership that lasted many years.[10]

---

and June Campbell. No doubt my mother awoke to some gentle pre-Beatles pops. Half an hour later, I was sitting in Glasgow's Central Station, listening to what I considered exotic announcements of names of British towns. I would be travelling on the West Coast Main Line, something of a misnomer, as it only skirted the coast between Lancaster and Carnforth. London? It sounded like The Emerald City to my naïve ears.

[9] Many think of big loveable Bernie as a bumbling hulk adding the *thick* factor to Carry On pictures. In fact, he was an award-winning graduate of RADA, and he was their *most promising* student; articulate and well-read. How unlike the public perception. It has long been my view that the role creates the actor, not the other way.

[10] For years Norman told me that we had met ten minutes before at a table at the far wall. He said I had walked over while he was drinking from a hip flask. I have no recollection of this whatsoever. Since he really hasn't had a

'I like girls,' he said.

'You like girls?' I asked, as if it had been rehearsed for this very moment.

'Yes,' he said. 'And do you know what I like best?'

'No, what do you like best?'

'When you get to the giggle band.'

'The giggle band? What's the giggle band?'

'I'll tell you what the giggle band is. You know that stretch of skin between the top of a girls stocking and her knickers?'

'I do. I do know that stretch of skin between the top of a girls stocking and her knickers.'

'Do you know why it's called the giggle band?'

'Tell me. Tell me why that stretch of skin between the top of the stockings and the knickers is called the giggle band?'

'Because,' says Norman, 'you get past there and you're laughing.'[11]

---

hand in writing this should I call it an unauthorised biography? He might indeed have been correct within his own memory, but as I remember it, so it is true. As I write these things I am reclaiming memory and fixing what has been a running stream. I certainly invite you to believe these things happened and are as true as I remember them. Perhaps I should just label it all *roman*.

[11] No doubt readers of this work – if indeed there are any – will be throwing their hands up in frustration. Why, they might ask, does it take so long to get to the pay off, and why oh why the constant repetition? A point that an old pro like me feels the need to explain. Music hall, for all its Victorian and Edwardian charm, had a serious defect in regard to the punters hearing the artiste. A rare few had voices that broke through the mob's racket. These voices were once described to me as being positively bovine. For the average human, repetition was the only answer. Saying the line several times ensured most of the audience heard. This obviously affected the writing of jokes and the telling of them. Anyone in the early 1960s would have understood that we were referring to the great music hall days. The repetition served us well because it gave the impression that there had been some rehearsal to our performance. From the very outset Norman and I relied on each other. From the moment of my reply to his first line he knew we were on the same wavelength. The only time we repeated such a

Dickie exploded while shaking his head in disbelief. It was certainly a top-class delivery of the punch line, but I thought it might be considered a bit crude for some.

'A little near the knuckle,' I said, pulling in my chin, and giving a knowing nod to Dickie.

'A little near the knuckle?' Norman came back again. 'I wouldn't like to be your wife.'

Just then Dickie was called over for a little tête à tête with bandleader Ted Heath. I noticed that he stopped to sign a few autographs for two girls with diseased bones. Courtesy costs nothing. Dickie was a gentleman. And that was it. That's how Freddy Foster and Norman Liddell met. At the start of those wonderful hedonistic sixties. And as I sat there, with his head on the floor in front of me, I did think fondly on him.

---

performance was on The Good Old Days television programme many years later. The advent of mikes and better acoustics killed off such types of joke telling. Praise the Lord, many would say. I would be one of them. If you compare the typescripts of stage performances years later you will see that they are punchier and more fluid. (See Appendix 1)

2

Present/1962
'What a city to loot!'
Dick Heldar, on London.[12]

Returning to my butchery the feet and hands were next on my list. As I took that little jig-saw to those talented feet, my own almost fell into a ball-toe exercise at the memory. Norman taught me to tap and I confess now it's the best thing he ever taught me. Of course, all of this was reciprocal as I soon taught him the art of seduction. This was something I told Norman I knew about.[13]

'Just get the bird as wet as an otter, then fire in.' Unfortunately, he tried this out on the lovely Alma Cogan, a songstress who had enjoyed many a hit-parade placing during those tumultuous 1950s. At the start of the 1960s, that strange breed of British entertainer, that included Dickie Valentine, was heading towards an exit door, foreshadowed by John Lennon's wailing harmonica at the beginning of *Love Me Do*.[14] Strange that her future lover should partly be responsible for that. Life is full of little quirks and coincidences. In 1962, though, she was like a real star burning brightest before the end.

---

[12] Dick Heldar speaking of London in *The Light That Failed* by Rudyard Kipling. A wonderful, though now forgotten, work by one of England's greatest writers.

[13] It was a lie; a rather pale one, but a lie nevertheless. I'd had sex twice before that discussion. Both of those times were fumbled and messy affairs. I truly believe those first experiences affected the rest of my sexual life.

[14] I met Lennon quite a bit in those days and he was always chatty He told me that he loved Scotland and had happy memories of holidaying there as a child. I do believe his eyes misted over at the memory. Flicking through an old journal I have also a documented verbatim conversation with him. (See Appendix 2)

We had approached her first in the wings of the London Palladium, as she was waiting for Mister Bruce Forsyth – now *Sir Bruce*, to introduce her as the night's star guest.[15] It had been a fine night for romance, humour, and spectacle, what with that American showman Stubby Kaye, The Moscow State Circus and Terry Hall and his Lenny the Lion ventriloquist act. There was also a surprise guest in the person of Michael Miles from television's hugely successful *Take Your Pick*. Truth be told, I wished I had been chosen for the Royal Variety Performance some months before. Jack Benny and George Burns came over for the occasion and I admired their acts and personas.[16]

Miss Cogan was tapping her foot to the sound of *We Got Love* when I offered my usual 'break a leg' to a fellow performer. She turned around: the lips were apart, deep red Max Factor gashes; the tongue was about to move... when Norman lunged at her, his mouth salivating at the thought of even a dry hump with Alma Cogan.

It is appropriate that I mention the night had not started

---

[15] I swear Boy Bruce, The Mighty Atom, has so much energy he will be in the running for a brace of Queen's telegrams.

[16] I have often been questioned on my memory. The fact is that I tend to retain the most useless of information. Were I to take part in one of those trivia quizzes that pollute public houses these days I would, no doubt, have shone. As a sickly young lad, I was just bright, but that had little to do with an exceptional memory. No, I believe my memory had more to do with my engagement in the world around me. I found this enjoyable, but it might also have been seen as a survival mechanism. Sometimes I stored away moments that I thought could be developed later for the act. For instance, once I sat in Bishop's Park in Fulham, feeding the pigeons. I had gone to see the memorial to those who fought for the International Brigade. My mind turned to a pigeon sketch. Before I got home the sketch had been written in my head. Of course, Norman objected: *I am not dressing as a fucking pigeon!* (Again, see Appendix 1) And he didn't for quite a while. It stayed in my notebook. Some years after it would be rejigged into a TV comedy sketch.

well. *Norman and Freddy* had become the first act of any sort to get booed off the Palladium stage. It was worse than a bad night at the Glasgow Empire. We arrived at the hallowed doors thinking this was the night that we would be initiated into the special circle, that luminiferous gaggle of entertainers that Britain had taken into the army for a few years and then spat out. The world was then their oyster.[17] Television was there, and it was theirs for the taking. And they took. And why not? Greed and fame spurred them on.[18] They were as protective of their careers as a mother towards her child. These cognoscente would have things pretty much sewn up for a lot of years to come.

At the Palladium that night we were the first comics up, and we died like no one had ever died at that theatre; before or since. It wasn't just that our jokes were bad, although they were. The gods just weren't smiling down on us. Then, to cap it all, Norman told a totally unrehearsed gag about a man who puts his spine out while trying to lick his own cock. He didn't say the word *cock* but it was quite clear to everyone what he was on about. That was when the booing started. It started low at first. No doubt some were embarrassed about booing in the first place. Being a heckler takes a certain kind of courage; one must have something of the frustrated performer

---

[17] It was interesting to note that many of them were just like their dads. It took my generation to buck that. Once National Service finished, they could no longer snatch away your youth. That was the real reason for its existence. Once it disappeared the young could have their day. And they did. It was all bright clothes and possibilities.

[18] I am being rather cruel here. Having a career and a place in life spurred them on also. No doubt the snapping jaws of poverty was also a spur. Celebrity and poverty often go hand in hand. It doesn't matter if that celebrity rides under the banner of show business or notoriety. The gangster will often push himself into the show business ring. Poverty is the club that both have escaped from. There is a mutual recognition, and often respect.

within.[19] A few daring individuals gave courage to the rest. A loud wave of booing and catcalls and whistles followed. We left the stage and made our way back to the dressing rooms. On the way, we passed a diminutive unfunny comedian who had made his name on the wireless:

'You'll not be needing the work then?' he asked. 'I don't know how you'll get out of that,' he said. 'Can't see them knocking on your door again, boys.'

He was wrong, though. He was very wrong.[20]

As for Norman's lunge at Miss Cogan, she certainly did not have a *giggle* in her voice that evening as she told him to 'behave'. We did not receive the after-show invite to her mother's house either. I had heard that the elite visited Kensington High Street, 44 Stafford Court, often. To mingle with Cary Grant, Danny Kaye and Tommy Steele would not have hurt our career.

---

[19] As indeed most British do. Americans too I would say. Europe seems to have less of this secret longing for the limelight. Most performers will be heckled at times in their careers. I find the whole thing vulgar. The sign of a great act is how you deal with it. As time went on Norman's fuse got shorter. Water off a duck's back was not advice he prescribed to.

[20] It could have obviously gone the other way. A couple of years later Tom Bell – one of England's finest young actors and drinkers – interrupted a dinner speech by Prince Phillip with the cry *Tell us a funny story!* That remark put young Tom's career on hold for some years. (And what a career! He had exploded onto the scene in Alan Owun's *No Trams To Lime Street,* a TV play brutally wiped.) No doubt if Norman had told his joke to Her Majesty he would have been sent to the Tower. There are unwritten rules to play by in this game and woe betide anyone who slips. At a Water Rats do some years later I remember pointing to Tommy Cooper and laughing: *I see the Big C's in!* The comment was akin to farting in the Vatican.

3

Present/1993

'I like to write when I feel spiteful. It is like having a good sneeze.'
D.H. Lawrence in a letter to Cynthia Asquith,
November 1913.

In Norman's flat, I caught a glimpse of myself in the hall
mirror. The shirt was splattered with blood and the look was
an advanced case of Alzheimer's. The face looked startled, a
man with his life behind him. My reflection was not a happy
sight for me. I have been troubled about this ageing business
for some time and it still does not sit easy with me. Norman,
on the other hand, never gave it a thought. He was either
unthinking or unafraid of ageing. To him it was the natural
march of time. He was afraid, though, of where his illness was
taking him. It was a hell he did not wish to enter.

It's as well I mention this early in my story for it looms large
over our tale, an ill wind that brought only pain.

'I'm a bit of a coward, old lad,' he had said. 'That's the
mark of it. I can't seem to reconcile to my future, Freddy.
How'd you like to help out your old pal? Eh?' I'd been busy
puffing up cushions on the chair and had only been half
listening.

'What are you saying, you old slap?'

From where he was lying on the couch his hand shot out
and he grabbed my wrist. An action he would not be able to
perform six months later.

'It's me, Freddy.'

Pulling my hand away with some force I straightened up. 'I
don't want to hear that, you hear? You look on the positives,
boy.'

'Positives? I must have missed them in all the croakers'

talks.'

'I won't stand here and listen to all this. You hear? You operate in fucking Normanland and nobody operates in fucking Normanland but Norman!' Before I knew it, I had my coat on and was heading for the door. 'I don't have to listen to this.'

'Last act of a cruel man,' he shouted after me. 'You always hated me.' The front door clicked shut on this. I could hear him still bawling, but the sound was muffled as I made my way to the lift. There was the usual smell of piss in the hallway, a stink that seemed to pervade my life at that time. The door opposite had a gate in front of it and a top and bottom deadlock. That was besides the Mortice and Yale. This wasn't the place that Norman had moved into, just the place that it had become.[21] At the far end, the door to the stairway had been kicked through. Between that and Norman's door were walls daubed with spray painted names, gang slogans and stains from Christ knows what. The floor was worn away and etched into it the scrape of boots and even bikes. In the corner to the left of the lift were discarded food trays, plastic bottles and smashed cider bottles. There was burnt tinfoil and even the lift doors were burnt, laying testament to an aspiring arsonist.

I stayed out a long time, well into the night. I have found walking a great stimulus to thought. I returned much later with fish and chips.[22] He was still on the couch, but the

---

[21] I see now that the building could become a metaphor for life and the ageing process – this life was not the one I entered, just the one that it had become. Is there such a thing as unconscious metaphor? I do hope so as Freddy could have such fun analysing his own manuscript.

[22] I actually had a slight altercation with the chip shop gentleman over the price of cod. Once again I harked back to my happier days, grumbling about I could have got into Annie Ross's club for 10/-. He called me an 'old fool'. I was more offended by the 'old' than the 'fool'. I also suspected he hadn't heard of Annie Ross, so he probably deserved the abuse that followed.

television was on. I didn't speak and neither did he. I remember we watched a news programme about anti-terrorist raids in London. By the end things between us were fine again. If ignoring a conversation can be said to be fine.[23]

'London's changing too fast,' he said quietly.[24]

'Aye,' I replied.[25]

So, I would say that Norman was not afraid of ageing or death. He was, though, afraid of the manner in which the end of his life would be lived. Maybe deep down that is the fear that all of us harbour. Not the death itself. As the Welsh bard said: *after the first death there is no other.* But how we approach that dying light is what makes us human.

Annie's Room was a favourite haunt of mine. It was run by Annie and her wonderful husband, Sean Lynch. When I met them both I told Sean that I had seen him earlier that day in the film version of the Wesker play, The Kitchen. Life is full of coincidences and synchronicity. Annie was pals with Billie Holiday, she went to school with Liz Taylor and her brother was Scottish entertainer, Jimmy Logan. Charlie Parker was the godfather of her kid. It is a strange world. It is the strangest of worlds. A world of connections and coincidences. It is everywhere, should you care to look.

[23] There were occasions when he carried it on. I have a recollection of calling him a nihilist one night in the heat of argument. I went on one of my long walks. When I returned he was still laughing.

[24] The truth was that I saw London as something of a sprawling mess. I'm not sure it hadn't always been so. Cities like London must be constantly in a flux. The pictures presented in the cinema bore as much reality to London as did the Western film to the Old West. London was creation. Sergeant Dixon wasn't always there to clean things up, give a salute and send you happily to your bed. The truth was that if you wandered the streets late at night – as I did often returning from some party or other – when the bars had died and the clubs had shut up shop, you'd see many a bundle of rags shift in the doorways. The NFAs (No Fixed Abodes) trying to wipe from their minds the true horror of their position.

[25] There were many quiet moments together. Me, reading the paper, Norman deep in the racing pages. I would comment on the news and he would ignore me. 'I see Deleuze has died.' Not even a grunt. 'Suicide.' More silence. 'Seventy.' His paper flicks. 'So much for transcendental empiricism.'

As I looked at my reflection in the hall mirror my face took on a look resembling anger. I could still get angry, I thought. There's hope for old Freddy yet.

4

1969
Freddy: I think I'm going through my mid-life
crisis.
Norman: You're optimistic.

i

Soho had a reputation that was well deserved. By the late
sixties, I had a small room off Beak Street, a notorious home
to the sickest porn shops and the dirtiest prostitutes.[26]
Bathsheba[27] – not her real name – my next-door neighbour,
had a smell of the farm about her. I had moved in out of
necessity as my flat in Fulham had been wonderful, but I was
trying to put something away and could not afford the rent.
The sixties only swung for some.[28] Norman and I hadn't
worked in three months. Well, we had worked, but it was
unpaid. We were writing a script as a vehicle for our particular
talents.[29] The story focused on two coach drivers taking a
party of school kids to Spain. It gave us a cracking chance to

---

[26] My previous flat in Fulham had been offering me little chance to save for
a mortgage deposit. I had future plans for my housing status. The Milner
Holland Committee had assured me affordable housing after the Rachman
debate, but 'affordable' means different things to different people. I moved
out early 1968.
[27] I actually called her *Doll*. She had told me a former regular client from
Glasgow had called her this. I just smiled. My thoughts were of *Doll Tearsheet*
as I'd watched many a *John Falstaff* lumber up the stairs and along the
landing.
[28] At the start, though, I could afford to buy myself a second hand 1961
Ford Anglia. My first car. Bought for £200 and 8/11d. Where the hell the
change came from I don't know.
[29] W. Somerset Maugham had said that there were only three rules of novel
writing; unfortunately, nobody knew what they were. Could I possibly
extend that *bon mot*, but reduce the rules to a singular?

laugh at both nations' cultural differences in a mixture of gentle probing humour and outrageous farce.[30] I really did enjoy the writing process[31] and Norman complimented me by noticing that my voice on paper was very different from my real voice.[32]

'It's like you've swallowed a fucking dictionary,' he said
'Fuck off.'
'I mean it.'
'Fuck off.'
'Is that how you talk in your head, you fucking ponce?'[33]

---

[30] This is how we both felt at the time. But I am not the man now that I was then. Norman would be. If he wasn't dead that is. Foreignness, different cultures, different skins and voices, were something to be mocked in British comedy at the time. It rankles with me still that I didn't see offence in some of the jokes. We would shrug our shoulders later and say that times were different then. No doubt Dr Mengele would use the same excuse while puffing on an after-dinner cigar in Brazil. Or not. Not everyone is wise after the event.

[31] Norman did not enjoy it so much, but he certainly had a way with a song. Not long after our first gig – at The Angel Pub – we were in a club booked by celebrity agent Grainne Mulhern. We got there hours before show for a tech and rehearsal. Norman was sitting hung over a piano with a cigarette burning in his mouth, much like Hoagy Carmichael. He was tinkling the ivories with one hand. It was slow and sweet as he half sung, half spoke *We're just a couple of guys, just swinging by…trying to bring laughter to your world…* I approached behind him and sung *So if you open your eyes your heart will follow…* He had it so completely when he sang confidently, *Yesterday's gone, forget about tomorrow.* What we created was the theme tune that would take us through our careers. (See Appendix 4.) My arms went around his neck and we hugged: a rare occurrence.

[32] A joke is the purest form of the written word and the idea. There is no room for baggage. Something it has in common with the poem.

[33] Norman was not just a ladies' man; he was a man's man. There were many in the business like him, and many in the business liked him for this. As for me, I was an original. I was always that bit different from the common herd. What I saw as my maverick temperament might at times have been a professional winner but socially it was akin to animal rape. The idea of the outsider is admired up to the point he becomes your neighbour.

He was sitting at his desk tapping heavy digits down on the Remington typewriter,[34] which had been liberated from the BBC two years previously. We had popped in on the off chance that someone might have a look at some of our newly written jokes. Shame on them that no one came down the stairs. There had been an atmosphere of tragedy about the building since a report had come in about a serious rail crash in south east London. Maybe that shock had left security lapse. An office door left open; an office left empty. I was in and out and pell-melling it down the street before they could say *licence fee*. Norman couldn't stop laughing. Where we laid it on his table is pretty much where it sat for the next few years. And that's where it was when we had the conversation about how I talk and how I write.

'You can take the boy out of Glasgow…but you can't get him to go against his nature.'

This was uncalled for as I thought I'd left all traces of Glasgow behind a long time before. Unfortunately, my reply did not carry with it the tone associated with great put downs:

'Say that again and I'll kick your teeth in.'

After that we both fell into a long silence familiar to those of us who are touched by the muse. At the end of it something happened that would change the nature of our act. We decided it had to develop. Norman told me that change was fine. I told him that I was looking towards more of a transmutation. Norman repeated that change was fine. He told me that he wanted me to play the fool, someone who

---

[34] Even the Remington was old, but compared to the Underwood we had been using it was pure gold. I was one of those people who always wrote by hand first and then transferred to the typewriter. All manuscripts to the BBC had to be typed. This excluded many would be writers. Partly through their financial situation and occasionally through societal roles. In certain locations the typewriter was seen as a *girl thing*. In Glasgow at the end of the 1950s my mother bought me my first machine for £2. She had to say that it was for my sister, Fran. I have never had a sister: Fran or otherwise.

listened to no one. He wanted me to be arrogant, blind to the sensibilities of others; he wanted me to be a snob, but quite aggressive with it. When it came down to it he really could deliver great ideas when need be. I really did relish the idea of playing a character so far removed from myself that I opened a bottle of Scotch to toast what I thought would bring proper fame and success. We had been together eight years and I saw this as a tough apprenticeship. We talked of getting new pictures to reflect the shift in the act.[35] Publicity photos were important as they offered the public the image that you wanted seen. You might be the cheeky chappies; you might be debonair wits; or you might be slapstick buffoons. Each of these called for a particular look and a particular lighting. I had always imagined myself photographed by a Clarence Sinclair Bull or a George Hurrell. I originally wanted a certain class, presented in the style of the Hollywood greats. I wanted a high key light and a face that was alluring. As it turned out we eventually made an appointment with wedding photographer, Colin Bone. He was cheap and we turned to him at the start of our career.[36] Colin *'Call me Col'* Bone had one set of lights that I assumed had been on loan from the MI5 interrogation rooms at Thames House.

'Smile, boys! I can see your star is just around the corner.' I hoped not from his shop – I wouldn't dignify it by saying *studio* – as he was just around the corner from a brothel. *Call*

---

[35] It was a shift in the act but was it enough? Was it really a new form? One day there will be something new, but not today. And I doubt tomorrow. Most seem to be either the old rebranded or dressed differently. This was a rather controversial theory in the early 1980s, particularly when I compared much of the 'new' comedy to The Crazy Gang of the 1930s.

[36] I had told Norman early on that Roger Mayne was taking pics around my front door the day we met. Imagine if we had procured the talents of Mayne! What a career boost! Name dropping a famous snapper into an interview would have been cool then. Shutterbugs were beginning to cause something of a stir in London town.

me Col's name was passed on to Norman one drunk-sodden night at a party late in 1962. I wasn't there and have no idea how he wangled an invite, but he swore blind it was my hero Tony Hancock who passed him the name. Whatever the truth of that, we ended up having our pictures taken by a short-sighted wedding snapper. The surprised look that Norman used from then on was originally the result of the close to nuclear flash. Norman's eyebrows went north while his face had something of a pained expression. Understanding that the camera always lies I wanted a Gable or a Cooper even. I ended up with a mugshot.

'Do you have high key lighting, Mr. Bone?'

'Call me Col. What's that you're saying?'

I could see that he hadn't a clue what I was on about. Norman muttered *Fanny* under his breath. I assumed at the time it was directed at *Call me Col,* but as I write now I am certain the name calling was for me. That night years later, when we toasted a change in our career, I thought of Colin Bone, wedding photographer, and the stardom that was just around the corner. It was not to be, although drinking together was a bonding that lasted up to the point I smashed his chest in with a 15-inch laptop. But that was in another room and an age away. If I had had the gift to see what fate would bring I would beg it to be gone. What a curse to see a life laid out in mediocrity, hope upon hope dashed on the jagged rocks of reality.

His lifeless body a few feet away, I stood at his window looking out on the black and murderous night. So, London, is this all that life can afford? A few large snowflakes fell softly on the rooftops and street.

'Norman,' I said quietly, 'it's going to be a white Christmas.'

The room was silent.

5

1969
Freddy: You're a glass half empty man.
Norman: I am with you in the chair.
The Dave King Show, Dec. 1969

ii

A few days after the talk and after more pictures had been taken I had a meeting, not far from the flat in Soho. There are times in our lives when we are offered a road. That road is the road to success and it is the only time we will ever get a chance to take it. That road often also has a toll and, if truth were told, in the end I couldn't pay the price. That is a hard truth for Freddy Foster to speak. Even now. Since the very early days of my Glasgow upbringing success was my raison d'être. I cannot speak for my partner here. Just performing and earning money seemed enough for him. And the girls, of course.[37]

I had been asked out to chat about *Norman and Freddy* hosting a Saturday night show. As I walked along Dean Street with the snow coming at me, I had two things on my mind: the first was to stay warm, as the temperature plummeted to minus three. The second was to give a good account of myself to executive producer Robert Rennie. For this reason, I didn't invite Norman. He would have ruined things. I admired him in so many ways; his persevering nature, his sense of fun,[38] his

---

[37] Oh, Norman, the many, many girls. Mostly showbiz, the dancers, the assistants, the stage managers, make-up girls, wardrobe mistresses, the wig girl. The people who understand something of that life maybe understand something of loneliness.

[38] Norman often told me that he couldn't do anything without there being a sense of fun in it. This seemed to fly in the face of what a depressing bastard he could be. But there is obvious joy in a lot of my memories. At a

32

generosity of spirit.

He could not sell us, though. Not if his career depended on it: particularly if his career depended on it.

The Colony Room had gained something of a reputation for attracting the *glitterati* of the art, literature, and showbiz world. Muriel Belcher, the proprietress, opened the club in the late 40s. She was renowned for her plain speaking: if you weren't liked you were called *cunt*; if you were liked you were called *cunty*; if you were especially liked she would call you *Mary*. The boys and the girls loved her. I had heard stories of Francis Bacon[39] dropping fifty-pound notes like old train tickets. He was fast becoming one of the richest artist's in the world and he wasn't aware of it.[40] The money was there when he went to the bank. It was in his pockets when he reached to pay for the champagne. He told Princess Margaret that he wanted to fuck Colonel Gaddafi and she stormed out vowing never to return. It was Lucian Freud laughing and Dylan Thomas vomiting magnificently over the puce walls. How do I know these things? I read the *papers*. I kept in touch with what was happening in the *arty* world. If you keep up with the gossip then doors can open. At this time, *Norman and Freddy* might not have been Morecambe and Wise; we might not have had a

---

harbour – God knows where – he jumped up onto one of those capstan gubbins and stood pelican-like on one leg while the other jutted out at a 90-degree angle, as though performing an arabesque. His hand shaded his eyes as he looked out to sea. It was the funniest of poses and I applauded him loudly.

[39] I have always been drawn to the avant-garde, in people as well as art. Perhaps I identified with the unusual, the exciting. Freddy was never a boy for cheap harmonies in artistic endeavour.

[40] I liked Bacon. I admired him. I spoke to him several times. Although I seemed to have had the correct impoverished background to garner attraction, I was not tough enough to appeal to his particular tastes. Perhaps for that reason we spoke easily. I reminded him of a story that he had booed Princess Margaret while she sang a Noel Coward song.

'It was Cole Porter she sang. The press: they always get it wrong.'

successful show, but we ticked over with the odd television spot and a constant grind of the clubs, some of which were nothing more than pissholes and shitholes. Is it any wonder I wanted to get out of the snow and into the warmth of The Colony Room? There lay the chance of riches.

The stairway was dark when I entered, and I can't say it was particularly fragrant. Although badly lit I could still see that the place was filthy. The stairs creaked loudly, and it crossed my mind that they could snap underfoot. I felt a sense of intimidation, not artistic joie de vivre. Maybe it was the darkness, as though someone was ready to pounce from the shadows.

When I got to the room itself, I was expecting to see the famous. I was disappointed. If the good and the great came to this room to drink and talk, they must have been having a quiet night in. Although I had never been in or even seen a picture of Muriel, I knew it was her standing at the entrance: she had a Jewish lesbian look about her. Beside her stood a very attractive black girl. A piano sat at the far end and art posters covered the Welsh vomit walls. Maybe the posters were there to hide the green paint. It struck me that for a notorious artists' bar, green walls and a green carpet hardly reflected a good eye for colour schemes. As I thought this, I caught Muriel saying to the girl beside her, I *know fuck all about art.*

Everybody seemed to be smoking and quite freely dropping their ash on the burned carpet. Although not as quiet as the huge Michael Andrews mural behind the piano the place was certainly much quieter than I expected.

Two men were standing at the low bar clutching long glasses filled with scotch and ice. One of them caught my eye; half smiled and waved to me. It was Robert Rennie. He was wearing a dark blue pin-stripe suit and blue tie, looking every inch the City gent rather than a producer of light entertainment. He leaned close to the man with him and whispered something in his ear. As I approached, the man disappeared into a group of flamboyantly dressed young men.

'Freddy!' he shouted. 'Freddy, come over!'

Every step that I took towards him my heart sank. I was already standing beside him when he said: 'Come over here, Freddy! Where's that loose cannon of a partner?'

'We don't do everything together.'

'Glad to hear it. Do I sense dissatisfaction with the act?'

Until he said that I swear I'd never considered a split with Norman. And even once the words were uttered I knew the idea was patent nonsense. Once you get your partner you stick to him till death you do part. *Oh, how very true Freddy Foster.*

It is very difficult for me to think of that night without regret and a tinge of real sadness. I don't remember how long it took me to answer Rennie but it did seem like an age.

'The act's fine, Robert,' I replied flatly.

'Glad to hear it. Particularly now.'

'Why now?'

'Because,' said Robert, 'he's just walked in the door.'

I swung around to see Norman wearing a light jacket darkened with melted snow. His hair was plastered over his forehead and he looked like he would kill. I got him an overpriced rum and coke immediately and stuck it in a frozen hand.

'I've just seen Janice. She's pregnant.'

6

1969

Norman: She was blind when I met her.
Janice: I was. It was terrible.
Freddy: That's awful. I'm very sorry to
hear that.
Norman: Yes. But with patience and
modern drugs she sobered up.
Aboard The Silver Princess, 1971

iii

Janice was Norman's long term, long suffering girlfriend. He had met her while we played The King's in Glasgow. She was a dancer and knew the business well enough to understand Norman's lifestyle. She was a wild girl and gave him a real run for his money. For every girl he fucked she would match him by doing the same with one of the male dance troupe, and sometimes the odd stage door Johnny. A modern girl who would move from the drug rush of purple hearts to heroin's ragged-arsed edge. And she survived. She moved through a particular period of our great country's history with real panache. She made her mark on life, and anyone who thinks that's easy then I've got one thing to say: you try it.

I ignored the rather melodramatic entrance and information with an exterior of perfect calm. I didn't want Rennie thinking that I was the excitable type. Television deals are rarely struck with that sort.

'How did you know I was here?'

'You can't keep a secret from me, Freddy.' In all but one instance, I thought, this was true.

Robert was very put out at this intrusion and looked

annoyed. 'You know,' he said, 'this is a members' club. Now, Norman, I set this meeting up with Freddy because Freddy is the man I want to talk to.' This might have seemed a little harsh, but it really was the only way to talk to someone like Norman. He was not a subtle man in his manner and appreciated the blunt approach when being spoken to.

'I'll give you a call tomorrow, Norman. Go home and have some rest. You look awful. I'll call. I promise I'll call. We're just sorting some business.'

Norman stared at Robert Rennie and, for a moment, I thought he was going to break the glass in his face. Instead he finished the drink off in one. He handed me the empty and walked calmly out.

'I was at The Palladium a few years ago when your other half put your career on hold. He hasn't changed.'

'That was a long time ago, Robert. A lot of drinks have passed over the bar since then.'

'Why do you stay with him?'

'You said it: *My other half.*'

He took me over and introduced me to the man he was talking to when I walked in. It was Larry Pringle, the newspaper columnist. He was preening himself and talking loudly to the young boys.[41] I had a brief correspondence with Pringle a year before. More of that later, perhaps.

'Of course, Francis is a realist; in his attitudes and in his paintings.' He spoke so loudly, as though his opinions must be heard by all. Perhaps that's why he ended up doing a showbiz column. His weekly words fell like showbiz manna and woe

---

[41] It has always been my thought that powerful people don't have to raise their voice. But Pringle was powerful in his own way. His column was full of gossip and innuendo and did not stop short of libel. 'Say it and be damned,' he boasted at every opportunity. There was something of the Dame Sybil about him. Or Joan of Arc. Many would have paid to see him burned at the stake.

betide anyone who got on his wrong side.

The picture at the head of his column must have been taken forty years before. This person standing before me looked close to seventy. His skin was a pale yellow colour with what looked like black streaks of shadow coming around the cheekbones. The lips were wet and red and the skin under his chin hung like the leftovers from a *brit malah* party. He looked absolutely stinking with corruption. The young men around were part of a pop group. They hoped to get a mention in Pringle's *To Watch Out For* section. They felt it would give them artistic credibility to be seen in The Colony Club.

I couldn't concentrate on the next few hours' conversation, so I steadily got drunk. I confess Norman's intrusion was bothering me. Now and again I would be brought back to the moment by a sharp burst of laughter or Robert Rennie's boozy face up to mine shouting that these are great days and they will not be seen again. I agreed. Deep down, though, I felt that *Norman and Freddy's* chance might have passed by. We were still reasonably young, but our material had not really moved with the times. During the height of the *hippy* era, particularly two years before, we had done one sketch that involved me in beads and an Afghan coat. The sketch ended with Norman clobbering me with a plant pot saying: 'You said you liked flowers.' It was the only joke we ever did about hippies, a movement crying out for the piss-take.[42] We seemed part of another generation of comedians. It was a generation that had no real connection with the young on any level. And youth was where it was at, *baby*. It was reflected in the faces

---

[42] If we believe everything is of equal value then those with nothing to say shall say it loudly. And those who can't create will package up anything and call it art. Many will get very wealthy out of this. People were no more stupid and gullible in the 60s than they are today. And young people sound just as vacuous now as they did then. Perhaps there was just too much of a focus on people who had nothing to say.

and bodies of the sad little twerps who stood before my alcohol fuelled head all those years ago in The Colony Club. I wanted to say all of these things out loud to Robert Rennie, but fear stopped me. I was afraid of my own truth. I was also afraid that I was wrong and so didn't want to blow everything completely. Something deep inside me, call it arrogance or ego, held on to the idea that we could still be big in showbiz – yet everything around me told me it wasn't happening: ever. Robert Rennie wanted to meet me in order to fuck me.[43] I think this was the truth of that night. It was not the fact that he wanted to fuck me that was of concern: I always take compliments when they arise. It was the fact of being used, sold, disrespected on a professional level. And how many young men and women have thought the same? How we can deny something so obvious in order to get ahead? I pushed it to the back of my mind. Somewhere where it was out of harm's way. And *harm's way* was in my thoughts. I didn't need bad thoughts to bring me down. A person in showbiz has to be *up*. Unless they wanted to end up like Hancock.[44] Depression is an easy state of mind to get into in this business. You spend most of your time fighting against who you are and playing out a public perception. You deny your

---

[43] Not long in Rennie's company I understood that he was one of those people that lacked empathy. Now, lacking in empathy is in itself not the greatest of human flaws, but, coupled with a genuine nasty streak, it is the most destructive of human traits. From someone else, male or female, the compliment that they wanted to fuck me I would have accepted gracefully.
[44] Tony Hancock had committed suicide in Australia in 1968. He had taken an overdose of vodka and amylobarbitone tablets. I met Hancock a year before his death. He was absolutely charming and very serious. His suicide note read: *Things just seemed to go too wrong too many times.* In those words held the mood of the man I met. His 1960 Face To Face television interview with John Freeman destroyed him in many ways. A human being should not be analyzed in such a way for public entertainment. I confess that I did hero worship him to a degree. His death left something of a gap in the heart of British comedy. We shall never see his like again.

true self for so long that when reality bites it really takes a chunk out of you. So, we deny the obvious. We push away the real to replace it with…with what? The paper moon and the cardboard sky? That was Freddy Foster at that time. Later, real life would enter and refuse to leave. It is often the case that serious illness becomes the wakeup call. But at that time, I was dreaming the good dream. I played a lot of showbiz games like this. Many did. Norman didn't. He couldn't have even if he had wanted. He was better than the lot of us. He was one of the finest men. And it shames me greatly to say that I wasn't.[45]

Larry Pringle's voice brought me back to the moment:

'Well, of course, writing a diary is a – what? Craft? Or sullen art?' He laughed with pursed lips after this comment. His head went back slightly and the skin under his chin flapped. The young boys had no doubt heard that voice in a hundred old films. It was the voice of *The Master*, *The Guvnor*, the man in charge. It was the voice of the one who gave the orders, who made the decisions. Whereas they were the boys who would be carrying George Arliss's bags to his room at The Ritz. But there might be a change in the air as he was actually talking to them.

'It's a subjective art,' he continued. 'Although if any of them had an honest bone in their body they'd admit all journalism is subjective. What?' And he laughed again, louder this time. He was enjoying the opinions that he could express without question. The boys looked as though their faces were beginning to cramp in rictus smiles, but one of them managed a desperate line:

'I read your …'

---

[45] I went to the BFI to see *A Touch of Evil*, a film I had missed on its original release. The last line spoken by Marlene Dietrich lends itself to Norman very well: 'He was some kind of a man. What does it matter what you say about people?'

'My column, dear boy, my column.'

'The people you…'

'Met them all. Rogues mostly! Haha!'

Robert leaned into me and whispered:

'Freddy, how can any of us die now? I mean, now. It's not possible.'

Larry Pringle was quite typical of the *entertainment* journalist: a self-important, self-serving, vain and foolish, gushing twit. Quite unaware that most of the public didn't consider them journalists at all.

'A funny thing,' said Rennie, 'these boys here are only about ten years younger than you, yet you look like their granddad, Freddy! But I like you.'[46]

At this everyone laughed. I laughed. I laughed even though I knew that Rennie often put people down in order to make them more vulnerable. And then I thought about Norman's words:

She's pregnant.

---

[46] He slapped my shoulder at this. The line was from a Dick Emery character called *Mandy*. The character had become part of British culture and it was referenced often in other programmes. Emery was one of the most successful television comedians throughout the 60s and 70s. Little is now said of him. He died of a heart attack at the age of 67. He had been living with his showgirl girlfriend, 30 years his junior. Obviously the five marriages hadn't been enough.

7

2004/Present

> *Norman: I don't think people are tired of double*
> *acts.*
> *Freddy: Well that's encouraging.*
> *Norman: No, they're just tired of this double act*
> *Billy Cotton Band Show, October,*
> *1966.*[47]

I kept a secret for a lot of years regarding Janice. It gave me a particular and perverse pleasure in my more thoughtful moments. Before Norman had copped off with her I'd been there and done the business. And I continued with that business right up until her death. The only secret I kept from Norman. If you're going to have an affair make sure it's with someone as close as possible to you. No one will suspect a thing, and if they do it gives you the freedom to react with angry indignation. You'll probably be applauded for doing so.

Janice was not one of the world's most beautiful women. Her hair was probably her best feature. It was short and dark with bangs.[48] She was a new generation's Louise Brooks. Or rather she could have been if she had acted. For a dancer, she was pretty thick set, with stocky muscular legs.

'I was never tall enough to be a Tiller Girl,' she'd say.

When she left the profession she really turned to fat. She was the only fat junkie that I ever met, and in this business

---

[47] This was a variety show. Even the term *variety* sounds dated now. But it was originally a term to separate it from music hall. I enjoyed Billy, which probably dates me. But there was lovely warmth from the cast of Kathie Kay and Alan Breeze. These days even names make me feel old.
[48] A lovely word that was being used a lot at the time. American, you know. Fringe was quite *square, man.*

you come up against a lot of junkies. Having said that she was also one of the most sensual and sexual human beings I have ever met. *She walked in beauty, like the night.*[49] She was a real trouper, and when Norman got his illness she nursed him day and night. Is that when we see the true stuff of a human being? When circumstances become extreme? She was the most caring human being anyone could meet. She got upset at other people's troubles. I remember she came into her flat when I was having a cup of tea with Norman. He was watching horse racing on the telly.[50] It was a worrying time all round. It might have been early days[51] but his foot was already dragging on occasions and he often sounded drunk. When she came in she was really upset, crying; the lot. She'd seen some boys set about a man just down the road. We knew who the kids were. Everyone knew. Just before the gee-gees Bush had been on talking for a while about a *war on terror*. But everyone knew the real terror was outside their door. No one gave a monkeys about bombs when you had lawless boys on your doorstep. They had nothing, were not worthy of the news, and behaved accordingly.

'Like a pack of wild dogs, they were. A pack of wild dogs, I tell you.'

I was going to phone the police. But why put up Janice and Norman's phone bill for nothing? Instead I took her into the bedroom.[52] Norman just stared at the horses entering the

---

[49] Byron! You wonderful rogue you!

[50] He was quite the armchair sportsman even in his healthier days. Sitting for hours watching the cricket; the Sunday slap of leather on willow, the crackle of applause. I couldn't bear it myself,

[51] Perhaps late 2003/2004. The disease did not appear overnight. It was a gradual thing and as such it was noticed gradually.

[52] I should say that upset as she was, and drenched by a London cloudburst, she got me going from the moment she entered. She was wearing a black top that was soaked through. Her nipples were jutting through the material

starting gate. Janice's natural animal smells, even at that age, could send me into paroxysms of lust. As I pinned her against the bedroom door, ripping at her blouse with one hand and trying to hitch up her skirt with the other, she was furiously pulling at Thor's Hammer.

'Bang me, Freddy! Bang me!' she said. And I did. But even with the lust I could rarely stop my mind from meandering to other times. What is all this intrusion? The more I concentrated the more the reality would melt.

A night there – was it there? – discussing the act and bitching about some upstart. They had been drinking. Not me as I remember. No, not me that night. And the argument flowed, cutting, uncaring about my presence. And she let fly:

'Oh yes, some man! Sitting up in bed with a post coital gherkin. Romance is alive and well and living at the Riddell residence!'

'I was peckish! Can't a man get peckish?'

'There are moments, buster, there are moments! I was used to finer things!' Bent over down a lane?

'You were never used to finer things. Your family were London's post war beggars. Most of them jumped at the chance of getting moved out the slum.'

'How dare you, you cunt!'

'Oh yes, I see the finer things reflected in the choice language!'

But through these memories my hips would automatically be performing like Etienne Lenoir's double-acting, spark ignition engine.[53]

Even in her pension years Janice insisted on wearing heels that were unsuitable for her posture and weight. They had the effect of pushing out even further her already large bottom.

---

so clearly that an Aldermaston marcher from many years before could have hung his wet duffle coat on them.

[53] The more I write this the more I understand that there are no borders on memory. Always it was the past living in the present. Always my feelings were of the moment; of the now.

The plus side was that they did give her the correct height for snatched moments of passion. As a result, on that particular day, we had the job finished in under seven furlongs.[54] That included my memories. Next door Norman cried out. His horse had thrown its rider at the fifteenth fence.[55]

I never felt any sense of guilt about my relationship with Janice. In fact, guilt has been something of a stranger to me. If anything, I think over the years I kept their marriage alive, particularly when Janice retired from dancing. She liked to laugh with the other girls, she liked to party, the attention of men, and all that goes with that sparkling world. It was the dancing she didn't like, which is no good if you're a dancer. (I might not have had any respect for our audiences, but I was passionate about comedy). Maybe at one time she had wanted fame. Maybe she had dreamed of it as I did as a child. But fame is a difficult fish to land. It turns and twists with the fashions. When all of that went, she could have gone off the rails and taken it out on Norman, but I think our furtive coupling, our clandestine meetings, served to re-affirm her love for my dear partner.

As I carried a pair of Wellington boots and Norman's feet to the front door I thought of Janice. I miss her: her moon face, pale as la Luna through wisps of evening cloud. What a romantic fool I can be even now. The mystery of the moon, its romance and power, was reflected in her sea green eyes. She pulled men to her like tides being pulled from the shore. And Norman fell, as all men should fall, completely and breathlessly. As for me, I thought that I had resisted her magic, thought I was in control of my life. But, of course, I wasn't.

---

[54] A reasonable thoroughbred should manage that in about one minute twenty-four seconds.

[55] I learned later the horse was *King's Fountain*. Norman went on about it all night.

I was perhaps the biggest fool of all. As I sailed through the years burying my faults under an ego the size of Everest, I would offer my tuppence worth on things I often knew little about. Oh yes, I met the creators but really didn't understand their work: the politicians, the artists, the actors, [56] all of them always slightly removed from Freddy Foster: comedian. But I loved their company. Norman did not. He had a total disrespect and disregard for the powerful. (I am not a powerful man, but I have known many powerful men.) Having power is a gift only truly understood by those that have it. Power seems to bring with it confidence. It also brings with it the unshakeable belief that you are right in everything you say. And you will have a say in everything. When I was growing up social ties were knotted less with respect and more with fear. People in positions of even relatively lowly authority could destroy families, and often did. A few weeks without a Public Assistance dole out led to the pawnshops first and the loan sharks second. Through this I learned at an early age that power isn't complete without power over the individual and as I went on in life I saw how it could be gained through sex. Some have been caught out in some scandal or another. For the politician[57] there might be the public apology to the wife, the House, the constituents, the country, Uncle Tom Cobley and all. They might ride it out on the *forgive me* ticket. The days

---

[56] There were often cases where I looked up to those who were certainly my intellectual inferiors. In company I would often try to make them feel good about themselves so they would look favourably upon me. Seeking approval, something that I can say Norman never did. In that he was a better man than me. In so many ways he was a better man than me.

[57] There are few certainties in my life, but there is one thing that experience has taught me true: the high and the mighty, the rulers and the leaders, have been never been fit for purpose. If given the slightest opportunity they would put an end to democracy by standing and defending the democratic rights of the British public. They are players, much like an Oxbridge student theatre production. Democracy does not roll easily on the tongues of the entitled.

of falling on the sword are well and truly gone. And what of me and these people? I made them laugh, regaling them with stories of the affairs and the bastard children of the famous. But I never mentioned *my* private life. That particular sub-plot would have revealed a pathetic hustling fraudster of little consequence.

I placed the Wellingtons by the front door beside a clutter of shoes. I didn't want to forget them in my present state of mind. While doing so I also tidied the shoes. Some of them needed a good clean, I thought. It was perhaps not the time to be polishing shoes, but I am a neat and ordered person and it has served me well all my years.

8

Present/1992

'Life can only be understood backwards, but it must be lived forwards.'
Kierkegaard

I always wanted my words to be celebrated. I wanted my
comedy to be important. Instead I became a daft old prat.
That's the truth of it. They can write it on my gravestone:
Freddy Foster – Prat. That's if I get a gravestone. Look at poor
Norman. Not even a memorial. His body parts dumped all
over London town. What was I to do, though? It was his
wish. At least he died in England. That's what he wanted. It
would never have suited him to breathe his last on foreign
shores, whereas I have no such qualms. Norman was an
Englishman first and last, so any consideration of last days in
foreign fields would have come with not a little anguish.

Perhaps I should say something of the practicalities of my
gruesome task. The first thing that I needed were several large
plastic sheets. This was to contain the body parts and contain
the bloody mess that would ensue from the chopping. I spoke
to Robert at B & Q – he had a name on his brown coat:
Me: Drains.
Robert: It's a very dangerous chemical if you don't take precautions.
Me: Well, I would certainly take precautions. What do you recommend?
Robert: Rubber gloves and goggles.
Me: I'll take them as well.
Robert: Better safe than sorry.
Me: I've always thought so.
My original intention was to use caustic soda to melt the flesh
*- o that this too too sullied flesh should melt, thaw and resolve itself into a
dew.*[58] But alas it wasn't to be. I tried it in the bath with one of

---

[58] *Hamlet*, Act one, Scene Two. I have to tell you?

the hands and almost blinded myself with the fumes. Murder is not really my business.

'What's this?' In my daily tidying routine I had come across a letter stuck down the easy chair. It was shortly after Janice had passed away.

'It's a letter from Dignitas,' he mumbled.

'Well that's going in the bin.'

'No, Freddy. It's to do with choice and dignity. I want to die, Freddy.'

It was the first time I had heard him utter those words and they had the effect of angering me. I took it to be a personal affront after all the time and energy that Janice and I had given him.

He continued, 'I want to die here, not abroad. That's how much this bloody government cares for its citizens. They'd rather we sneaked away under the cover of dark to another country. Perish the thought that people die with their loved ones around them in their home.'[59]

'Haven't you noticed? I am your loved one. Only me.[60] You don't have anyone else. Such is the life of the great Lothario.'

These were harsh words, but he did get my goat up. How dare he tell me that he wanted to die? What a slap in the face to someone who has given so much. Do people realise the effect that has on those that love you? I think not. Or maybe I'm being selfish. Trying to save a life. What happened to '*rage*

---

[59] I really needn't have worried that he was going to go through with this, as the cost of a personally timed death was way beyond his means.

[60] Indeed, this was true. It seems that in show business you must have lots of friends. This is only so to the outsider. The truth is often very different. The nature of the business is that you are travelling so much making close friendships is difficult. There might be a lot of colleagues and associates but that is not true friendship.

rage against the dying of the light?'[61] (Norman would have understood this reference as he recited it to me – much to my surprise – in the early 60s.)[62]

'There's no fucking rage left. Well, only at you.'

'You're an ungrateful bastard,' I replied.

'I want my pride. I want my dignity. And it's something else, Freddy, I want my dues.'

'Your dues?' I said in an inordinately high pitch. Under any other circumstances it would have been comic. 'Your dues, you cunt?[63] Your dues are being paid every time I empty a pisspot or wipe away dribble from your chin. Your dues are given you in every bath and every shave.'

He was obviously up for all this and had been thinking about it a long time.

'Where's the dignity in that? I was a boy about town. I was a fucking player. Look at me now. I'm a burden. I was a burden to Janice and I'm a burden on you.'

'Don't you give me that shit, you selfish fuck. We would have walked over hot coals for you. That's what partners do. You're with a man or you're not.'

'Help me die, Freddy. If you care as much as you say you do then give me that.'

'Well I didn't know you'd turned into Bertrand fucking Russell. When did that happen? It's fucking obscene, that's what it is. *You're* fucking obscene. I didn't realise you were a quitter, Norman. I thought you had more in you.'

'Everything I had in me is going. It went on the way here.

---

[61] At a theatrical *do* the director of the Shaw Theatre told me that Dylan Thomas was good on the first few pints but after that the stories fell away too much: the *green fuse* blown.

[62] Dear reader, I can only say he was full of surprises. Outside the back pages of a tabloid I rarely saw him read anything but our scripts.

[63] Although something of a logophile I did revert to the most base of language when riled. But I have always loved language and the written word; the word without a god.

Let me fall away without any more loss. Lying about gets you to thinking a lot.[64] I've been thinking about things.'

'Well, you've managed to avoid that all your life. Why start now?'

An anger rose up in him. It must have taken all the energy he could summon to utter his next tragi-comic slur, like a film hero stuck in slow motion.[65]

'Because every man has to face himself one day. And this is my day. Maybe we spend our lives running away.'

Where did all of this come from? It didn't sound like my partner of all those years. Or maybe that was what he'd hidden away from me and Janice. Maybe that was why he fucked his way around the fringes of the entertainment world. What annoyed me was his use of the word *we*. I wouldn't have it; I would not fucking have it.

'I faced myself every fucking day of my life. I faced myself when I jumped on a train to London fifty years ago. I faced myself every time I walked on a stage. I thought that was what it was all about.'

---

[64] From my many days in bed as a child this was something I recognised. The moment that he said it an image entered my head of my Glasgow days. I saw the window above the sink that looked over the back courts. The cooker to its left with the coal fire to its left again. The living room and kitchen were one; not open plan, just *there*. Through the door to the cramped hall and facing my mother's bedroom door and my bedroom door. I thought of pushing my door open slowly to see a young me in blue striped pyjamas, tousled hair and bottle white face, undernourished, sitting up in bed with a book in my hand. These split-second memories were common in much of my conversations throughout my life. I believe we are all like this and we have learned to push them away tout suite. I shall not interrupt the flow of the story in hand by relating them all.

[65] As the disease progressed Norman's speech got worse. There were problems, certainly, but I could understand him. The stage he was at in speaking was dysarthria. He had been told that this could end in anarthria, where speaking would be impossible. When I first heard about this I shed some quiet tears.

'Maybe that's what it's about for you. You think I did any of this in order to face myself? Gizza break! I was poking the fire to brighten the room![66] The past was where it belonged. Didn't anyone ever tell you that it's all about the hiding? If you think anything different then you were the one who was wrong, Freddy.'[67]

All of this was more than an argument about the act; I realise now. We think we know people but I've learned the best we can hope for is to know something of ourselves.[68] The voice we hear daily in our heads will never be heard by others; it will rarely get a line. Norman must have heard himself very loudly over the months as he discussed the pros and cons of being alive.

'I suppose we learn something every day.'

I said this as I was tearing the letter up, but I didn't really know what he was going through. How could I? Damn it, Norman, how could anyone truly understand such a thing? Did you really expect me to? I could feed you, dress you, wash you and wipe your arse. Wasn't it enough that I gave you these things? I wanted to take your illness away. I wanted to heal you. But I'm no fucking Jesus. I wanted to give you success and fame in the beginning, but we were forgotten. We were overlooked by the profession that we gave our life to. It can suck the soul out of you and leave you nothing. You didn't care, did you? I don't think it ever meant that much to you. But to me, Norman, it was everything. You never knew how much I gave of myself, how much I humiliated myself. I

---

[66] Reader, please do not ask.

[67] The past is different for different people. Mine is much like ice under a winter sun. It dissolves slowly and flows into memory. And so my past has thawed into a pool, to be scooped up, in cupped hands, running inevitably through my fingers, never still.

[68] I do remember the yesterdays, which is strange, for I was certainly someone else.

fawned over people who weren't fit to lick our boots. And all you gave me was grief at every turn. As so often happens these thoughts gave way to a churlish reply.

'You probably got the disease just to torture me.'

But we say stupid things in the heat of argument. The revelation that Norman had motor neurone disease had come into our lives like an emotional avalanche. There was little it did not touch and little it did not destroy. It didn't affect our careers as he had basically retired some time before. By that time it was really just *my* career. Something has just popped into my head! Isn't this process a wonderful thing? I remembered while writing this that once a very long time ago Norman told me that he was looking for resolution. I mean, what was that about? Resolution? From what you may ask. But that I can't answer. What had this man done that needed resolving in his mind? I never did find out. Was it about how he treated Janice? But I never thought that bothered him so much. Perhaps we all need some resolution in our lives. Doubts amble silently in our minds and answers often arrive on shifting sands. Is that the true nature of the human beast? A cigarette burnt my fingers while I gave thought to that paragraph. How little it takes for me to drift these days. Yes, I was pressing on. What else could I do? If our double act was a damp squib then my solo years were a hurricane of humiliation. Thankfully, I might say that this was short-lived. I became something of Norman's carer as the disease progressed, particularly after the death of Janice. True love was not soft kisses and whispered words. It was not the rush of warm breath on a cheek. Nor was it the desperate clutching at a body during love making. It became the bathing of a body that was reeking of sweat and piss and excrement. It was the wiping of an arsehole with hard bits of shit sticking to the hair, the not showing disgust when lifting the balls and running a warm cloth underneath. When Janice was gone, I did not hesitate at performing these duties. Instead I attacked them with vigour and proficiency. It should be said, though, that unlike Janice, I wore a pair of strong rubber kitchen gloves. No doubt performing such tasks would fill many with revulsion. I can only say, my dear reader, until a loved one goes through such a time you have no real worthwhile opinion.

And so there shall be no box sets of the great Norman and Freddy. Success that even into older age we hoped was just around the corner was replaced by disease and death. Now who could have written that? Our comedy is all but lost. Many of the recordings have been destroyed by television stations making space on their shelves for compilations of people falling off roofs, dogs driving cars, brides slipping on the dance floor, to fill another evening's *entertainment*. Shall these words that I tap out now be the only evidence that we walked this earth? Or shall this also be *wiped*? It's of no great matter.

These memories are having a physical effect on me. I have suffered slight dizzy spells throughout this writing. Thoughts of my death have entered my head and I have turned from them. It is not me to dwell on these things. I have always held to life.

The letter from Dignitas was never mentioned again, but assisted suicide was.

9

1969

Norman (throwing back a whisky): Just killing the worm.

Robert Rennie lived on the edge of St John's Wood. Until that night I had never been there, but I had heard of it. One of the most surprising things for me was that it wasn't a wood. Regardless of the state of my mind at this point, I filed away some of the stories Robert told about his famous neighbours. There was a boast to everything he did. The year before he had taken me to The Liberal Club and bragged that the refurbished staircase had cost the public £150,000. He introduced me to the actor Sidney Tafler, also a guest, his usual haunt being the The Savage Club. Fred Emney was there too, lumbering amongst the tables with a fat cigar stuck in his face. I enjoyed it all. Somehow, I thought that these things might help *Norman and Freddy*. That's the thing with me. I was always working. And I was always working to make us the best in Britain. Norman just sat back and waited for things. The only day that I saw him get off his arse to get his career moving was that first day that we met. He never really understood that, or if he did he never mentioned it. So, while I was sucking up to every bastard that might open a door he was down the pub with his thick as shit mates.[69] Or he was having a few days in Spain with or without Janice. I never

---

[69] He once turned up at my door with these crapulous ruffians looking for a night cap! I gave them all the sharp edge of my tongue and sent them on their way. My relationship with my neighbours was never the same afterwards. Mrs Kopeykin wouldn't even enter the lift with me. Perhaps she had visions of what the Cossacks had done to her grandmother, a tale she had told me over a mug of *sbiten* when I moved in. It was horrific. The story, not the *sbiten,* which was sweet and fruity. I will not relate the story as this is a memoir, not an exposé of Cossack atrocities.

really tired of it, though. It's what kept me going. It was the challenge, I suppose, and I really did like the hobnobbing. Only a liar would say differently.

So, while I was schmoozing in Robert Rennie's palatial home, Norman was, I assumed, sitting in his damp little flat contemplating lot and life. It's just the way of things.

'We're pretty close to John Lennon's house,' Robert said while threading an eight-millimeter piece of pornography onto the projector wheel. At this one of the pretty boys –Dean or Clint or Dana or Storm or whatever name was the flavour of the day – shouted out in a *trying too hard to be at ease voice*:

'John Lennon? Coooool! I like The Beatles.'
Saying you liked The Beatles was like saying you liked to breathe or shit.

'You know The Beatles?' piped up another of the pretty boys, who looked like he hadn't hit puberty. I thought if I was into pimping I could make a small fortune out of him in some of the more private clubs.[70]

'Met them through George Martin who was producing Peter Sellers at the time.'
Robert's dick probably grew an inch with every dropped name. Unfortunately, Peter Pan had a look on his face that said *Who's George Martin?* And probably *Who's Peter Sellers* as well? It struck me that there was a generation coming up that would have to have everything explained to them; every single cultural and political reference explained to them. They would have that same fish look and would be measured by how far they were prepared to sell themselves for a moment of fame.

---

[70] Do not for a moment confuse these young victims as bohemians. They were never that. They were addicts, or soon would be. Of alcohol often, and of drugs; but mainly it was a fevered and desperate grasping for fame. Of that foul mistress perhaps I shall say more later. But also within that we shared a common goal. It is what thrust us all forward. I should not really emerge from this story as in any way better than any of them.

My stomach began to turn over at the thought. Robert Rennie must have noticed colour drain from my face. He pointed towards the toilet and I moved to it with a purpose.

When I returned to the lounge the lights had been dimmed and the film was tickering away. The black and white images on the screen were grainy and the performers looked tired and broken. Probably a few of them wanted to do Shakespeare with Gielgud or Olivier, but they had walked into the wrong party, and sometimes there's just no way back. I saw them daily, as they walked the same streets as me, like hungry dogs. Where would they go in the future? They should be taken care of, given shelter, warmth, food. Somehow I couldn't see that happening.[71] What was happening in Britain? The *keeper of the cloth cap*, Callaghan was Home Secretary and Wilson was at Number Ten: both were obviously too busy sending troops into Northern Ireland to bother about what was happening a couple of miles from their front doors in St John's Wood.

The screen didn't interest me that much – maybe something to do with my Scottish Presbyterianism coming out. I liked the real thing. I liked to think I could fuck women till my knob was a raw point, if I wanted. I say *if I wanted* because my sexual activities were few and far between, even the case with Janice. Those kinds of films just left me bored. Not so, obviously, for the audience on that night. The pretty boys, though, had lost something of their shine and I could see one of them openly wanking.

Robert Rennie stood in front of me with a stiffy in his pocket. He was stroking the material while holding onto a whisky and coke.

'Well, Freddy, you really want this show?'

---

[71] I know, I'm getting on my high horse here. But something in my background forced me to see what others just didn't. People were living their lives buried under the crumbs of success. Or is it with hindsight I see this?

I was very drunk but managed to stand up and push him gently aside. 'No,' I said simply. And that was that. I left them all to it. I would never see those boys again. Fame is not only fickle; it is sometimes downright offensive.

Giant snowflakes floated and fell in the dead black night of Rennie's driveway. I walked to the side bushes and picked up a heavy stone which I launched at the lit upstairs window. It connected and the glass shattered.

'Villain!' I shouted like some 19th century melodrama hero. Oh Freddy Foster, what were you thinking?

The large oak door swung open and there stood a rather louche looking Rennie. He had a drink in his hand and there was a bemused look on his face. He spoke without anger:

'Go home, Freddy. You don't belong here.' At this a young man's arm fell around his neck and pulled him back. The door closed.

I walked four and a half miles back home in the snow and wind. When I got there I rapped a few times on Bathsheba's door. There was no reply. I lay in my cold bed for a while thinking about her. And then I thought of Norman and Janice. I picked up the phone and dialed Norman's number.

'Hello?' he said, sounding totally awake.

'Norman?' It was quite obviously him, but I wanted time to formulate some kind of question. I had sobered up on my walk home, but I was still trying to work out the damage the night had done to our careers.

'It's you. What is it? I thought it was Janice.'

'It's not Janice,' I said.

'I fucking know it's not Janice, unless she's been necking fucking hormone tablets.' Sometimes his aggression to those closest to him really did take the biscuit. 'Listen,' he continued, 'I'm going to marry her.'

And what could I say? 'You've got to do what you think is right, Norman.' Of course, there were other things I could have said. Marriage has always been anathema to me. My show business world was my wife. I could never put so much time, energy, and effort into a relationship. But for other men their wife was the only rock in a very stormy sea. I could have told him that I'd butt-fucked her down a lane around the corner from The King's Theatre in Glasgow. But, of course, I didn't. I repeated:

'You've got to do what you think is right.'

'Yes. I thought so,' he said, his voice sinking.

'Hey, Norman,' I said. 'How'd you fancy the cruise ships?'

'They're not The Palladium.'

'It's travel. It's sun. It's a laugh.'

10

Present

Captain: Wait a minute! You mean you travel with a
chimp and a lion?
Tarzan: I have my reasons.
"Tarzan and the Great River."

To watch a great dancer, you really have to hold your hands up and say, 'That is talent.'[72] I've always been an admirer of successful people. The secret is hard work, dedication, perseverance. And luck. It was the last of these that *Norman and Freddy* was shortchanged on. Of course, some would say that you make your own luck. I say *bollocks*. For anyone to say that is insulting. I did everything in my power to keep our act together and successful. Our career did not bear the fruit that I might at one time have hoped. This does not mean that we were unsuccessful. We tasted more than most and for that I'm grateful. It was just the potential I felt that was left untapped.

I pulled Norman's old golf bag out of the hall cupboard. It had his name in gold lettering on the side. I ran my hand slowly over the lettering: *NORM*. The bag was thirty odd years old. I know this because I had bought it for Norman as a Christmas present not long before we hit the high seas. As usual he had complained.

'It says *Norm*. Who the fuck is *Norm*? Norman-fucking-Wisdom? Are you Mr.-fucking-Grimsdale?'

I thought of this as I turned the bag upside down, letting the few clubs clatter to the floor, and took it through to the living room. Occasionally I have played golf and fumbled slightly

---

[72] Mister Lionel Blair had this in abundance. And a career that spanned fifty odd years to boot! I met him several times and thought that he looked something like a young Conrad Veidt.

whilst returning the club to the bag. Slipping a pair of bloody legs in presented problems of its own. They are very unwieldy, particularly because of the bending of the knee. When the mission was complete, though, I had to admit that it was a neat and snug fit.[73] It is curious how many perfectly normal objects around a house will accommodate the disposal of body parts, as if they were made for that very purpose.

As I worked it struck me – not for the first time – that his flat smelled. You could even see it. Great patches of damp, like someone had used the walls as a urinal. It was raining and water had collected in a small puddle on the inside of the window ledge. The window frame had come away slightly from the wall due to it. Norman pointed it out to me two years before. A man from the council had come around. He was a youngster who didn't look at all official but tried his best to look efficient. He was wearing an open-necked shirt with a beaded necklace tight around his throat. The denim clad lad called *John* looked at the window and walls and said *damp*. He then left, and that was it. No one else came around. I've always wanted to know who these people really are and whose boxes they really tick. Their existence seems to be some kind of preliminary, but one without any follow-up. You acknowledge their existence and that is all that's required of you. That in itself becomes its purpose. All books written, all paintings ever painted, every piece of music ever played has had a unifying factor: to show us ourselves. When I think of the council I think of Francis's *screaming popes*, something deeply tortured and without any means of expression, except a scream. We just want our existence acknowledged.

---

[73] As something of a merchant in irony I did think of putting head covers over the stumped lower leg end, but Norman only had the novelty sort. There was something disrespectful about pulling on a *Tweety Pie* or *Elmer Fudd* woollen image. Norman himself, I'm sure, would not have minded as he had a childlike love of Merrie Melodies and Looney Tunes cartoons.

R D McGregor

After two years the smell had not shifted. Norman was not the tidiest, or indeed most hygienic, of men at the best of times. Towards the end, when Janice had been gone some months, it was at its worst point. But then I must carry that blame. When the diagnosis was final – and this itself took some time and many tests – I wanted to be strong for him – as had Janice. When life deals a blow such as that it doesn't so much take the wind out of your sails as sink your ship. I have no doubt that the illness did something that I would have considered impossible: it brought us even closer together. Our lives since that fateful day at the Brittle Bone Society Dance in 1961 had been linked through the troupers, the camaraderie of shared dreams and dashed hopes. We shared digs and meals as much as we shared the stage. That is what having a partner means. We were as comfortable with each other as we would have been in our own company. Often more so.[74] When Janice retired from the business just after we returned from the cruise in 1972 the three of us became closer. Perhaps it was being away from Blighty that did that. Maybe we were just getting older. We were in our early thirties. When in rooms together we could easily stay silent and behave as though alone. Norman would settle down and watch anything on television.[75] I would read or write. I was always trying to perfect our act. From a very young age I developed the knack of closing out all sounds when I was doing my own thing,

---

[74] It is only with hindsight I can understand that Norman had to have company. All the affairs, the nights in the pub, the man at the centre of attention, was all because he could not be alone. I don't know what makes a human being tick; I don't know about all the Freud gubbins. Whatever the reasons, my partner needed others around. Was there something of self-hatred in him? I always had a hunch that his lifestyle made him loathe himself more. A thousand lifetimes and we could not unravel our own selves let alone that of others. Why try?
[75] Norman told me that he watched shit television in order not to think. I told him it was working.

62

building a buffer between me and an extremely noisy Glasgow. If it wasn't the Luftwaffe disturbing my night's rest as a toddler it was the city council destroying the slums to make way for a bright high-rise future. Janice was always baking. Although I wasn't living with them, it was quite the family unit for a while. A very long time actually. Thinking back now, things went downhill not so much at the beginning of Norman's illness, but rather at the start of Janice's.

One of the first things I did when we got back to England after the cruise ship was buy a Cortina MK 3 and investigate house prices. I was using my money wisely, while Norman, with assorted hangers on, went on a month long bender. No one could get through money like my partner. He was incapable of holding on to it or investing it. For him money was for the moment. By the time of Janice's death the flat reflected his poverty. Dirty dishes would be left stacked on tables for days on end, mould growing over dried egg and beans; green liver spots floating on the dregs of tea like small islands. For a man that had little to nothing to do most days I thought that there was no excuse. I did what I could, but I still had something of a life left.[76] As I said, with Norman, there was no point in beating around the bush.

'Your flat is a pisspot,' I told him.

'Well, don't come 'round then.'

Of course, I had no choice as he wouldn't visit me. He said that it was too dangerous to cross his front door after three o'clock in the afternoon because of kids. Sometimes, he said, they look up at the window and put their hand to their temple as though holding a loaded pistol.

'Why don't you come around in the morning then?'

'That's when I try to get some sleep.'

---

[76] So, I decided to move in. He could not take care of himself and this realisation made me angrier with him than he deserved. Reader, you may have guessed thus far, I am not a perfect man.

Sleeping at night was nigh on impossible because of the thumping music. And then there was the knocking, he told me.

'What knocking?'

'The knocking on the door,' he said.

'Who comes to your door at night,' I asked.

'Well I don't fucking answer it. You think I'm mad?'

He told me that he had heard terrible noises. He thought the kids were throwing live animals off the roof.[77]

'One time I went out. Early on. I was quiet. Put the landing light on. I went to the stairs. I had my stick. But if I'd lifted it to clatter someone I'd have fallen. So, I opened the stair door. I tried to look down but it was dark. I just felt there was someone there with me. And then the landing lights went out. They're on a timer, see? And the door came back on me. Gave me a fright so what did I do but drop my stick. I couldn't see it. I just felt my way along the wall to my door and locked and bolted. My heart was banging in my chest. Next day you found the stick leaning on my door.'

Norman looked frightened when he told me this, but he said that it was the lack of sleep that got to him. Plenty of sleep now, Norman, I thought as I dragged the golf bag to the hall cupboard.

There was, at one time, a full set, but he had sold some off in the mid-80s. That was a particularly impoverished time.[78]

---

[77]. There was silence in my Chelsea home. I walked in silence from one room to another. The living room to kitchen. The boiling of a kettle piercing the quiet, a dropped knife, its clatter on the floor. My silence was a given. It was an eternity of such. It's what I paid for. Perhaps in the night there would be the turn of a taxi engine, a distant swish of car on puddled roads. Money buys this kind of quiet. Norman did not prepare for future calm. Those that crave silence spend their nights listening…listening…

[78] It hit Norman particularly hard. My small investments for rainy days paid off, if not handsomely then adequately. I did offer my partner money many times at this period. Each time he just looked at me angrily. When I

The only work coming in was from the student circuit. A tour of Britain's universities: this was a time for people to have a cheap laugh at *Norman and Freddy*. Within the shortest of times cynicism had become the rule rather than the exception. I do blame that little prick Ben Elton. The truth was he wasn't fit to lick our boots, and within the history of British comedy he and his ilk are fucking nonentities. And don't try to tell me that we were stale and part of a different generation. I say to that: funny is funny. Something is either funny or it isn't. That prick wasn't funny. He was so unfunny it physically hurt – but I'm running ahead of myself.

It was especially difficult to think rationally whilst engaged in such an odious task. I wrote down what I could and when I could. We had been doing this weeks before his death, and I tried to continue.[79] Whatever task I set myself I do try to tackle it in a professional and dedicated fashion.[80] A long time ago now Les Dawson[81] said to me:

'Freddy, why don't you set the record straight?'

Should anyone enquire after the true history of Norman Riddell and Freddy Foster I will have it to hand.

---

eventually moved in to take care of him he demanded rent. I expected nothing as his carer.

[79] I have many of these pages and notes to help me with this now.

[80] I pride myself that I have been so governed all my life, whether it be performing, joke writing, or indeed socialising.

[81] Les was an absolute gentleman and an absolute stand-up genius, regardless of the fact he told me he was 'drawn to failure.' Well read, talented, and gifted way beyond most of his contemporaries; Norman and Freddy included. I had been complaining to him that Norman and Freddy had been overlooked and our material was better than many others who were enjoying fruits more than us. I was lying though, to perhaps impress him. I think Les knew but was just being his kind and polite self. On Norman, Les was pretty astute. He said to me that Norman's 'main aim in life appeared to be to make love to every woman in sight.' As for Norman – a man not given to compliments – he said of Les in 1993, 'He was a fucking Prince that man.'

11

1970

'An elephant…hmnn…an elephant…'[82]
Norman Riddell's last words before
boarding the Silver Princess, July 1970

i

The leaving behind of the 1960s was to be welcomed by some. It had left a sour taste in the mouths of most, though. A generation came crashing down to reality. Some never recovered, like the '50s acts who couldn't make the '60s leap. But when Robert Rennie had said that these were 'great days', little did any of us realise that they were ending and *Norman* and *Freddy* would spend the first two years of the new decade on a boat.[83]

There is something of the idea of punishment on the cruise ships. There is a sense of failure in every entertainer's heart. You cannot get bookings in your own country and so you are

---

[82] Norman had just learned from The Stage and Television Today that Dickie Henderson's sit com *A Present For Dickie*, in which Dickie starred alongside an elephant, was to be dropped by ITV. The intention was to launch the entertainer into the new decade. The show not only flopped, it would ultimately end Henderson's TV career. Mini the elephant did not capture the public imagination. Some years later Bernie Winters would replace his partner, and brother, Mike, with a St Bernard dog called Schnorbitz. It was a huge success. The brothers had been partners for over twenty years. Possibly Mike's replacement was the greatest insult in comedy duo history. That's showbiz, folks.

[83] Actually, there were several ships. We picked up another in Australia, and another in the U.S. This took much time and planning on my part. Obviously Norman did sweet F.A. All the reader has to know is that we were at sea for a couple of years. If anyone wishes to find out more about the ships might I suggest a maritime volume of cruise ships of the 1970s?

cast adrift to contemplate that failure in a limbo that is closer to hell than heaven.

The cruise company knocked up posters that somehow nailed our humiliation to the mast. *Sunshine Tours In Association with Sunfruit Proudly Present Stars of Stage and Television Norman and Freddy… With The Lovely Janice.*

And there we were, staring out, our heads floating in yellow starburst. On the left, my face long, with eyebrows raised, eyes looking to the sky, mouth seriously pissed off – in an exasperated, humorous kind of way. And then Norman: that cheeky smile; red face; exaggerated wink. The truth is that we were both working at it and hoped that the punters wouldn't see the desperation. When I think of that poster now, I am surprised that no one came looking for us with murder in their eyes. The shot of Janice was separate on the lower right, cheesecake, full figure, glitter, high heels, big smile and breasts thrust out. She looked great considering she'd lost the baby well into her second trimester only a few months before.

Norman's face in the poster seemed to connect with Janice. It seemed to be saying: *I'll be having some of that.* The whole thing was naughty; it was cheeky, sexually playful and teasing. Looking back, it so much belonged to another time. But then it was all about family viewing smut: Praise the Lord! Over the years my view on comedy had changed dramatically. I came to feel that I wanted to reflect something that was going on in society, maybe something more erudite, or dare I say *edgy?* It wasn't going to happen on a cruise ship, that much was certain. We weren't *comedian's* comedy, and we were rarely *people's* comedy. Deep down I still despised our audiences, maybe more so with every tortuous year. The public take you as you present yourself, and that's you pinned down forever in their consciousness. They were stupid and ignorant and laughed at words like *boobs* and *wee-wee, how's your father,* and *cobblers,* and a hundred other trigger words and phrases that tried to brace up a thousand unfunny stories. Before we left for the cruise Peter Cook[84] was being interviewed on some telly show. At one point he said, *What? Like Norman and Freddy funny?* That got a big laugh. I turned it off, sat down, and wept.

---

[84] I really admired Cook. It went beyond the respect given to a fellow professional. There was an element of envy in my admiration. I envied him his lifestyle which seemed more modern than I could ever be at that time. I envied him the crowd he was part of and the ground that I saw he was breaking. While Norman and I were delivering a tired gag to Dickie Valentine he was opening up The Establishment Club and really nailing down political comedy in our country. Ben Elton and some of that crew thirty odd years later should have taken a leaf out of his book. He had style, intelligence, and good looks. All I could say was that he had a different kind of comedy. I went twice to The Establishment Club. The first time was after an invitation from Cook himself. There was some confusion about this invite as I believed it to be an invite to perform. It was not. It was an invite to just come along. I believed it to be an error of misunderstanding and did make it along on the night that Lenny Bruce was playing. Even with Peter Cook laying a path, Britain had never seen or heard anything like Bruce in full flow. There was a great element of the improvisational about his performance. It was something that I didn't really take to at first and found the genius American difficult.

12

1970

Life is a tragedy when seen in close-up, but a comedy in long-shot.
Charlie Chaplin

ii

NORMAN: *I've been on a cruise before.*
FREDDY: *You've been on a cruise before?*
NORMAN: *That's right. How'd you know?*
FREDDY: *You've just told me.*
NORMAN: *When was that then?*
FREDDY: *Just there.*
NORMAN: *Where?*
FREDDY: *Here. Here, just now. You told me you'd been on a cruise before.*
NORMAN: *I was too, y'know. Well, it was a booze cruise.*
FREDDY: *What's a booze cruise?*
NORMAN: *It's a night out drinking on a boat.*
FREDDY: *And how was it?*
NORMAN: *Didn't know I was on a boat until I went for a taxi.*
   Enter JANICE.
JANICE: *Hello, boys.*
NORMAN: *Hello, Miss. Are you lost?*
JANICE: *No, I'm one of the dancers. Do you dance?*
NORMAN: *Not much, but I bet I could show you a few moves.*
JANICE: *Oh, you're a cheeky one.*
FREDDY: *Right, bright spark, show her your moves.*
NORMAN: *What? Now?*
FREDDY: *Yes. Go on. Show the beautiful girl your dancing. I'd be interested in seeing that myself.*
JANICE: *Haven't you seen your friend dance?*

FREDDY: *He can't dance. He was only saying that to impress you.*

NORMAN goes into a gentle tap routine in the background.

FREDDY: *He can't dance. He's got two left feet.*

FREDDY turns to see NORMAN pick up speed and perform a short and frantic tap dance. NORMAN stops at the end and offers JANICE his arm. She takes it and they exit, smiling lovingly at each other.

FREDDY: *Thank-you, ladies and gentlemen and welcome to Sunshine Cruises brought to you by Sunfruit. My name is Freddy. The one that walked off was Norman. And the beautiful gal was Janice. Welcome, welcome, welcome to Sunshine Cruises and we hope – we know – that you're going to have a ball. You're leaving the grey skies of England for some of the most beautiful views this planet has to offer.*[85]

And that was the very first sketch that we did on a ship. It was July 1970 and Britain still looked like post-war fucking Berlin.

---

[85] This was the actual script. I kept all of our material for many years. Although no longer with me I remember huge sections of our career material. It is interesting to note that it belongs to another age as much as the early repetition of lines in jokes. The history of civilisation can be shown through the history of the joke.

13

1970

Freddy: Laughter is the greatest medicine.
Norman: I hope there's no one sick in our audience.
First show on a cruise ship, 1970

The cruise creates a world of its own. It is a world I didn't
particularly take to. Every day I would long for when we hit
land. I hadn't realised just how much of my world had been
taken up with schmoozing with the famous. I enjoyed the
clubs, the parties, and the company. Norman could quite
happily sit in the same pub every night for the rest of his life.
On land or sea. As long as the barmaids changed he'd be fine.
Janice could have stayed at home with her recreational heroin
until she had been sold a bad lot. Me? I just craved company.
I also craved the news. Although we got news it seemed
second hand. And I didn't seem part of it. The ship was
torture of a particular kind for me and I had no one to talk to
about it.[86] One night I sought out a sympathetic ear with
Janice. I had slipped into her cabin in the pretext of
borrowing a pair of nail scissors. She was alone and sitting on
a chaise longue with a scotch in her hand.

'I just came to see if you had a pair of nail scissors. Not
disturbing you? Is he here?'

She snorted and swung her glass around. The cabin was
quite large and had a large bed with an unmade satin quilt on
top. The drinks cabinet was fake tigerskin and some dirty

---

[86] There is something that no one ever says but is as true as the earth: travel
is a sad business. It really doesn't matter where one may travel; the process
of the journey is akin to heartache, but we ignore it. Why is that, I wonder? I
shall make a pencil note to remind me to give this more thought. I think it
has something to do with loneliness, and man's place on the earth.

glasses sat on top. I wasn't fussed so I poured a drink without asking.

'I'm glad I caught you alone. Needed to bend an ear.'

'Secrets, eh?' she said low with her head shaking. 'Freddy and Janice with their secret world.'

'I just wanted to say the ship thing isn't forever. I'm working on things. Things for when we get back.' This wasn't a lie as I worked most of the time. But with the ship it was a different matter. We weren't gone more than a few days and I was homesick. It consumed most of my thoughts and kept me awake at night.

'Get back to what, mister? The rag-bag life we've been living?'

'Come on now, Janice, all artistes have to struggle.'

She was still staring into her drink, still shaking her head. I confess I hadn't really heard a negative Janice before. For that, Norman was your man. He was capable of sucking the song from a lark.

'There's no get out of jail free card now, Freddy boy. Our moment's gone and we're scarpering for cover. If we don't wake up this'll be our Titanic, I tell you.'

I had tried to talk with Norman and Janice about the loss of the baby, but they had shied away from those conversations. All Norman had said was it was *not meant to be*. And that was it. Since then Janice came off stage and was another person. She only shone in front of the audience.

'Tomorrow I'm going to start again. I'm going to be young Janice again. I'm going to be full of spirit and fun and pretend I'm young again. Isn't that the way to be, mister?'

'Well, I never trust anyone who's constantly up. They're either a fool or a liar. Maybe they only think of themselves and close their eyes and ears to the world. I don't know. I do know that I want you to be happy again. I want that old Janice back again.'

She fell into a silence while I sat down beside her. What I had left behind. A career? Something of that certainly. Maybe if I had played my cards differently and been more 'accommodating' with Robert Rennie. Maybe also if I had straightened Norman out with his attitude and with the booze. Maybe if I hadn't been seeing Janice on the sly. I've never been one for regrets. Never.

'Secrets,' she mumbled.

It struck me that maybe she had let her mouth run away with her. Maybe the cat had fled the bag and the game was a bogie. Maybe Norman was party to every clinch we ever had.

'You haven't told him about us?' I tried to pull her close to me, but she stood up quickly and staggered over to the dressing table.

She had her back to me but I could see her front reflected in the mirror. Her face was wet and her stage eyes had smudged and run. She hung onto her drink like a bus strap, swinging around trying to keep her balance.

'Secrets, Freddy? I have enough to open my own secret service. You don't know half of it, do you?'

'I'm thinking of Norman,' I lied easily. I was and I wasn't. I did consider him, but in the long run I had more selfish motives. Her body sank into the dressing table stool.

'Ah yes, little Norman. You wouldn't want him hurt, would you? Maybe the two of you should be lovers.'

Panic set in but I tried not to show it. I spoke calmly and quietly: 'What have you said?' Her reply confirmed that she had said nothing.

'Said? About what?'

'It doesn't matter. I just came to talk to you about everything that's happened. About where we are.'

'Well, we seem to be on a big boat and will be for quite some time. Gets us away from that fucking country for a while. Puts the hems on you waltzing around like an Aunt

73

Fanny at every piss-poor party that every bottom of the bill holds. Keeps all the world's secrets contained, eh?' And then she wagged her finger at me. 'Or so you think…'

I stood up to return my empty glass to the bar. Janice's body had slumped over, although she had not fallen. Her glass was tight in her hand.

'I could've been a different person…with a baby…Someone to look after…A little life…'

'Yes. I'm sorry. It might have changed Norman too.'

Her body was pulled up as though on strings: 'Him? Oh yes, it would have changed him!' She started to laugh. 'Me having that kid would certainly have changed him. You see, Freddy old chap, he's a bit of an old fashioned old cuss is my husband.' At this she tapped the side of her nose. 'Know what I mean?'

I really didn't like to see and hear Janice like this. But she came closer to me I saw the pupils like pinholes.

'How the hell did you manage to score on a ship?'

She turned away towards the bar. 'Where there's a will…' She held up her glass.' You want one?'

'No. I'll just…'

'Scurry away will you? Just scurry away like a rat? Well, mister, let me tell you what happens to rats on sinking ships.'

'I believe they desert them.'

'Yes. That's the word. Desert. Treacherous rats desert their ship. And the ship keeps her secrets.'

'You should go to bed.'

'That's part of the problem. I went to bed.'

'Where is Norman, anyway?'

'Where the hell do you think? Planted between the legs of some top deck floozie. Providing her bit of cruise rough.'

I thought I would change the conversation.

'I thought of another joke. Might be able to do something with it. It's for Norman.'

And she laughed. She threw her head back and laughed *at* me.

'Is this any sort of life for adults?'

I just ignored this and charged ahead:

'An Englishman walks into a bar and orders a pint of ale: an Irishman walks in and orders a Guinness; and a Scotsman walk in and orders a whisky. All night long they do not meet. What a waste.'

She raised her drink clutched arm in the air and blew a raspberry. I stood to leave, uncomfortable.

'You leaving?'

'An early night. A boy needs his beauty sleep.'

She repeated the line in a mocking tone. I was at the cabin door when she called me. I turned to look at her. She was pointing her finger, rather like the witch in Snow White.

'Truths and lies, little man. Truths and lies.'

I left.

14

1970

Freddy: You'd be lost without me.
Norman: I'd be successful without you.
                    The Sacha Distel Show, 10th November,
                    1968

The lack of fresh air below deck on ships is sickening. Even with air conditioning. When I left Janice I needed some fresh air so made my way to the deck. It was a warm and beautiful evening but it was ruined by the vulgar noise of some families. I decided to have a cigarette and retire to my bed. An elderly couple I later discovered to be Ethel and George McAuley from Prestonpans said hello to me. Ethel said she was looking forward to the next night's show. I informed her there was no show as we were docking in the early hours and the passengers would no doubt want to explore the Greek town during the day and evening.

'You're not the passenger who took her TV on board because she didn't want to miss Coronation Street?'

She looked surprised until it dawned on her I was teasing.

'Oh, you…' she scolded, tapping me on the arm.

I turned to George:

'You've got your hands full here.' He just smiled.

'Oh, George can't speak. He's got cancer. We came on the cruise to enjoy ourselves; see something of the world before he dies.'

'I'm sorry to hear that.'

'Oh, we have Christ's comfort.'

'What?'

'We know he's going to a better place.'

My sympathetic look was as much for that delusion as

George's illness. I finished my cigarette. The original warm breeze had turned chilly and I rubbed my hands.

'Well, I'm going inside now. Catch your death here.'

We said our goodnights and I went indoors. It wasn't until I was inside I realised what I had said and started to giggle. I returned to my cabin and went to bed with a very large whisky and a biography of Max Bygraves.[87] I awoke in the middle of the night with the dark figure of Norman hanging over me.

'Bastard,' he said. And then he left.

---

[87] As the years went on my reading habits were eclectic to say the least. Biographies I loved, and the classics. But I could occasionally be seen with a gardening book in my hand, even though I have never owned a garden. The biographies were, of course, lies. They were built on what you knew and what you wanted to be true. Not one of your favourites was as portrayed. And although you knew this deep down, when made public after some scandal, the truth would be akin to finding out that your parents were Fred and Rosemary West. You would perhaps feign betrayal, or perhaps you would build an Everest of absolute denial. Well, dearest reader, you might say, it's only one person's opinion, but might I point out that the truth cares not a jot for opinions. Dare I attack even my own readers? Heavens! And say many of you got what you deserved? For you got what you helped create. So early on and Freddy has distanced his audience. But surely only a money grabbing little shit would care about that?

15

1970

Freddy: Remember The Go Between? The past is a foreign country.
Norman: So is Latvia.
                    The Silver Princess, December 1970.

The passenger capacity of our ship was just over 2000. It was over 1,000 feet in length with a beam over 100 feet. I had read this information several times from various information points around the lower decks. Had I been banged up I would have had the bricks in my cell counted within a week.

Even on a ship this size it was surprisingly easy to avoid avoid each other for the first couple of days, and apart from meals and performances all three of us did this. Maybe it was the actual shock of leaving that made us crave our own space and our own time. I was hurt beyond belief that this was not like the holiday I had envisioned; it was more of a banishment. I loved Britain so much. But Freddy can be a realist and so he soon accustomed himself to a life on the ocean wave.

Likewise, Norman seemed calmer and happier. Janice looked resigned to it all. We each had our own coping strategy.

It was the early hours when the ship maneuvered its way into the port at Piraeus. Somewhere in my dreams I heard the ship's bulk creak into place. I had intended going on deck for this but sometimes sleep can be preferable to experience. I would imagine most of the passengers were caught up in a similar situation. I cannot speak for Norman. He was an irregular sleeper at the best of times. *A waste of time*, he would say. I'm not sure that the time he saved was any more productive than rest.

And so we all awoke to a different smell, a different sound and a steadiness underfoot. The engine's thrum had been silenced and voices were more audible as a result. It was those voices that helped raise me from my comfortable scratcher and into the shower. I was dressed in a jif and heading, ravenous, towards the breakfast room. The only difference between the breakfast room and the dinner room was the menu. It was the same room but with an ornate card outside identifying it as a morning, midday, or evening meal. As I entered, I saw Norman sitting at a table with a tomato juice in his paw. Some passengers recognised me.

A morbidly obese man stood in front of me:

'Are you Norman or Freddy?'

'Freddy.'

'Thought you weren't the *lovely* Janice!' His laughter exploded as he looked to his family for reaction. I recognised his laugh from the deck noise pollution. I smiled indulgently as I often do in those circumstances, and refrained from telling him to fuck off.

As I was getting my prunes and orange juice, I thought about questioning Norman about the night before but the thought of a morning argument was sour in my head.

'Mind if I sit?'

He just grunted and looked at his drink. I realised he was not undergoing a revolution of abstinence. The drink he held was a Bloody Mary. He smelled of stale booze and stale cigarettes.

We reviewed the previous night's show. We always did this, and old Norman could often get quite animated. There was rarely an argument, though. We both knew what worked and what didn't. We discussed what needed cut or what needed work. All of this was dictated by audience laughter, and our instinct. The first of these is one of life's great mysteries. No one actually knows why we laugh, why the body reacts in such a way, why the hahaha sounds come out. We can explain most of our human actions and reactions but not that. How could I not be interested in such a thing? The second cannot be taught, it grows out of the years you work the stage.

After this chat, I returned to the breakfast bar and got both of us scrambled egg and toast. He didn't ask for food but forked at the egg and stuffed it between two slices of bread. It was gone in seconds. Looking after Norman did not just happen when the MND took hold.

'Janice was ill last night,' I offered.

'Ill?'

'She's back on something. Didn't you notice?'

'I didn't see her.'

'Did you row?'

'I didn't see her.'

I suggested that he go back to his cabin and see her. I also mentioned a shower and change of clothes. He put up no resistance to this request but got up and left the room. I lit a cigarette. I heard the fat man laugh loudly in the corridor. Before the door closed.

16

1970

*Freddy: One thousand and one cleans a big, big
carpet for less than half a crown.
Norman: Her majesty will be pleased.*
            The Lulu Show, 20ᵗʰ July 1969.

It was near noon before we reconnoitered on the harbour front. I was alone sitting at a *kafeneio* sipping on a delicious coffee.[88] It was served in a demitasse cup, strong and rich with the grounds left in. Before having my second cigarette of the day I sampled a couple of Koularakia cookies. The sweetness of these buttered biscuits took away the taste of my foul morning prunes. The waiter, a young boy with a friendly or flirtatious manner gestured that I dunk the savouries: so, I dunked. If I hadn't been watching my waistline I would have sampled more. Physically I have always been *wiry*. I have to work at this. Norman referred to my body shape as '*a streak of piss.*' I left the *kritsinia*[89] in the breadbasket as my nicotine habit was crying out for its fix.

From where I sat, I could see layer upon layer of narrow streets rising skyward but at the same time rooted by age and history. Cobbled paths folded into each other and on each layer a row of shops, houses and bars waited for another invasion of tourists.

---

[88] Sitting at a table people watching with a coffee or a wine is surely one of life's greatest pleasures. In the very early days the café where Norman and I met had a great Gaggia machine. Steam poured from it like a geyser. It was probably then my lifelong love of coffee was formed. Although these days it comes at a price: my bones tend to stiffen up. I feel that rigor mortis is setting in early.

[89] It has been my routine in life to jot down words that are unfamiliar to me, whether that is in a foreign language or in my own tongue.

I pulled hard on my cigarette and let the smoke fill my lungs before exhaling. A Mediterranean breeze blew coolly but it couldn't cut though the sandy dryness of the midday heat. I thought how far I had travelled from my home in Glasgow. My cream coloured trousers,[90] sandals and blue shirt, topped off with a Panama hat might have presented a *tourist* but from where would be a matter of debate. The houses with their terracotta rooftops might have been older than the tenements of my childhood, but coats of whitewash gave them a sun-bleached beauty. The houses of my upbringing were dark, heavy spaces that seemed set out for the sole purpose of crushing my young spirit and youthful dreams.[91]

Norman and Janice poured off the ship with a hundred others. Ever the one to be the centre of attention he was physically picking her up while she screamed like a banshee, clutching on to a large straw hat. The hat was similar to one Bardot had been pictured wearing at the time.[92] Norman was wearing what seemed to me to be a golfing cap. Although we had seen sunshine in the last few days his glow was more alcohol blast than ultra violet rays. Janice looked as fresh as Doris Day.

'You two look happy,' I said as they approached. Janice was

---

[90] In a few years' time all of my light-coloured slacks would be given to a local charity store. The prostate has inadvertently contributed to the feeding of many starving children.

[91] Now, as I read that back, it seems very revisionist in some ways, or perhaps more knowing. I have many memories of those times, the slow days and dark nights; muffled underwear onanism; a cupped hand to the toilet, a creaking floorboard and cold lino. Of such things are growing boys made.

[92] Janice was very much the opposite of Bardot in looks but certainly admired her style. This was often reflected in her choice of hats. For some years she always wore a similar hat to that which Bardot wore in Vie Privée. And then a cowboy hat that BB sported in the ludicrous western Shalako. This film was adapted from a Louis L'Amour novel. I had not read the novel. Life is far too short. When the French starlet went off the celebrity radar Janice took to wearing berets for the rest of her life.

dressed in white shorts and flip flops and a surprisingly high-necked orange coloured top. She looked lovely. Norman was wearing a Paisley pattern shirt, khaki shorts, and sandals.

'You look like a prick,' he said.

I whipped off my hat and asked if it was too much.

'No,' he replied. 'You just look like a prick.[93]

On that mildly humorous note we went off to explore the town.

On the second level street, I made something of a fool of myself, and Norman would tell the story for years to come. I had been admiring the Greek plates and pottery on sale. Most of the designs depicted ancient Grecian history and mythology; men in battle, swords, and spears at the ready. Janice was looking at what she was told was Hellenic reproduction jewelry and Norman was being his usual flippant self.

'For that price, lass, I want new.'

While they walked ahead I went indoors where a selection of plates had been hung on the wall. I was glad of the chance to get out of the sun if only for a few brief moments. It was cool and dark, which didn't, I believe, show off the plates to their full advantage. In the corner sat a grey haired, nut brown old man. He was in the process of filling his pipe when I entered. He stopped what he was doing and I nodded to him and said *gamoto horia sou*.[94] He nodded and continued pushing the tobacco into the bowl of the pipe.

---

[93] This *humour* of Norman's I called *doing a Fanny*. It referred to the rudest, most offensive person ever to grace the television screen, Fanny Craddock. If she hadn't committed career suicide on Esther Rantzen's *Big Time* in 1976 someone would surely have crème bruleed her before long. To put the icing on the woman's undead credentials she refused to visit her partner of thirty-five years while he went through the latter stages of cancer. I'll speak no more of the woman but to quote her long-suffering Johnny: *And if you follow the recipe, all your doughnuts will look like Fanny's.'*

[94] A greeting I had learned from the friendly purser.

Some of the plates, I felt, could have done with a good dusting. I was, though, quite taken with a particular design of a Greek water carrier – a beautiful brunette who would not have gone amiss in the London Go-Go scene. I was removing my purse from my waistcoat pocket ready to barter when Janice appeared at the door. She leaned in and hissed at me, all the time through apologetic smiles to the old man.

'It's not a shop.'

I froze. 'What?'

'It's not a shop. It's someone's house, you berk.'

Behind her in the brightness of the street I could see Norman's head going up and down like a nodding donkey, and I could hear his laughter like an actual braying one.

I was flustered and kept repeating *gamoto horia sou* to the homeowner, who stared at me as he lit his pipe. Outside Norman was slapping his knees laughing loudly. We all held hands and ran down the narrow streets laughing like children.

Mid-afternoon we stopped at a beautiful tavern. Before eating we polished off three beers and a bottle of wine. With no show that evening drunkenness was inevitable. We forgot all and let the alcohol take us to a safe place; a place where we could put away our petty cruelties for a few hours. Janice returned from several visits to the toilet brighter than when she went in. Whatever her current drug of choice was it certainly wasn't heroin. Norman seemed to notice nothing. He was too much occupied telling the filthiest stories to anyone who would listen. The noise and the drunkenness drove its way deep into the night and early morning.

17

2004

'Comedy is an escape, not from truth but from despair; a narrow escape into faith.'

Christopher Fry, *playwright.*

March 25ᵗʰ

I still feel giddy thinking about that day at the hospital. In the waiting area, a mute television was tuned to the news that Blair was having a meeting with Gaddafi. Images repeated again and again and subtitles formed letter by letter. He was offering the 'hand of friendship' to the 'mad dog' of the Middle East. Muammar al-Gaddafi's terrorist activities across Europe would be buried in the desert sand, and the 'rats' and 'cockroaches'– as he called his people – would be silenced. No one except me was watching. The news ticker at the bottom of the screen had my attention. We only waited five minutes before being called in. God bless the NHS.

I got up with Norman and Janice and behind them towards the door. As they entered the young doctor blocked my way.

'Mr. Foster?'

He sounded like an autograph hunter.

'Yes.'

'Could you perhaps wait while I speak with Mr. Riddell and his wife?'

'Yes,' I mumbled. 'Yes, of course. Of course.'

The door closed and I returned to my seat. Moments before Norman had been staring at the floor; Janice had been clutching a handkerchief in one hand and his hand in the other. They had been leaning into each other like knotted fingers. It's how I pictured them as I sat again and watched the news roll round.

Man: Doctor, doctor, I'm tired all the time!
Doctor: Lie down and tell me about it.

Man: Doctor, doctor, I can't lift my foot properly when I walk.
Doctor: That's a bit of a drag.

Man walks into a bar and orders a pint. Barman pours the pint. Man struggles to lift it. Turns to the barman: "I know I asked for a heavy, but this is ridiculous!"

Man: Doctor, doctor, I have shlurred speech.
Doctor: What?

Man: Doctor, doctor, I keep tripping up and I'm clumsy. What can I do?
Doctor: Have you considered joining the circus?

Man: Doctor, doctor, are the test results back?
Doctor: Yes. You've passed. I'm sorry.
I turned my gaze from the screen. The news wasn't good.

Here I am, milking my memory, my shifting memory. Let me describe. The sun is beating down outside, and a breeze comes in from the coast. A Panama hat lies on the bedspread. I sit down and write. I stand by a window watching the sleet come in from the west, cold and miserable, and think of a child and his mother standing on a beach doon the waater, freezing, with the laughing sea creeping up his shins. Different locations and different times. What is this thing I do? This Freddy? This Norman or Janice? Or this mother? What is this thing I do?

2

18

2004

A man goes to the doctor for a bowel check-up. He's asked to drop his trousers and bend over. He does this warily, for he is not a man used to such positions. The doctor snaps on a pair of surgical gloves and pulls them up tightly to the fingertips.

'Now you might feel a bit of discomfort here,' the doctor says as he slides a long middle finger slowly into the man's rectum. 'Do you feel anything?' the doctor asks. The man slowly turns his head and says 'Yes. I think I love you.'

Catalan joke

Medication. Woe betide anyone who talks to me about medication. Riluzole, Phenytoin, Carbamazepine. Hyoscine Hydrobromide, Glycopyrrolate, Atropine, Morphine, Gabapentin. And what about the botulinum injections? Tizanadine. This was soon replaced by Dantrolene, and then back again. Then there was the Gabapentin when the physio wasn't enough. Benzodiazepines he seemed to get hooked on. Who the hell was I to argue? It seemed like the last years were a constant routine of drugs of varying sorts. Some we were told might have side effects. My dear Norman experienced all side effects. I'd seen him vomiting, falling down; I'd felt his heart as it beat hard and fast in his chest. I'd seen him sit on the toilet trying to squirt a piss from his bladder and cry as only a few drops trickled down. He cried as well with the pain of constipation. Janice would rub his arse while he sat on the toilet, trying to massage and ease the bowel movement. This is the humiliation that life brings to us. It serves up the foul and disgusting, yet there are many who say it is a gift and should not be taken away.

'Would you get me some water, Freddy?'

The atropine which he had tried in pill form was now being injected but it was drying up his saliva glands. His skin as well was looking bad. Janice had been rubbing Oil of Ulay into his hands and face to counter this but the side effects were working at a quicker rate than the cream.

'There's your water.' I carefully handed him a small glass. If he couldn't hold it I would have guided it towards his mouth, but he seemed fine this particular day. Sometimes his coordination was poor – again a result not of the disease but of the medication. His big mitt could still wrap itself tightly around a glass. As he brought the water to his lips the concentration on his face was total. He took the drink in small sips. Between sips he would say *aaah* quietly. I couldn't take my eyes off him. I didn't know what to expect. Maybe I thought he was about to keel over.[95] Maybe there was a God after all and he was benevolent when he could be bothered. Maybe Norman's heart would just stop beating and the misery that the disease promised wouldn't be forthcoming. Maybe I would be left alone to get on with the pointlessness that I considered life. Maybe Janice would come home a widow and be released from her caring duties. But these maybes relied on the benevolence of a non-existent deity. There would be no respite, no reprieve, no escaping the cold light of day fact that this disease offered nothing in the way of hope, or indeed rest.

'I was told my voice would go.'

This was a statement intended to draw me again into a discussion about assisted suicide. The law of the country was very clear on that: you would be treated as no better than a

---

[95] There are some that associate themselves with death in quite a perverse way. They hear of someone dying, someone they barely know, but at the end of the night they'd be best friends and want everyone to know how upset they are. I have tried to avoid them. As I have tried all my life to avoid sickness. The truth is it sucks the life out of you caring for another person. It's like an act of killing. The stink of sickness sticks to your clothes; it shows on your face, and how you hold yourself.

criminal, a murderer no less, and you would be dealt with harshly. No argument about love and caring would be considered. No discussion about mercy would be entertained. Under our law suffering would not only be allowed, it would be encouraged. Our caring society. It was a cloak to hide the cruelty of the law. Did it take me that long in life before the veil was lifted from my eyes? Yes. Quite simply, yes. I was sixty-four years old. Sixty-four years walking this planet, blinded by the irrelevant, admiring the callous and the cruel; looking up to a perverse ideal of success.

Aaaah…

It wasn't just the medication. I took him down to the clinic twice a week at first. The funny thing about that was when we started it was as though he was going to get well again. There was some hope. But the physiotherapy wasn't a cure; it was a way of easing the muscle cramps.

'What this is all about, Mr. Riddell, is trying to optimize your physical ability. To keep you moving and as normal as possible for as long as possible.'

Those words were from Norman's first physiotherapist, Jacqueline Stoddart. She was the cocaine to life's regular dose of mogadon. How she stayed positive in her job was beyond me. A daily routine of the dirty rag of illness of strangers would have done for me.

'I get help at home.'

She looked up at me smiling from the bamboo chair she was sitting on:

'Hello. You're Mr Riddell's partner?'

'Over forty years. For my many sins.'

'I think that's wonderful. Those must have been difficult times.'

'They were good times, lass.' And Norman gave her his best lecherous wink that carried with it an unspoken acknowledgement that there were stories to be told.

She giggled as she addressed me: 'Well…'

'Freddy,' I offered.

'Well, Freddy…you play an important role in all of this. You will be handling Mr Riddell —'

'You can call me Norman. If shandy pants here can get away with first name terms. Tell me, what do you mean by *handling*?'

'You spoke to the doctors. Your mobility, your functioning in normal daily tasks will…'

'It's all going to deteriorate. That's the long and short of it. We were told. We can cope.' I was choked up as I blurted out those sentences. Norman sighed and looked at me. I didn't know what the look was.

'What?'

'It's about safety. For instance, when you might be bathing – '

I had to stop the girl there. In those very early days of the disease natural resistance to the basics of palliative care was at the forefront. It takes time to put the self on the back burner.

'Look…'

'Jacqueline. Jacqueline Stoddart.'

'I'm just really here as a chauffeur today. I think that sort of thing can be dealt with by Janice.'

'Janice is my wife.'

I must confess the look on Jacqueline Stoddart's face was a picture True to its farcical situation, and more Ben Travers than Molière, Janice arrived on cue from stage right:

'Sorry I'm late. Those buses…'

19

2004

> *Norman: There's only one thing wrong with our*
> *act.*
> *Freddy: What's that?*
> *Norman: Our act.*
>
> University of Glasgow, March, 2001.[96]

I was a stupid man for most of my life. Of course, I told
myself that I was a cut above the ordinary. Wasn't I well read?
Couldn't I converse with the golden ones; the chosen ones?
Those that luck and chance isolated from the common herd?
Those that I admired – no, worshipped. I worshipped those
people. Was that my mistake? Did they all sense in me less of
an equal and more of an idolater? Were they stringing me
along all that time? Was the joke on Freddy Foster? Is that it?
Is that what I'd left my home for? My journey was directed by
the vicious laughter at my expense? Oh, Norman, your voice
is echoing now. I hear it. Were you the one who was right all
the time? That lack of respect that you held for all and tawdry
sundry. No one made an impression on you –

'At that time only Ken Dodd, lad. I was at an
impressionable age. But he just seemed to be his own man.
Later, maybe Les Dawson.'

You were your own man, Norman. I was never my own
man. Never. I was shaped by others. I was guided by others. I
was influenced by others. This whole broken life.

Aaaah…

---

[96] One of seven supporting bill to a one hit wonder. Getting Norman and
Freddy must have been seen as a joke. This might have been Norman's last
performance.

What is it that makes us? What shapes our destiny? I thought it was meetings and kowtowing to a show business elite.

Aaaah…

A fraternity that measures its pride in the cars owned, houses bought, holidays gained. It was never the work. Most of them were whores trading out their meagre talents to the highest bidder. They bent with the wind of change, if they could bend. They went with the flow of fashion. Grasping at the money at every opportunity.[97]

Aaaah…

'It took me a long time to appreciate water…'

He'd finished his water and delivered me from my thoughts. They seemed to be taking over a lot of my time then. Is that when I started writing this memoir? Maybe it was then that my life started to be less structured and ordered and I had to get it back in shape. I'm reminded of the Stravinsky quote about living by memory, not by truth. And my memory has been a strange fish.[98] It is the actions of the past that interest me. Perhaps there is something of the primitive artist in me. My past is much like the cave paintings of animals in movement, rather than the still life of the Dutch or Flemish School. My past is the movement of people and the change in places. How wondrous and beautiful memory is.[99]

---

[97] We all saw it. We see it still. On television, the grasping, desperation for more cash. We ignore it or maybe have come to accept it as something that goes with fame. We saw it early on in films. That style of acting, seemingly natural, easy going, *bloke-ish*, with Connery and Caine. It owed less to Stanislavski and more to poverty. Those constant turns of the head, looking back as though some little shit might creep in and steal their savings.

[98] I should warn you that I have the most precise memories of incidents that have never taken place. How we can ruffle the feathers of truth.

[99] In writing this I am trying to get to the truth of the matter of our lives; all of the matter. But where is that truth? I am beginning to feel it is less in the words than somewhere between those words. I say, above, what is this chapter's purpose? I shall admit defeat in an answer.

'Remember what you said about getting me into a swimming pool?'

'Throw in a few ice cubes.'

We both laughed. I remember placing my hand around his head just below the ear. I never touched Norman. But this was a gesture. It was the most natural thing in the world. He placed his hand upon mine and we said nothing.

20

2009

'Blimey, Doctor Livingston, I presume?'
Terry, when confronted with a black doctor
in the first episode of Terry and June,
October, 1979.[100]

Norman once described me as fastidious in my habits. I do like things to be just so. For this reason, I left Norman's torso on the living room floor and stood at the kitchen sink washing the dishes from our last meal together. We'd had carrot and coriander soup with wholemeal crusty bread and butter. Well, I had the bread as Norman's swallowing was poor. The soup had been entirely homemade. Some years before I had rejected all processed food and focused on the healthy and the fresh.[101] It had been instigated by Janice's cancer scare in 2004.[102] She had a breast removed in the summer of 2005 and by the spring of 2006 looked so fantastic I kidded her that she looked twenty-five again. She didn't, but she did look great. All three of us were over the moon at her recovery. I cooked for both of them many times. Janice couldn't cook and had to be nagged to eat fruit of any kind.

'A bunch of grapes and an apple wouldn't have saved my breast, Freddy.'

No, but maybe if she had eaten better she'd be with me

---

[100] The end of the 1970s and the casually racist joke could still get a laugh on British prime time TV.

[101] Even as a child I was a fussy eater. I couldn't eat liver until my mother convinced me it was *velvet steak*. I had aspirations from a young age.

[102] This was a matter of months after Norman's diagnosis. I must confess my agnosticism was rapidly giving way to rabid atheism. These were the only people that I had in my life. It's not as though they were by any standards old.

now. A few weeks ago, she could have helped prop him up in bed, as I did, and spoon-feed him that beautiful soup. Perhaps if she had been here things wouldn't have happened as they did. But we could fill this world with *maybe* and *perhaps* and I'm really not sure it would make a blind bit of difference to anything.

My mind is full of a million stories of Norman and Freddy. I liken it to a scrapbook – the one I never kept, but Janice did – where the pictures are not stuck in, but left on the page. When the book is picked up the pictures fall out. Such are my memories. Such are my ghosts. I am trying to keep our lives together as clear as possible. Even then I felt that someday soon I would want to account for my actions. And I want to tell our story accurately, for if I don't then who will? Even if that story condemns me.[103]

Thirty-five years was no mean feat. Sure, we had our ups and downs but that's how we survived. We would often mentally spar with each other. I ridiculed him for his Neanderthal thinking processes and he would in turn attack me – although with little verbal *finesse*.

'You mean *prig*, Norman,' I told him in a dressing room after a gig to celebrate the inspiring – for all *wannabe gals* – victory of Margaret Thatcher in 1979. That lady not only had intelligence, I believed, but she had grace and strength of

---

[103] My account is not a day in the life, to see the life in one day, although one minute slowed to several hundred pages would no doubt tell us much. Rather, this presents sections of a life that might give some substance to the life of those depicted. Perhaps by the end the reader would like to know more of Ethel and George McAuley and the cancer that prompted his cruise; perhaps more of my former neighbour, Bathsheba; or maybe Mrs Kopeykin? But I focus on those closest to me even though I do not subscribe to the idea that one should write about what one knows. On the contrary, we should all of us concern ourselves with what we do not know.

character.[104]

'I said *prick*,' he retorted while spitting out bits of vol-au-vent that he had filched from one of the club tables when we arrived.

'No,' I persevered. 'You mean *prig*. As in *I'm priggish in my behaviour*. That's what you want to say.'

'Don't tell me what I want to say. I know what I want to say and I say it. You are a prick, mate.' He was stabbing a finger at me while speaking, the finger punctuating the sentence. There was really no point in arguing with him when he was in this state.

Later, cracks began to show in my support for Thatcher. The first time was when we were discussing Norman's finances, or lack of them.

'I don't have a sausage.'

I had not long put my deposit down on a lovely little flat in Chelsea. I had saved. Norman had blown everything as soon as he got it. I considered this something of a mental illness.

'What? Didn't you put something by for a rainy day?'

'Come on, Freddy, lad, this is England. Every day can be a rainy day.'

'What are you going to do?'

'I'll turn my pockets out and present myself as a deserving case.'

'To whom?'

The word *whom* was probably asking for his mockery. For an Englishman, his use of his mother tongue left a lot to be desired.

'Whom? Whom is it now? Whom? I'll tell you *whom:* anyone

---

[104] For those who wish to criticise me for this fawning stupidity feel free. I was often blinded by the times I lived through. My background poverty is no excuse. Freddy is no hero in this memoir. If he is then he is indeed *flawed*. Or perhaps *failed*. And always be wary of a man who speaks of himself in the third person.

that'll listen and drop a penny in my – wait a minute, lad, let me say it – *hypothetical* cap.'

'Social Security?'

'There's a fucking misnomer.'

'You think the world owes you a living?'

'No, not the world. My country. Because I'm British I want Britain to take care of me. I took a chance with this profession. I sowed seeds –'

'I won't argue with that one.'

'I sowed seeds. There was no harvest.'

'Well, poor fucking you! You want to be a whining scrounger!'

At this Norman struck under the belt and not only winded me but wounded me also. I think his words shook me more than most things he had ever said up to that time. It's a truth that we can only really get to the people we know. The closer we are the more pain we can inflict. And he came up physically close in order to ram his words home steadily. He held my head in his hands and looked directly into my eyes:

'You think you remember where you came from, but you don't remember, lad. You don't remember. You only remember where you wanted to go.'

I suddenly had a memory of my mother crawling out of her scratcher at five in the morning to get to her cleaning job. I remembered her tucking me in with rough but warm blankets:

There you go, my son. Mammy will be back soon.

And she would leave me alone for hours. And I would fall asleep again and forget to get myself up for school.[105]

The cosy nostalgia couldn't protect me from Norman's words. I felt the chill of reality.

'I remember,' I replied quietly and sat to apply some colour.

---

[105] I have found several letters that my mother sent me over a period of years. There were many. I only have a few. I have included them in *Appendix 5*, should anyone be interested.

So, we had our ups and certainly had our downs, but when things were at the wire Norman Riddell was there for me, and when he needed me I would be there. In the early days I knew this, but little did I know then just how much my sweet friend would need me. The first sign of this was not through the motor neurone disease but through our fall from any kind of public grace. Nothing happened to us overnight – not like some bastards that I could mention. Our slide was from a certain kind of mediocrity into the elephants' graveyard of the business: pubs and panto. I'm not talking about the major pantos where a star carries a show; I'm talking about the small town, low budget embarrassment. The show that everyone in the business knows about but has the manners not to mention. These performances were beyond any jokes. We had been slipping over a period of years and both of us felt that maybe we needed a bit of R&R. Well, as much R&R as I can put up with. I'm not, and never have been, one for sitting around doing nothing. We had lost contract after contract as things were cancelled before we had a chance to put our moniker on the dotted.

The reasons were obvious: the world of comedy was changing before our very eyes. The heyday of Britain's good old boys was finally over. They all scampered back to their houses with the indoor heated pools and the Jags and Bentleys in the driveway. They had it sweet for so long. A new generation came up behind them and bit their arses. But they had their house, the architectural monument to all that they had worked for, or cheated for, and lied for. The house was the pinnacle of success. A car can be stolen or on loan; but a house? Maybe it's a Queen Anne Grade ii listed detached? Built maybe in the early 18th century? Maybe it has a double volume entrance hall and double reception room? Its own pool and private fucking cinema? Maybe you could invite the elite of society and tell them every penny was earned through hard graft. And you wouldn't be lying, would you? And you would just be speaking the truth when you'd say *maybe these out of work layabouts ought to get on their fucking bikes,* like Mr Tebbit senior had done in the 1930s? Dare I say that I would have happily been one of them? Oh, hang your head in shame, slumboy Freddy. Would Greco-Roman columns outside your front door have protected you from the sense of betrayal? Would your poor mammy be birling in her grave? We shall never know. As for the rest, their hatred for everything that made them would be slow in festering. They would be mocked by the new wave of youngsters and this would anger them. I sided with them totally. Well, you don't shit on your own doorstep. But had an element of complacency crept into their careers? If so, then it was understandable. There was nothing else and nothing entered television without going through them. Yes, there was the odd freak experiment, but that was never at peak viewing time on any day of the week. The upset came from a new generation of audience, tired of the well told joke. From what I could see they were tired of jokes *per-se.* They didn't want to escape their lives; they wanted the humdrum thrown in their faces. While the miners' strike tore the country to pieces, jokes would be made about the situation.[106] When the country had to pull together there was a so-called comic faction intent on disruption and poor satire. This was madness. It was not comedy. It was bile spewed forth by humourless individuals. Instead of fighting it the old guard ran for cover or tried to join the bandwagon.

---

[106] It is a strange turn of events but the very thing I complained about would slowly lift a veil from my eyes and I would see the country in a very different light. I was once told that a man starts off a socialist but with age and experience moves further to the right. I seem to have been the exception to that rule as my age headed north and my politics appeared to have caught the bus east. The new generation didn't have the class, or wit, or intelligence, of the Peter Cooks of this world.

Some scarpered with their undeclared tax, feeling lucky that they reached the finishing post without having been caught out. There would still be the golf three days a week; there would still be the girls, the lunches and the charity events. Most of them would still take a fee for these personal appearances, regardless of the needy cause. Not all of them, though. Of course, the new lads would have some of this cake too. What they didn't have, though, were jokes.[107] They had no respect for tradition either. One who sent particular shivers down my spine was Ben Elton: an un-funny man. I would watch him on television ranting on about politicians and missing all of the targets. This wasn't comedy; this was soap box oratory of the very poorest kind. Where was the craft in any of this man's work? Why didn't anyone just jump up and knife him? What that boy needed were lessons in gratitude, humility, and golf. There were moments, of course, when a shard of hope would break through. As when he interviewed, and was courteous, civil, and, some may say ingratiating

---

[107] Norman was good at listening in pubs and crafting stories to a couple of punchy lines. He came around to my flat once – once? Too many bloody times – three sheets to the wind. 'So', he said. 'How do you know a Hackney girl is having an orgasm?' I was in my dark red, louche, gentleman's satin finish pyjamas, if my memory serves me. I looked bewildered as he had woken me from a much-needed sleep. The question was repeated with the answer nailed on at the end. 'She drops her chips!' He told me to write it down as he would forget before he got home. I closed and locked the door and returned to bed. Moments later I got up and wrote down the joke. We could change the location depending on where we played. I returned to bed and was about to fall off into a deep sleep when the doorbell rang again. I knew it was him. 'It's three o'clock in the fucking morning, you drunken bastard.' If my annoyance even registered it was ignored. 'What does a Hackney girl use for protection?'
'I don't know.'
'A bus shelter.'
I closed the door for the last time that night. The jokes could never be used in our act. I often thought that Norman wasn't really near the knuckle; he was the knuckle.

towards one of our finest storytellers and politicians, Jeffrey Archer.[108]

I saw in the mirror Norman had stopped jabbing his finger in the air.

'Things aren't good, Freddy.'

'Things aren't good, Norman.'

For some reason he saw this reply as a piss take. It wasn't meant to be the beginning of a routine. He got up to walk out of the dressing room. As I remember it was Bernard Manning's Embassy Club[109] in Manchester. As Norman pulled open the door there was a large man with a shaven head standing before him.

'Norman and Freddy? You're on in five,' he said.

He stood there until Norman closed the door and opened his heart for the first time since I had known him. For this reason I do remember it verbatim.

'Look, Freddy,' he began, 'I've known you for a long time now.'

'Twenty odd years,' I chipped in.

'Shut the fuck up, I'm trying to tell you something important, he snapped back. 'You're such an irritating little tosser sometimes, Freddy. I want to talk about me for a minute. The past is gone. I don't know what I'm doing, why I'm doing it, and who I'm doing it for. The thing is I've not been feeling good.'

The past is gone? I thought that my ugly-beautiful partner was about to announce that he had the big C, but I was

---

[108] I jest, reader, I jest.

[109] Bernard Manning's World Famous Embassy Club to give it its full title. I truly thought Manning's act was often racist, sexist and homophobic but his quiet acts of generosity to many minorities hid a different side. He could be funny, but taken as a whole his act made me uncomfortable at the time. I think less of it now.

barking up the wrong disease. It was our act that was bothering him. It was about where we were and where we were going. And it was where he began.

'I met you when I was twenty-one years old. I was a hungry young kid with a sharp suit and a bag full of gags. Seven years before I saw a man who was to become a legend. That man was Ken Dodd, and the place was the Nottingham Playhouse. My mum and dad had taken me along as they did every now and again. That night I decided that I too wanted to be a comedian. I wanted to make people laugh. No, it fucking wasn't that. It was the fucking thrill of it all. It was the adoration. I'd never even kissed a girl. Imagine being adored by all these people. I decided that night that I wanted to be on the stage, not in the stalls. I wanted stardom and success.'

'Me too, Norman.'

I rolled up a Kleenex and batted it into a corner bin.

'You're missing the point, you little fossneck!'

'Now, Norman, your language really does need cleaning up.'[110]

At this point his hands clasped around my neck and the grip was tightened. I tried to push his arms outwards but it seemed to me that my partner was the victim of some kind of supernatural possession. He put his full weight behind the murderous attempt. I fell backwards off my chair and he followed on, breaking it as he fell awkwardly. I was trying my best to tell him that we had a show to get on, but it came out more as a strangulated muffle. Had the gentleman who had been at the door not returned I truly believe I would have lost my life that night. Such are the passions that professionalism can drive you to.[111]

---

[110] I made the assumption the Nottingham vernacular was a swear word. It was worse.
[111] I am usually prone to dramatizing situations to the hilt, but Norman's behaviour that night was extreme. I should have shut up and listened for I

'Couple of minutes, gents. And if there's any shirt-lifting[112] shenanigans in here you'll be out the front door 'fore you can say *boomps-a-daisy*.'

Norman looked at him, still strangling me, smiled, and said calmly:

'We're pros, you fucking gobshite.'

Before leaving the gentleman did warn us that Mr Manning would probably dock the price of a chair from our fee.

'Well,' said Norman, 'there goes our wages.'

When the door closed, Norman released my throat and fell over me crying. Bubbling, he said 'What's happening to us, Freddy? What's happening to us? Why can't we get the big gigs? Where did we go wrong?'[113]

I struggled to my feet and fixed my clothing in silence; my emotions were racing. Before I left the room, I looked back at him slumped in a chair:

'Full of sound and fury, signifying nothing,' I said as I closed the door behind me.

---

think he was obviously at breaking point. I found out much later he had dumped a girl that he had got quite attached to. One night stands were one thing but love affairs he thought were a proper betrayal. Norman did not seek a Mary Kay or a Dinah May. He loved Janice.

[112] The homophobic rhetoric of the average punter was a disgrace. In the business, many kept their preferences quiet lest they lose lucrative careers. I knew them all and respected their decisions. As they respected mine not to speak of my own relationships.

[113] Was it dearest Bob Monkhouse who said comedians suffer more than most because they are more in touch, they feel the pain of living? It took me years to understand a miner, or a cleaner, feels as much.

21

2007/Present[114]

*'I asked one half of the comedy duo, Mr Freddy Foster, how he would
describe the attractive new member of the now threesome.
"Rondo allegro," he replied dryly.
Striking a few comic notes you can catch Norman, Freddy…and Janice
this Friday on The Des O'Connor Show, only on ITV.'*
James Grafton, The TV Life, December 1973.

Where did we go wrong? Now there's a question that I have often
considered over the years, and the answer is very simple. We
were successful, but just not *as* successful as others. If success
can be measured in longevity, then Norman and Freddy were
indeed successful. We might not have been in the public eye
constantly, but we were known by both punter and performer.
That elusive key to the kingdom was, alas, not to be ours. I
thought of this while I stood at the kitchen sink washing
blood and bits from my hands. A red dry stain smudged
across a small scar between my middle and index finger. (A
flashing memory of a night in Sunderland. What was it
Shakespeare who said of scars reminding us the past was real?
Of course, he didn't have the benefit of a cuttings library.)
Some bits of flesh were stuck between my fingernails. I
fanned the fingers out and cleaned them. Strangely, that was
the first moment that I felt any sense of nausea. It was the

---

[114] I smile while writing this word: *present*. But, dear reader, you do not know
where I am. So you cannot imagine a table or a desk, or a wall or a garden, a
window or a door. I am inclined to go on in this mode for a while longer. It
is unfair and naughty of me, I know, but give your narrator this indulgence
at the very least. Let my story unfold in its own time. Let me revel in this
control that bit longer. If I was being interviewed by *The Paris Review* I would
tell them that unlike *Papa* Hemingway I write sitting down. There, enjoy that
morsel.

slightest of flesh pieces, no bigger than a maggot stuck to the skin that brought the swoon to my head and the churn to my stomach. I have removed a head,[115] hacked off feet, dismembered legs. And now I felt sick at the quotidian task of washing my hands. Something about the process reminds me of standing as a child at the sink, my mother washing my hands. From the window of that slum kitchen I could look over the absolute hopeless desolation that was Glasgow at the time. People packed in and told to make the best of it. Was it then I decided that was not for Freddy Foster?

Norman's flat was close to spotless. I worked through the night cleaning. It obviously needed some paint and a bit of plasterwork; it needed some windows replaced, and the pipes bled. Some things were done immediately following the terrible act. Food was scraped off and the plates washed. The soup pot that had always sat on top of the hob was shoved under the kitchen sink; I didn't know then it would be used soon enough for a gruesome broth. When I was pulling up the pillows a thought came of a time when he could hardly speak. Janice had been gone just under a year. He was lying down with his hand clutching a marker pen and the small whiteboard I had bought him.

'Fff...yay...' he said, or gurgled out.

I came close to him and turned the board up. It said *keep smiling*. I thought of that time while I puffed up the pillows. A Proustian moment, or was that just with smells? I could smell Norman in every part of the flat as well. It brought things

---

[115] I read over this and the memory came to me of that awful evening. I became the night sky; I became the running water. Was that perhaps shock settling in on my mind and body? Or perhaps closing of the distance between myself and the soup pot and head. We could be one. It was at Vauxhall Bridge. I had gone down to the bank so that I wouldn't be seen. apart from the eyes of a woman carrying a sheaf of corn. Carrying it through Pimlico I remember thinking Beardsley, Churchill and Joseph Conrad had walked those streets. Sans soup pot and head.

back. Bits of conversation, words, laughter. I asked him how he was and he told me he'd much rather be skiing.[116] He then pulled a crooked smile. That was so recently. Someone there and then not there. How do any of us contemplate such a catastrophe?

But it was clean. I should have done this when he was alive. I slid the suitcase with Norman's torso out of the door, along the landing and into the gaping lift. I pressed for the ground floor and waited. The door across from Norman's opened and a pale-faced girl appeared. She looked at me. I smiled and pushed the ground button again. I assumed the lift was out of order. There was no way that I was going to get the suitcase down to the river anyway. It was far too weighty. Then I remembered that Norman had a shopping trolley.[117] It might still be in the flat. The girl pointed to the empty milk bottle outside Norman's. She then disappeared inside.

I left the case in the lift and went back to get the trolley. While getting the key out of my pocket I looked down at the milk bottle. Inside there was a slip of paper. I picked up the bottle and teased the paper out. I confess that what was written on it shocked me to the core. It said *Are you a keen golfer?* The smash of the dropped bottle echoed. Then there was a shuddering sound and I turned just in time to see the lift doors close. I moved quickly to it, slamming my hand against the door's open button, but it was too late. The lift started to descend.

Halfway down the stairs it struck me that there was no reason to rush; apart from the pale-faced girl few would be up in this drug-addled hell hole. I finally got to the ground floor and there, at the end of the corridor, the lift doors with the

---

[116] This was a reference to Stan Laurel's last words to his nurse. When she said *I didn't know you skied, Mr Laurel* he replied, *I don't.*

[117] This had been bought prior to his illness. I had suggested it was only used by old ladies when out. He had suggested I stick it up my arse.

suitcase as I'd left it. I would return to the flat and get the trolley device. I would take the torso another night. Maybe to Janice's grave in Brent.

This business was no good for an old man's heart.

22

1970/2006

'You didn't have to die in the streets you were born in.'
Freddy Foster

The mind is racing today. I won't get it all down. So many stories, so many thoughts. I am eating a croissant and sipping coffee.

Now some of you young whippersnappers might think that the '60s was modern Britain. Surely the swinging bedazzling '60s, the free love, the pill – greatest invention since fire – the second wave of feminism, the television, and the films. It was Michael Caine, James Bond, The Avengers, Mary Quant, and Rosie Boycott. Modern Britain? There was something older still that underpinned the country, though, and kept it rooted in tradition. And it was this that fought for, and in some corners, won the battle for the hearts of the people. Harry Palmer was fighting for the British way, James Bond was a hired killer, for Queen and country, John Steed was an old-style gentleman who would join you in his club for a whisky and soda, and a chat about the test scores, Mary Quant was a top girl whose freedom gave men a better view, Rosie Boycott was a thorn in the side of the old school but not really dangerous until Spare Rib at the start of the following decade.

Behind it all though was poverty, and it was desperate poverty at that. As performers travelling about the country, Norman and I were better placed to see the truth of the swinging '60s than many. The poverty was rarely reported.[118] Why was this? The world's camera was pointed at glamourous London? Instead we saw, as though on a loop, a young

---

[118] My mother commented on this several times in letters mostly lost. One I have managed to keep she touches on the subject.

bearded fellow flicking through a rack of vintage army uniforms: polished brass buttons and blood red material chosen as day wear.[119] But 'poor' London didn't get the coverage. And it was there, as much as it was in Derby, in Manchester, in Cardiff, in Newcastle and Sunderland, in Dundee, Edinburgh and Aberdeen. No one city was untouched by poverty's whorey old grasp. When the histories were written, the masses would be forgotten. What were we to sell the world? Families sleeping with the lights on to keep the rats at bay? Decaying houses with no hot water, gas, or electric? In the middle of a swinging Britain? David Bailey V Nick Hedges? Lies or truths? By the late '70s sides had been taken. You either made it in the preceding few years or you were well and truly fucked. Much like the start of the decade before. Britain was a nasty, unforgiving country. You could see it in the faces of those that filled the Employment Offices, and that poured out of the gates of the comprehensives. We could still turn out the cannon fodder should the need for cannon fodder arise again. In fact, at the start of the '70s – or when I returned from other lands – some of the youngsters I saw about the streets looked shell-shocked, as if a war had been fought and lost. They looked let down; betrayed. And of course, they had been sold down the river by every politician. And I certainly knew those bastards. I spoke with them. I heard them laugh. And I told some of the jokes that made them do so: *What's the difference between a minister and a supermarket trolley? A supermarket trolley has a mind of its own.* They were from good schools, all of them. They learned to believe the lie at an early age and repeated it with swagger and arrogance. When caught *bang to rights* they would fraternize with their pals in the media: *It's a two-way street, it's quid pro quo, it's give and take, you scratch our back we scratch yours. Tell your*

---

[119] Mick Jagger wore one of these in an early '60s pop show and the trend started then. Let no one tell you different. Freddy was there.

dandruffed scum to stop sticking their snout in our trough. Of course, I was a shameless toady, for most of the time I spent in the glare of the dull. I hate myself now for the Uriah Heep humbleness I affected. I never stood a chance. The old boy network crossed all parties. You got into Parliament, you got into a good thing. *Rock the bloody boat, don't sink it.*

Having said that, when 1970 trundled in and I was about to board a bloody boat, I was heartbroken to leave my beloved country behind. I became a Brit abroad. I could pretend it was another, easier time, a more decent time. That's the thing with ex-pats. They live in another age, or they pretend that the sun never set on the old Empire. The sole topic of their conversation is the country they left behind. And they all have an opinion of it. Going to the bloody dogs, they'll say. Glad I'm not there to watch its decline. They hark back to a time when people knew their place and role in life; a time when an accident of birth nailed you to your future for ever. A time when Freddy Foster would have been working in a job totally unsuited to his temperament and his natural skills. That's the truth of the matter. I was that first generation that to a certain extent took, as given, that I could do what I liked. Those maybe ten to fifteen years older, may have breached the bastions of power, but it was my lot who took it all for granted. I was born a few years into the war, conceived during the Clydebank blitz as German bombers hit the munitions factories and shipyards that snaked along the Clydeside. I arrived on Guy Fawkes night in 1941, wearing a mask even then.[120] The echoes of the German bombs echoed down the Clyde from the shipyards to my cot. The war changed things, my ma said. The next generation were offered the Keys to the Kingdom. Sons and daughters, like me, didn't have to doff our caps, no longer went into 'service'. We didn't have a place

---

[120] My mother always told me that I was born without a face. I later learned it was a caul.

in society and so we wandered wherever we liked. We didn't have to die in the streets that we were born in. But then, when things went wrong we looked back to a more defined and structured time, Blighty that was gone.

Norman and Freddy were aware of all of this. I say this as in a sort of *Norman and Freddy Inc Plc* sort of way. For what I really mean is that Freddy Foster knew all of this. I was the one who got out talking to people, reading the papers, listening to the news. Norman couldn't give a damn, it seemed, about anything but having a good time. He would be the one laughing in the short documentary before the main feature. There were many made, along the lines of *the young and the old can enjoy the swinging sixties. From flares to flat caps, London is the capital of the world! A Look At Life*…for some. And truth was I was part of that '*some*' that did enjoy it.

I think I saw more than Norman. I was the one who spoke for the act and got the bookings: I was the manager. We did have an agent at the start of our partnership – George Bloom Associates, from 1962 until 1963. In the beginning, I was unsure of so much. Nobody in those days moved anywhere without an agent, and it was Norman who put in the right words with George. He met him one night in the Prospect of Whitby. The truth was George Bloom was the only one who would touch us. He said he'd represent us on a yearly basis. He had been a property man in the '50s, and rightly saw show business as a more lucrative market, if he could strike the motherlode. George didn't speak too much about his days in property.[121]

'Some tough boys in property,' was all he said. He did,

---

[121] He did help me find somewhere to live a little better than Southam Street in Golborne. I didn't know London when I arrived and had very little savings. The room I acquired was in a slum and therefore cheap. Like many parts of London these slums were demolished, and the area now finds itself on a money roll. George got me a small flat in Fulham.

though, occasionally let drop that he had dealings with Rachman and indeed Rachman's mistress, Mandy Rice Davies. This was well before her 'slow descent into respectability'.[122] I never prodded him in any way towards speaking about those people. Everyone is entitled to their privacy. All that really concerned me was could he be of help to Norman and Freddy. He had us travelling all over the country, small venues and large, where we were admittedly lower down the bill.

'Exposure is the name of the game, boys.'

Wherever we played I made a point of getting to know the right people. I had a little black notebook to jot down names and numbers. I also had another for ideas and such. These were the tiniest of books that slipped easily into my inside jacket pocket.[123] If I had an epiphany I'd shoot off to the nearest loo for some thinking privacy. Maybe something told me that one day I would be acting as agent and manager for Norman and Freddy. The fact was that I wanted to know everything about the business I had chosen as a career.

Perhaps that's why I didn't get stage fright then. I really didn't know what it was. The stage and the studio floor were where my feet were on the ground. I dreamt of stepping on them as I lay in my bed as a young boy. I wanted to escape the Glasgow post war dump, to move away from the ragged arsed poverty and taste the finer things that life had to offer. Rationing had only ceased in 1954. That's how bloody modern Britain was. So when the '60s came in it was, for some, the biggest party the country had seen. And we celebrated new figureheads, the ones that gave hope. There were the working-class boys and girls that had a few bob in

---

[122] Sweet Mandy's own words.
[123] I have a collection of notebooks that have travelled with me through the years. Much of what is written in these pages comes from those books. I cannot guarantee the accuracy, though, even of incidents that might have been recorded moments before.

their pocket to be spent on fun. For them, the weekly wage packet in the brown envelope, the tickertape tax receipt, the few pounds, the few coins –

That'll be seeing you through 'til next Friday then?

– wasn't enough. They wanted real success. And that success was judged by the house, the car, the holidays, and the money, not just in the pocket, but on show. The gold watches and bracelets, the diamond rings. These things could be grabbed. And although Norman didn't read the papers, he knew this all too well, that he was one of the lucky ones. He had come from a family of miners; back breaking labour, the body aching at the end of every shift.[124]

'I swear that when I saw Doddy he was like Jesus fucking Christ to me. He was sent from God to save a Nottingham boy from pit life. There was no need to get your hands dirty to earn real brass. No need.'

I was never the nervous sort; I was cocky, confident; I had a bit of the gab. And onstage? I took to it like a duck to water. If you get stage fright then go back to your day job, I would say. There's plenty would swap. That's what I always said. Until I got stage fright. Not back then. Never back then. When I was much older. When I should have been able to do it all in my sleep. It was September 22, 1994. Norman couldn't go on. The bastard was doing it to me again. And again, just before we went on. But I didn't argue this time. Right, I'll go on and fucking slaughter them. And from the ashes of his unprofessionalism this phoenix would rise. And Norman would lick his lips and phone me in Newcastle or Birmingham and tell me that he wants some of that. Because when it's in your blood it's in your blood.

But then…

---

[124] I can only imagine this as I get into my Ken Loach mode. I have had to carry little in my life but my memories.

I found myself in a room alone. Not a dressing room proper. A room with pile upon pile of student magazines. We'd been doing these types of gigs since the mid '80s,[125] but this was the lowest I'd felt. Maybe because this walk out seemed horribly final.[126] I could hardly manoeuvre around the magazines to see the small mirror propped up against the wall. I was a professional and wanted to apply my makeup. I knew the lights would show up my sweat, they would bounce off it and I'd look like a Christmas tree. A girl entered. She looked about twelve.

'Hey what you doing here?' The breaking voice revealed it was a boy. 'This is a private area.'

I turned and faced him. A badge on his left tit told me he was the *Ents Convener*. The look on his face told me that I wasn't looking my best.

'I'm an artiste,' I said softly. 'I'm Freddy Foster.'

'It's the real ale night. They're going to tear you apart.'

The little turd looked as though he hadn't done a hand's turn in his miserable fucking life. And what was worse he looked as though he never would. I stared in the filthy mirror.

A stupid young person needn't become a stupid old person, but looking at my reflection I realised there are no guarantees.

The troubles started there and by the time I went on my hands were sending a shake along the mike that could be seen at the back of the hall. The voice held though.

'Well,' I said, standing in the spot. 'They say things can only get better. Looking around here tonight I can only fucking hope so.' The insult worked and they laughed briefly, perhaps at a memory from Saturday nights in with mum and dad. 'I'm going to be full on tonight. Full on, Freddy. It's the age of insult and humiliation; it's the age of Care in the Community

---

[125] I have included a few of these at the back of this story. One I have found in Janice's cuttings I've included in Appendix 6.
[126] It wasn't.

TV. Invite them into living rooms up and down the country, from Scrabster to Land's End. And then mock and destroy them. What's that got to do with the price of a pan loaf, you might say. Well, my children, comedy should reflect the times we live in. Which is why I say to you – the great unwashed – get a job.'

'Cunt!' The word was thrown from a mass that I could not see. I puffed out my chest like a little bantam cock, stepped forward, and said:

'Is that an insult or an invite, sonny boy?'

I shook through bad to worse. George Bloom would never have booked us into such a place. But in the thirty years that separated him from 22 September 1994 so much had changed.

George died in a car accident near Saddleworth Moor in Yorkshire. He had booked us into a pub in Oldham and was coming up to discuss an 'important career development' for us. That was late 1963. After that we didn't bother trying for another agent.

I had learned a lot in a year from old George, and I charged zero per cent for my work. Norman and I always split our fees fifty-fifty, and our expenses the same. Norman trusted me with all the finances. I would no more have stolen cash from him than I would a joke: it just wouldn't be done. As for George, that 'important career development' died with him. After that we didn't bother trying for another agent.

As we travelled Britain in those days we made a fair bit more than the average wage, but the motherlode – as George had called it – was always just tantalisingly beyond our grasp. The fact is that we had to work hard, and damn hard at that, to live in a decent address in London, and to be seen at the right places. Of course, there were the free parties and award shows. These were the perks. But most of the restaurants and bars and clubs had to be paid for. They didn't come cheap.

'How much?' was an oft-heard Norman refrain. Of course,

he was going through an absolute fortune with his drink. I, on the other hand, squirrelled a lot of my cash away in order to save something for a mortgage, a nice little flat in Chelsea perhaps.[127] The rum and cokes could have bought a place in Knightsbridge. But we were of the sort that either had money and blew it all or saved it. We weren't *moneyed*. Going back to where we came from coloured everything. The families with money occasionally lose that money only to have it restored to them within a few years. History is my witness to this. For anyone who still believes wealth is a result of hard work and an astute business sense, put this story down now. I've suffered many fools in life, but I won't allow them to read my thoughts.

'You won't find the answers in the bottom of a glass, Norman.'
'Fuck you.'
'I rest my case.'
'I drink to forget.'
'Forget what?'
'That you, my Jock partner cunt, are still glued to me.'
'You'd be lost without me.'
'I'll drink to that.'
I have always presented a passive outward demeanour, but let me say now that it's not all easy. As you might have gathered, our relationship was fraught. Maybe that's what made us unique. Perhaps those tensions manifested themselves in our act. Many double acts had problems, but none built hostility into their performances. Morecambe and Wise, Cannon and Ball, played with exasperation, but there was an undercurrent of nastiness to our stage banter. You

---

[127] The first flat I ever owned was in Fulham. It wasn't what I had in mind, certainly, but it was a good little buy. The small flat in Chelsea did materialise, although some years later.

might have thought Norman couldn't stand me. Maybe one of my problems was that I thought about everything too much. I thought about money and success, I thought about our next show. And I thought about the places we often played that really weren't fit to have such an act as ours. This is not me getting all *uppity* as once described in a magazine.[128] It's facing plain facts. I have never turned away from the harsh realities of my personality. I am as honest about myself, faults and all, as I am when considering anyone else. Human flaws and frailties are part of the price we pay for walking this earth. Let me say now that I have been less than perfect in my behaviour. I have said and done things that I now regret, and I regretted at the time of saying and doing them. In my defence, all I can say is that I did what I thought, for whatever reason. It is this that kept my head above water in the most awful days. How can one do otherwise? We were aspiring to be a shining moon, but some of the newcomers were glints of light on broken glass.[129] We were dated, romantic, rose-tinted, the remnants of the warboys, tail-end Trinders and society sycophants. Underneath my polished professionalism, I yearned to be the Footlights iconoclast, ignorant of how only graduates of the dreaming spires were allowed that particular spite.

In the end I did the right thing. When Janice passed away I was staying in my own flat. My daily routine at this time was pretty simple. I would get up and have some breakfast – usually toast and orange juice. Then I would get dressed and walk to the shops at the end of the road. A decent little bistro

---

[128] I threatened to sue. They printed. I didn't sue. Some years later someone else did and put the little bastards out of business.

[129] I am referring to the great Chekhov here: 'Don't tell me the moon is shining; show me the glint of light on broken glass.' Reading the greats really is a boon.

had sprung up, so I'd buy the morning paper and sit sipping a strong coffee with usually two or three cigarettes while reading. Then I would jump on a bus to Norman's.[130] As the bus approached his area I saw the almost daily disintegration of the streets and buildings. Sometimes kids would push past me getting off the bus. Even on hot days they would wear jackets with the hoods pulled up. I confess that I found this threatening. I even found the way they wore their jeans threatening. Fashion as a means of intimidation? There's nothing new under the sun. Ask the Mods, The Rockers, The Teddy Boys.

Once inside the flat and relative safety I checked my friend was still alive. He would always either be lying in his bed, as I had left him the night before, or on the couch watching morning TV. God knows how long it took him to get there. If he could have gotten to the pub that way he would have.[131] Every morning he would say disdainfully:

'Get here, then?'

This time he was on the couch. I went to the kitchen and opened the window to air the place.

'You were up smoking all night again? I'm surprised people across the river in Neasden didn't phone a fire brigade'

'Nah, it was Princess Margaret.[132] I asked her around for a

---

[130] My car, a Citroen Visa, was becoming more trouble than it was worth. It was in the garage after the exhaust fell off. Then it was the clutch. Then it was the radiator. Then the electrics. The only reason it wasn't junked was so that I could take Norman to the hospital. The advert some years earlier had it flying off a warship like a jet. By the time I bought it third hand the machine had certainly been though the wars.

[131] By that point Norman's mobility was slow, but functioned.

[132] Royalty never impressed Norman. He once greeted Princess Diana with 'Aya gorrim wi ya?' He was obviously referring to the next in line to the throne. She just smiled at him. I don't think she had a clue who he was or what he was saying. I met her twice. The first time was early on in her celebrity. It was quite clear to me immediately she wasn't the sharpest tool in the shed. I will give it to the press, they did manage to carve something

quick fuck. Can that lady smoke.'

'She's well dead now.'

'Thought she was a trifle unresponsive.'

You had to hear Norman often in order to tune in to his failing speech. The sentence sounded more like:

'Yat eee awaif ryl unreeonsi.'

I shoved the kettle on. After that I stood in front of him and pulled him up. Throwing his arms over my shoulders I dragged him to the toilet. I could have helped him step by step but we both preferred to get this bit over quickly. In the toilet, I pulled his pyjama bottoms and pants down. Each day he would say the same thing.

'Can't stand.'

'I know,' I would say quietly and lower him onto the seat. The same bit of conversation every day:

'Will I leave you here in peace?'

'Yes.'

And I would close the door.[133]

---

new from so little, and embed it forever in the public consciousness. I told her that she was gathering more publicity than Norman and Freddy. She laughed and told me she'd gladly swap. This was days before the disastrous marriage. The next time we met was after the divorce. She looked as mad as snakes. No doubt the lies and deceit, bullying, and being worshipped had taken its toll. Why Charles allowed himself to be forced into a marriage he did not want didn't reflect well on the chappy at all.

[133] Norman's bladder and bowel functioned normally throughout the disease. He did have the occasional painful cramp and constipation, but most of the time he only had problems when trying to get to the loo in time. If anything, it was I who had problems in those departments. For a year my bladder was having some laughs at my expense. Often, when I was standing over the bowl or urinal, my *numero uno* seemed to have completed its function. No sooner, though, had I shaken or pinched off and zipped up then a late trickle would make its *riverrun past* – no, couldn't resist that! But it would make a last dash down the urethra to settle most uncomfortably in pants or shorts. It would spread across the material and emit a distinct fishy smell that only those with anosmia could fail to notice. My answer to this embarrassing problem was two-fold – neither involving a trip to a **GP**. The

The same routine every day.

While waiting for the kettle to boil I sorted out his pill drawer and took out those pills needed.

'I saw Lionel Blair the other day,' I shouted. 'Looks great. Still light on those pins.'

The voice from beyond the toilet door replied:

'Prime Minister can dance? No end to his fucking talents.'

'No, Lionel Blair, you deaf bastard. He looked years younger.'

'Formaldehyde.'

'He asked after you.'

'Good kid.'

The kettle boiled and I slipped a teabag into his beaker. I then went through and got him wiped and cleaned. After that I sat him upright in his wheelchair.

I was going to make him toast but to my surprise there was no bread in the breadbin.

'What happened to the bread?'

'I gave it to the pigeons.'

'A whole loaf?'

'Meant to give a bit but I let go. I was leaning on the sink.'

'Never mind. Here's your tea.' I placed the beaker on a tray and set it across the arms of the wheelchair.

'Sugar.'

'How long I known you, Norman.' I leaned over and started to spoon the sugar into the mug. Norman grabbed my tie tightly and pulled me close. He rasped the words into my ear:

'I want to nudge towards the inevitable, lad. The darkness

---

first idea was to be seated while micturating to apply pressure to the bladder in order to drain totally. The other way was just to dab the head of my penis afterwards with some soft tissue; much as the opposite sex does. These attempts at a solution were only partially successful. A couple of hours later into the day and I'd be smelling like Billingsgate again.

that waits for all of us.[134] It's all our nightmares. Kill me, Freddy. It's every sweating black dream, every monster in the closet. It's the falling off a cliff, the jolt in the night. Kill me, Freddy. It's every bad dream we have. Life's end. That's our greatest fear. We can win though. Take it so's it don't take you. Embrace eternity. Kill me, Freddy. I cannot live through this daily torture knowing how it moves, how it will cut me down. I am too scared to live on.'

He had a tight grip on my tie, his knuckles straining at the skin, his face red.

'Norman, I'm here. Let me take you through it all. Give me that.'

He relaxed his grip and let my tie fall; his head lolled back in the chair and his eyes looked towards heaven. This time the words were broken, anguished:

'Kill me, Freddy...'

Some days I have too many thoughts. They fight for air – or to be aired – on the page. They all fight to be remembered, to be seen, to be acknowledged. Some will be edged out half way through telling, but none, I hope, too painful to face.

---

[134] Now there's a line I wouldn't let touch a fiction!

23

2006

Freddy Foster: The way to great office is by a winding stair.
Now, where's the little boys' room?
Jeffrey Archer: Past the Picasso, left at the Matisse.
At the London penthouse of Jeffrey Archer, April
1999.[135]

In the supermarket, I walked slowly up and down each aisle. I wanted to get not just the essentials but the luxuries as well. I wanted to get him things that were almost symbolic of the extras that life had to offer. Things should not be hidden from the poor – and Norman was indeed poor. Was I being an idealist, a utopian even, in believing that a society should give the old[136] the freedom to eat, drink, live how they want for at least one day a month? Of course, I was being a fool about political reality. Deep down I understood that the old were little more than a fiscal headache. I chose a mixture of cheeses, a few baguettes, three bottles of wine, six bottles of real ale, a pineapple, and a few pork pies: a bloody feast, indeed.

When I was a youngster I went to the butcher for meat, the baker for bread, the dairy for milk. Now one shop does it all: from socks to raisins all under the one roof. As I queued up I spotted a sign that said *Bargain of the Week*. It was a computer. Norman and I had spoken of them before:

---

[135] This was to discuss a charity event. I was under the weather and spent most of the hour looking out over the Thames. I was slightly embarrassed about asking directions to the loo.

[136] My dear Norman was 66 years old. Where did those years go? I just remembered that on the way to Tooting in 1961, the fateful day I met Norman, I was singing in my head 'Don't You Know It' by Adam Faith. What a strange thing the memory is.

Doesn't write the bloody stuff!

I made the purchase there and then. It had all the bells and whistles that such things could have, most of which I didn't need. Norman and Freddy had hit the modern age. It was 2006. More than this: Norman and Freddy were going to write our story. Well, Freddy was going to write it, with anecdotes from Norman. With the money that would roll in we'd up sticks and get over to the South of France, tout de suite. There, I thought, he could live his life out in a deck chair enjoying the sight of beautiful people playing on the beach. I was, of course, in total denial of the situation. Norman was no Aschenbach and his disease was no cholera. People can survive cholera.

Norman told me once that he was going nowhere, that everything was over his shoulder:

'Bit of a train journey where eventually you forget the destination. Looking back all you see is leaves on the track.'

With my bags of shopping I went along to a letting agency to make arrangements until such time that I wished to sell my flat. Such was the rush of blind enthusiasm I had for the future. Was I going to allow us to slide into a shabby death? I had always knocked at life's door, always pushing at life. Be strong, Freddy, I told myself again and again. *Be strong.*

Words had brought down civilisations, tipped governments, toppled leaders. But some words ignite the spirit. A few hours before I had heard such words:

'Kill me, Freddy.'

I wouldn't be killing Norman; I'd be living with him.

24

2006

'It looks a bit black over Bill's Mother's!'
Norman Riddell[137]

I burst into his flat with a head full of news and hands full of shopping.

'Norman, you have a lodger.'

'Hope he's paying.'

'Look, I bear gifts.'

'You're not a…a…'

'A Greek bearing gifts? No.'

'I was going to say arse.'

The disease did not blunt his sharp wit although his comic timing you had to wait a bit for. Over the years I had fed Norman the funny lines. I was the straight man, the feed, but never the stooge. My lines would often get the laughs. It was a position I enjoyed. In many ways, it did suit my disposition and bearing.

Norman's reaction to the idea of a biography was predictable:

'Who the fuck wants to know about us? The Yanks? They have their own failures.'

I told him that whatever we were we were not failures. I wouldn't accept this, particularly when I was on such a high. We adapted to situations. I told him that it was never too late to grab the Keys to the Kingdom. After the first bottle of wine he was semi-convinced. He was also semi-conscious. I

---

[137] Norman said this a few times when things were bad. Each time I would look at him as though he was mad. This one he fired at me many times. It referred to using language above your station. He would also say "Bill Mather's".

told him it could raise our profile. I could go out and do interviews. It would be a sort of comeback.

'You have to have been somewhere to come back.'

'It'll be our story. We have things to say. You get to the heart of a man through anecdote.'

I opened an Old Speckled Hen for him and convinced him all over again. By the time he had finished the ale he was tired so I got him ready for bed.

'Could you give me a scratch, Freddy?'

'Sure, my friend.'

I laid him out on the bed naked and scratched him lightly all over his body. I then got his pyjamas on him and covered him up.

'Goodnight, sweet prince.'

'Up yours,' he mumbled and laughed quietly.

I sat up all night drinking a bottle and a half of white wine while jotting notes on a piece of paper. I would take delivery of the computer next day. I would collect my clothes and knick-knacks. I would make a few phone calls to see if there was interest in a Norman and Freddy biography. Once again, I had the energy and enthusiasm of a twenty-year-old. What a mystery the days are.

The sun had been up an hour or so before I heard the first bus. I lay down on the couch. Norman would not be up until well after midday. No thumps on the door or screams of animals leaving the roofs. I closed my eyes. Nice. Côte d'Azur. Keep the eyes on the prize, Freddy.

A Couple of Guys

25

2007 and before

'The cheaper the crook, the gaudier the patter.'
Sam Spade in The Maltese Falcon.

I came to sitting on the floor in Norman's kitchen, staring through the open door into the living room. I really don't know how I got there, but I can only gather that the atrocities that I committed made me ever so slightly giddy. My back was against the sink cupboard where I had earlier pulled out the large soup pot. How strange human beings are. I chose, in my career, to have them laugh at their actions, but I could just as easily have made them cry. Ladies and gentlemen, please welcome Mister Freddy Foster, tragedian!

Now, Freddy, calm.

How many times have I said that to myself? On nights when things had got particularly bad. Weighed down by nauseous memories.[138] Norman seemed in some ways to be stronger than me in that respect. Or maybe it's just that he buried the humiliation and the pain deeper. Up and down this bloody country again, and again, and again. And you had to take the insults, the hecklers.

We played in *Heilan Johnny's Bar* in Edinburgh – a haunt of the lowest of society's low. As we walked off, taking care to avoid the broken glass, Johnny himself came running up to us.

'You havnae finished yer fuckin' act, ya cunts.'

'Now look, Johnny,' I said trying to calm him, 'You wouldn't talk to Mike and Bernie like that.'

'Fuck they cunts,' he replied.

---

[138] I might not know the weight of a house, or a country, or this earth; but I am certain none compare with the weight of memory.

Norman's face was red and sweating. 'Look lad,' he said, 'they were throwing bottles.'[139]

'I'll be the one throwing bottles, ye ken?'

'Now look, Johnny,' I tried to reason, 'it's not in our contract that we deal with a physically hostile crowd.'

'You insulted them. Mean Scots jokes don't go down well in this place.'

'Freddy's Scotch, duck,' said Norman.

'Scottish, Norman. *Scottish*,' I chipped in quietly.

'He sounds like an English cunt tae me. And whit's wae the sexy stuff? We've got a classy clientele of the capital's finest. Dae ye honestly think they want tae hear why Scotsmen wear kilts? Because sheep kin hear a zip a mile away! Do they fuck, laddie, do they fuck. Ye ken?' He then suggested in the strongest terms that we leave *Heilan Johnny's* immediately, *sans* payment. People have to understand that the public face of an entertainer is never a true one. We had to make ourselves look, to a certain extent, tame. In our *away from the public* world Norman and I were very aware and used to Heilan Johnny's sort of behaviour and we acted accordingly.

As we dragged Johnny to our dressing room Norman kept punching him on the back of the head. I hit him a few times on the jaw and throat.

'You fucking cunts,' he was screaming. 'You are fucking dead, ye ken? Deid!'

Strangely, I have always found it enlightening we Scots can so easily fall in and out of the Queen's English. *Dead* or *deid,* the words meant the same to my wonderful partner and me.

---

[139] We have several times in our career had bottles and glasses chucked our way. I can think of few other acts that have had this audience reaction so often, if at all. I would like to say that it made us better comedians, but that would not be the case. In my more perverse moments of thought I think of how Noel Coward would have reacted to the odd glass. Possibly he would have said something witty about champagne and sauntered off. But even Coward's flashes of wit would have been drowned out in *Heilan' Johnny's*.

They were threats.

In the dressing room, we rammed him head first into the mirror, smashing it and the few lightbulbs that framed it. Do you think the sheep heard that then, Johnny? I ripped at Johnny boys' jacket in order to remove his wallet and liberate our fee. A job well done.

Afterwards, with the cash secure in my pocket, we had a nightcap in a lovely little hostelry in Leith. We laughed a lot but truly took no pleasure in the night's activities. Although there were a couple of scribes from local papers in the bar that night no one saw fit to slaughter us in a review. If we had been Mike and Bernie we would have been splashed over the front of every paper in the country. Johnny had a wee bit of clout with these hacks. I can only imagine he exerted some and stopped word getting out. But you can't keep a good story down. A year later, in London, a notoriously thick gangster came up to me in a club and said:

'You stepped on Heilan Johnny's toes?'

How you handle such a situation can make the difference between a good night and a visit to accident and emergency.

'His toes?' I said. 'No, his nose.'

We laughed and drank a drink together before I made my excuses and left.

I picked myself up from the kitchen floor with difficulty; and executed a Chaplinesque skid, set right by flailing arms. The blood would have to be mopped up before it seeped downstairs. I imagined my old flat with Mrs Kopykin looking to her ceiling with an anthesis of blood spreading like some nightmare Torah vision of the coming Cossack apocalypse.

I knew none of Norman's neighbours. They never opened their doors wide enough for light to fall on their faces.

26

2005

'A bird in the hand is what you want on a Friday night.'
Norman Riddell.

At heart, I always considered Norman and Freddy gentlemen. Yes, I will say if asked, we were too good for the venues. Yes, the world of entertainment did lose out on what could have become a classic British comedy act. I truly believe this. The fact of the matter was that the material was not quite good enough and we should have bought in some jokes, some routines. But, where was the money for that? No, it wasn't just the money. Norman and I considered ourselves writers as well as performers. From the very first moment of our meeting that was pretty much taken for granted. In the first year after he had been diagnosed, Norman suggested that he might write his memoirs.

'What would you call it?'

'Maybe *Flying Solo*.'

This was a slight too far and I told him so, but he moved me with his reply:

'Freddy, I'm talking about this illness. I know you're with me. And now Janice being ill[140]...I don't know. But there's something about it all that...it's difficult to describe. It's something I have to live with inside my head twenty-four hours a day. I feel it in my body every moment; every twitch, every itch, every movement that I want to make but can't. I

---

[140] Janice had discovered a lump on her left breast in December 2004. No final diagnosis on this had been made by early January 2005. We took this as a positive sign. It was almost a year to the day that Norman was diagnosed with MND. Surely life couldn't be cruel enough to inflict two major blows in such a short time?

sometimes feel so lonely.'

His memoir came to nothing, and a year later he had no interest in my plan to write our rags to rags tale.

Something in the illness curbed Norman's vicious tongue. I won't say that it softened him because he was a hard man in too many ways. But he certainly started thinking more, even although I didn't always like the thoughts.[141] After Janice passed away the request to end his life was almost daily.

'Be doing me a favour. I can't live like this. It's no life for a man. Not for a man like me. I don't want this, Freddy. If you'd done it when I first asked. That would have been easier. Then you could have said it was suicide. Now I can't do it myself. They'll know that. But there's ways they wouldn't ever know.'

'Why didn't you take your own life when you could?'

'I was frightened. That's the truth of it, lad. I needed you. Janice wouldn't have.'

'But you thought I would?'

'I did.'

'Well, the law's the law.'

'A mercy killing.'

'It's still murder. I'm not spending the years I have left banged up for murder.'

'That's if they found the body.'

I stared at him. This is what life had brought us to.

So, it was Norman who first suggested dismemberment and the disposal of the body. He told me that I could make the parts unrecognisable. It was he who planted such a horror in my mind. At what point does life change irrevocably? What is it that we lose on our journey that can bring us to this? That's what I thought as I put on my coat. I didn't want to be anywhere near him. I swear if I heard any more of his shite

---

[141] One of the oft repeated insults that did get to me was when he would say, 'And whose opinions do you have today?'

my cakehole would be frothing.

'I'm going out.'

'Might not be here when you get back. Might pop down the local Palais for a bit of jitterbugging: *'jittobuygn'*. I had to hand it to the man. He must have had steel alloy balls. If the roles had been reversed how would I have coped?

As I closed the door I heard him howl, like a dog being thrown from a roof.

In the lift going down a young man entered smoking a joint. I did the strangest of things: I took the joint from his mouth and took a toke. I returned the joint to him not wishing to Bogart it.[142]

'Had better, son,' I said as the lift jolted to a stop. When we got out, he headed for his hooded pals sitting on a wall while I walked towards the bus stop. No doubt the young man told the group his story. He lingered by the wall but the others walked with purpose towards the road. By the time I stepped on the bus they were certainly agitated. I took a window seat and stared them out. Someone once told me that anyone travelling on a bus after fifty years of age is a failure. I remember laughing. Now I would tell him to fuck off. I looked beyond the gang, at the windows of the dead flats. Lives behind the windows. Were they the failures? I felt as close to them now as I did with any celebrity. The group made their way back to the wall with a swagger more articulate than their vocabulary. And what happened to Freddy Foster that he could do such things?

A mercy killing? Can killing ever be considered an act of mercy? Maybe we make excuses to ourselves to justify a crime. Are we ever one hundred per cent sure that the reasons are what we say they are? That thought has been with me most of

---

[142] Note my familiarity with the drug culture parlance has reverberations of another time. Old men don't change their language. It dates them as much as their faces.

all, that uncertainty. It smothers me to sleep; it drags me awake. The past, the past, the past.[143] As a child I thought I could remember my father;[144] as a young man I tried to forget where I had come from; in middle age, I remembered what might have been; now I contemplate that life. People like me never had a present day and so enjoyed little that life had to offer.[145] As the bus headed to town I thought of Norman's words. What he was asking me was to wipe clean a lot of my past. He was asking me to destroy memories.

It was raining as I got off the bus and headed towards Theatreland. This was one of my favourite pastimes. I walked past The Palladium along Argyll Street onto Marlborough Street, swung left onto Regent Street, took a few steps along Coventry Street and I was playing with the puddles and the cracks like a child. I thought of doing a Gene Kelly gutter to kerb along Suffolk Place but there must be a point childish behaviour borders on care in the community. And then to the Haymarket, home of Fielding, of Gielgud, of John Sleeper Clarke (the brother-in-law of John Wilkes Booth) who fled America after the assassination of Abraham Lincoln. A billboard now advertising a revival of *Seven Brides for Seven Brothers*, the musical based on 'The Rape of the Sabine Women', the painting which is housed in The National Gallery a few minutes' walk away, which is seconds away from The National Portrait Gallery, which only last year bought the beautiful David Cobley painting of Ken Dodd, who performed at The Nottingham Playhouse in 1954 in front a

---

[143] Whitman's 'unfathom'd retrospect'. But here am I exploring crush depth emotions in that very retrospect.

[144] A bloody impossibility as it turned out.

[145] Everything seemed to be 'oh, do you remember…?' 'Whatever happened to…?' Is this the heart of our failure? Was it a failure to be in the present? Was there something of the copycat about Norman and Freddy? Did we too often emulate rather than originate styles and delivery and content? But surely success can be found through imitation? Or is that a dry well?

wide eyed Norman Riddell, and on it goes. I sneeze my way
onto Pall Mall – that's a left; then a left again onto Trafalgar
Square. A left, a right, a left. St Martin's Place, Place again, and
then Lane to The Duke of York, where Puccini sat and
watched *Madame Butterfly*, and where hundreds of children
stood up and clapped their hands to save Tinkerbell's life, and
where only a few months before I sat in the stalls and watched
Michael Gambon in Beckett's *Eh Joe*.[146] Let me wander in the
rain, towards Hop Gardens, Great Newport Street, Charing
Cross Road and a left to Shaftesbury Avenue and The Palace
Theatre where Sarah Bernhardt and the Marx Brothers trod
the boards ; and my head clears with every step, every
memory. Onto Earlham Street, Neal Street, Shelton Street,
Endell Street to Bow Street, left to Russell and a right to
Catherine and The Duchess Theatre. I feel like a young strip
of a boy, the legs instilled with a youthful sense of spring and
urgency. Ah, The Duchess where I saw the first stage
performance of *Alfie* in 1963. I stand for a moment and
thought of the film, a few years later, where I got a brief walk
on part, but alas no credit.[147] Norman called me a mug, but
while he was making the beast with two backs with some
floozy I was enjoying a cup of tea with Michael Caine. I'll let
the reader decide who the mug was. I stood under the arch
having a cigarette and thinking of all that had passed. He had
said *if they found the body,* so he had given it thought. His days
must have been spent in thought. Time has made us one on
that old friend.

---

[146] I find life occasionally absurdly apt. Something in me must have
recognised this *inner voice from the past* and recognised something that speaks
to me. Tears ran freely down my cheeks for the 30 minutes duration, and I
understood *that penny farthing hell* that was spoken of. I was sixty-four years
old: how could I not have done?
[147] My sole appearance was walking through a hospital ward door while
Michael walked past me. Hardly Shakespeare in the park, but I did watch a
great deal of the outdoor filming, much of which was done close to my flat.

I needed you.

No, I could not dwell on his words. Aldwych, Waterloo Road, and to The Cut to The Old Vic, the history of which could not fail to impress any lover of theatre. From Kean to Gielgud, from Olivier to Jacobi. All these names would fill my head in order to keep out the name I treasured most: Norman Riddell. And then to cross Waterloo Bridge. Still rain. Still cold. I could not have imagined that I would soon be dropping his feet over that scenic spot. It was a slower walk over the bridge towards the Lyceum, where Irving and Terry had walked through that magnificent portico.[148] And so these places and the exercise got my heart pumping.[149] Walking around a great city in the rain has got to be one of life's sweetest pleasures. You take in great gusts of cloud fresh air and it sharpens the mind: flanerie gets you everywhere. My mind might have contained a hurricane of thoughts, but I walked on, fixed on shedding the anger that I had left the flat with, to leave space to contemplate the enormity of his request. The London theatres had calmed me. He wanted to die. Why shouldn't he crave an end? Janice blew into my thoughts in the rain. What would she have done? Cried, certainly. Would she have helped him? I cannot say that she wouldn't have. How I missed the sweet girl at that time. No doubt Norman missed her terribly too, but we rarely spoke of her.

'Yaa fuchdurrr!'

He repeated, 'You fucked her!'

I looked down at him lying on the couch as I'd left him.

---

[148] I attended a performance of *The Lion King* there just after the millennium celebrations but left at the interval. Enough was e-bloody-nuff.

[149] If any readers who are familiar with Theatreland might suggest my route could have been faster, might I suggest that you shut your mutt? Freddy walks his streets as Freddy will.

'Do you want a cup of tea?'

'Bastard…'

'I'll make tea.'

Over tea Norman told me that he'd known about our relationship since the cruise ship. She had told him. He couldn't get hard for her anymore. He couldn't let her go, but he loved her, and so they used me to give her comfort. During this he said the most curious thing:

We had moments shared.

The whole situation I found more vulgar and tasteless than my 'cuckolding' of Norman. There seemed to me something rather morbid in their sexploitation. I felt aggrieved. A seam of lust and cowardice opened up through the relationship I'd had with Janice. When truths are spoken or the hidden is brought to light, when sores and wounds are open, salvation is not always the result. More of that later.

'Scratch my legs, Freddy.'

I pulled down the elasticated jogging bottoms that he was wearing and scratched his legs from top to bottom. As I did so a tear slipped from the corner of his left eye. It ran down his temple and around his left ear. Quietly he said:

'We would go swimming…'

'Wha…?'

At the start of the disease I would take Norman down to the Bickley Lido pool.[150] It was here he first spoke to me of assisted suicide.

'When I go under just do me in, would you?' I hardly had time to react when Janice arrived and the conversation changed. She would come down to the pool rarely. She said that she was embarrassed about her body.

The swimming helped the ROM,[151] but Janice would do the

---

[150] Norman always referred to it as the Southland Lido, its old name. And I was actually wrong as it was now properly a health club with an indoor pool.
[151] Range of Motion exercises.

more difficult joints in an order given out by the physio. Each day each joint would go through its paces to stop it seizing up. These were the passive exercises, but she would encourage him to do a lot himself:

'Come on, darling, three hundred and sixty degrees,' she'd shout as though a sidelines sports coach. We made room in the living room by pushing the table, couch and chairs back to the wall. There were ups and down, setbacks and some moves forward. Sometimes a success might be enough movement that we could more easily wash under his arms. That's how limited positives the disease offers.

'We would go swimming,' he repeated. 'I know where I'm headed now, lad. I know where I'm going.'

'Why did you think of the swimming?'

'You held me. You could have let go.'

'But of course, I couldn't.'

If the great British public had known of our infighting, the bickering, the harsh words, the triangle, they wouldn't have allowed us into their living rooms. It was the same with most of the gang – apart from Eric and Ernie.[152]

---

[152] The bile, the spite, the infidelities, the drunkenness, the contempt, the greed, the insults, the jealousies, mean spiritedness, the vulgarity, the self-loathing; they were all kept from public view. There was a putrid centre to it all, covered in gauze and glitter. Turn on your TV on a Saturday night. Watch the sham. But remember, you're hiding from the same things as we are.

27

2006

Emperor Augustus, while touring France, comes across a man who bears a striking resemblance to himself. Curious he asks, 'Was your mother at one time in service at the palace?'
The man replies: 'No, your highness, but my father was.'
                                    1ˢᵗ century Roman joke accredited to Augustus.

'Plug it in.'

'I have.'

'Switch it on.'

'It is on. Can't you see the light? That's a blank page in front of us.'

The computer had arrived. It had been unboxed and set up by a man from the store for an additional fee. This was also paid for.

'Hit the key.'

I gave Norman a look that said clearly I would hit him. I typed out *Norman and Freddy*. How apt that the first thing I wrote was our names. It was the most exciting thing that had happened to us in years. We were old men in wonder.

The day had been a to-ing and fro-ing affair.[153] Things were organised with the letting agent. Rent would go into my bank account – minus the letting fee. I had packed a few belongings and boxed my books, my notebooks and anything I did not want to leave for strangers to poke around in. I was told that they could have someone suitable in within a week. How easy it was to change my life, I thought. Was it always so easy? Had I made life more difficult than it really was? The years in Glasgow creating the new me, the years in London

---

[153] There was a meeting with a film man who had heard that we might be writing our story. But more of that later.

creating…what? This? It must be a gift from the gods to be born in idiocy. I feel sometimes that thinking was my downfall. I should have stayed in poverty-stricken ignorance;[154] happy in my own bit of shit.

Weeell we gluuuuep…

I had asked where we should start our story. I had read a lot of showbiz biographies and knew they always seemed to start in the present then jump back to the beginning. Or sometimes they had a little prologue: this had a lot going for it. But then who do you start with? Was our story going to open in Glasgow or Nottingham?[155]

'If we do it chronologically, Norman, there will be a pull towards mentioning everything. People will say what happened in April 1965. Things like that.'

'What did?'

'Well, we'll think about it. Churchill's funeral. That was the start of the year.'

'God, that's right. Seems longer ago. Why'd we say everything seems like yesterday? It never does.'

---

[154] Harold Wilson famously said he couldn't tell the difference between hock and burgundy. He was proud of that gap in his knowledge of the grape. Perhaps he thought that it kept him in touch with the working man. As did his constant references to the clogs that he wore to get to school. I would have none of it; I could tell the difference not only between the wines but between the wine glasses as well. Wilful ignorance I could not abide.
[155] This whole thing is beginning to get complicated. If Janice had told our story it would be different. How would she have seen us? How did she see us? What went around in her mind for all those years together? What did she think of me? Of Norman? What did Janice think of herself and the times that she lived through? No doubt a very different tale. And so the past cannot be fixed. It is never just so, it shifts and with each shift another thing altogether is brought to the table. As Sartre says, an infinite series of nows. This is my story at this moment from where I am. And I am already beginning to find autobiography an absolute waste of time. Let us consider it a Bildungsroman, an educational tool; a warning if you like. Or, if you would rather, imagine an empty bag. Imagine emptying all of these words into it. And then dropping it in the river. I doubt it matters a jot to me.

'Not even yesterday.'

This was just a throwaway line but Norman started laughing which led to a bad coughing fit. When he did this his whole body shook terribly and he turned a scarlet red. If he was lying on the couch I'd have to hold him up and give him sips of water. If he was in his wheelchair I'd lean him forward. I always thought he would choke to death when I was out.

Once he calmed down he said:

'Hey, not long before I have my NIV, eh?'[156]

I made us both a cuppa and kept him entertained, sharing my vision of us living in the south of France. We had been there during the cruise. I talked about the bars, the girls, the sun, the laughs. But I could tell he didn't believe any of it. And neither did I. Sometimes we need our lies. It was dreaming that the illness didn't exist, or would go away, or a miracle cure be found. But none of that was going to happen. Norman would never sit in a chair in the south of France. He could barely sit in a chair in his living room. My friend was on the way out. It was written on his face; it was written on his body. There would be no last chances. There would be no rolling back the carpet of history on this one. And he had resigned himself to it. But what I wouldn't allow was him going out thinking that his life had been a failure.

'You didn't get your hands dirty, Norman. Not like your dad down a mine. You lived your life in the slipstream of showbusiness. There was never dirt under those nails.' This was all part of the routine of keeping him 'positive'. Something one doctor had advised: Positive?

The doctor looked about sixteen, with a face like a cross between a well slapped arse and a pig.

---

[156] This was a non-invasive ventilation system that the hospital had mentioned on his last visit. It could relieve breathlessness, thus help his quality of life. But eventually the breathing muscles would be too weak for even that.

'I'm not handing out a wonder drug, you know that. I'm saying that he must be kept as happy as possible. Get him reminiscing? Get him working on a new project?'

'I thought about getting him a girl but that really wasn't on the cards.' The boy-doctor coughed and warned me off such a thing. Perhaps an older man would have recognised the humour.

'My father saw you.'

'On stage?'

'Yes. Years ago. I told him that you were attending. He told me to mention it.'[157]

'Tell your old man thanks. It's nice he remembers. Would he like an autograph? Maybe a bit old for that.'

'A bit.'

'Yes.'

'I don't think I've seen a comedy act outside the telly.'

'The art is gone.'

'Make 'em laugh, eh?'

He wrote out the prescription, tore the script and handed it to me.

'Thank-you for making my dad laugh.'

'Positive, you say?'

'Yes.'

'I'll do that.'

Where to start the true story of Norman Riddell and Freddy Foster was a problem. The words we have in our minds are like snowflakes, but the fall upon the page is heavier, dirtier. Things get buried under it.

---

[157] The Hippocratic Oath obviously didn't stretch to family.

28

2006

'…nothing's amusing that isn't spiteful.'
Leo Tolstoy, Anna Karenina, part 2, chapter 6.

'Weeell we gluuuuep…' he repeated.

'Where we grew up? Glasgow and Nottingham. That would make for a very long read, Norman.'

'I don't think I did that much until I met you.'

The bastard could bring a tear to a glass eye sometimes. I agreed with him, though. People would want to know us as a double act. Something of the familiar, comforting.

'Your mum's death. Remember I went up to Glasgow with you?'

'Yes. Hey, maybe we should be calling it Norman, Freddy and Janice?'

We were silent for a few moments. This biographical excavation could be more painful than we imagined. And then we talked and reminisced. What I'd forgotten he would fill in the blanks. There was nothing wrong with his memory. As for me, mine seemed to work in reverse perspective. The closer I am in time, the smaller the image; the more distant, the larger. We met, I told him, at a charity cancer do that we'd both gate-crashed. He corrected me and told me it was a Brittle Bone Society Dance. At first, I thought he was taking the rip, but then I remembered the yellow banner stretched high across the room.

Afterwards we had gone to the pub together, both quite wary of the other. We had invited Dickie Valentine but he politely refused, laughing that he'd be on thin ice with his wife if he hit the boozer.[158]

In the pub, we talked about great double acts – Flanders and Swann, Eric and Ernie, Mike and Bernie, Naughton and Gold, Nervo and Knox – without imagining ourselves in that relationship. The more, though, we talked the more sense it started to make. We seemed in many ways to be opposites. I was certainly more erudite, while Norman was more down to earth. We were from different countries, although both British. The dynamics, I began to think, were there. This could be an exciting new act. There was something, though, that was never said at the time: the act was born of fear. London was and is one of the earth's great cities. Norman put forward that Glasgow and Nottingham hardly stood up to it. I immediately agreed with him about Nottingham. I had to tell him about Glasgow's immense history in the medical and scientific fields and its great shipbuilding past. Norman countered with Liverpool and Belfast's shipping industry.

'A Belfast fella hears about the Titanic going down and says, "It was okay when it left the yard!"' That evening was punctuated with jokes. What we did agree upon was that everyone had to come to London to make it. As an afterthought, he said:

'Did you insult Nottingham, you prick?' he laughed as he went to the bar.

While I waited, I took stock of the man that was about to share the next fifty years of my life. He was tall for that time, just under the six-foot mark I guessed. (I remember it crossed my mind that he might be wearing lifts. He wasn't.) Inside the dark suit was the body of a young, fit, boozer. It was one of those frames that would carry weight well; sure, a paunch might

---

[158] While listening to the first issue of the *Sergeant Pepper* record I read that Dickie and his wife were divorcing. It mentioned that she had been an ice skater. I had a chuckle while reading. The thin ice comment was his private joke. No doubt six years later he didn't find it so funny.

appear in his forties but he could handle it. He had the swagger of the boot boy, the cornerboy, who would shout an insult and be prepared to back it up with a fist if you remonstrated.[159] He placed his pint on the beermat and looked down at my G and T.

'You know something, Mr Foster? The only time I usually buy someone gin and tonic is when I'm out with a girl. And a girly-girl at that.' He delicately put the drink in front of me and sat down. I had to nail it on the head straight away.

'How about we go outside?'

'Oh no, lad. Me da told me about men like you.'

'How about we go outside and I stick this G and T glass in your face, you thick as shit cunt?'

'Now-now, no violence on public house property. Cheers, duck.'

He held his glass out. I eyeballed him for a few seconds until a broad smile spread across his face.

'Aya gorra mardilipon?'[160]

I had obviously passed the first test. Although I wasn't happy about it, I smiled anyway, and clinked glasses with him. He took a mouthful of beer and sat back.

'I hear,' he said, 'that you've come down from Scotty Land?'

'I heard the streets were paved with gold.'

'Well, I've not seen any gold in the year I've been here. I'm doing a little stint in a pub in Swiss Cottage. Along Finchley Road way. It doesn't pay. They give me a few beers in the evening. Outside that I'm general cleaner in a brewery in the

---

[159] For those people the decline into old age is hard to come to terms with. The loss of physical power in your day to day dealings with the world is catastrophic. I had no way of knowing as he made his way back to the table that his would be much greater than that.

[160] For years I kept a notebook of Norman's Nottingham sayings. Sometimes when he was drunk he sounded like he'd stepped out of a Lawrence novel. Of course, I had several notebooks in which I'd scribble some thoughts or lines.

East End.'

I was certainly impressed that he actually managed to try out material on an audience. I had done enough in Glasgow but no doors were opening in the Big Smoke. I asked if he wrote his own stuff.

'Mostly. When I can. Sometimes someone will tell a joke and I'll elaborate on it. Polish it up if you like, Jock.'

There are many insults and put downs that you have to suffer in life. *Jock* I didn't like.

'Here,' I said, leaning forward. 'Here's a joke for you. A Scotsman walks into a bar in England and asks for two pints of ale, two whiskies and a packet of crisps. The barman says: "Two pints of ale, two whiskies and a packet of crisps. No problems, Jock." The Scotsman calls him back and says, "What did you just call me?" The barman answers: "No offence, Jock. It's just what we call you down here." The Scotsman says, "I'll tell you what, let me re-order: Two pints of ale, two whiskies and a packet of crisps, you English cunt – No offence, it's just what we call you up there."'

Norman looked at me and exploded with laughter. He finished off his pint in double quick time.

'I like you, Freddy,' he said. 'Another?'

'Joke or drink?'

'Both.'

'You're an alcoholic.'

'Arthur fucking Seaton me.'

'Here,' I said taking a pound note from my wallet to save any mean Scots jokes later.

'And get me a pint. I'm just developing an affectation with the gin.'

'Lost the use of your legs?'

'I saw you eyeing up the barmaid. Thought you'd like another trip to see her.'

He smiled and winked and pushed his way to the bar. From

where I sat I could hear him shouting *Darling!*

A few drinks later and a few stories swapped we got down to business.

'You want to try partnering up,' I said. 'I liked that joke you told Dickie Valentine. We could give it a year or two and if it doesn't work out we'll call it a day.'

'Suits me, lad. Take it *Jock and Cunt* wouldn't get a booking?'

'Only from the boys in blue.'

'How about Riddell and Foster?'

I thought that sounded like a firm of undertakers.

'It needs to be more inviting, more open and friendly; like you've known us all your lives. Norman and Freddy.'

He immediately liked it. No doubt he also liked that his name came first. It just came out that way. But it did have a ring to it. We said it a few times. *Norman and Freddy. Norman and Freddy. Norman and Freddy.* As I said: a ring to it. So, we had an act. All we needed was material.

Outside the pub that night we arranged to meet at a café in Brixton, near Norman's bedsit, the next day. It was dark and raining. The lamplight cast a white glow around us. A red-faced soaking policeman trundled past us as though he had piles. I watched him and said to Norman:

'Material can come from anything. Be observant.'

We shook hands, said goodnight and walked our separate ways. After a few moments I turned and saw him in the distance.

'Norman!' I shouted.

'What?' he shouted back.

'Who's Arthur Seaton?'

I heard his laugh and watched him disappear into the night.[161]

---

[161] Arthur Seaton was the main character in Alan Sillitoe's *Saturday Night, Sunday Morning*. The film had come out a few months before. It was possible Norman had seen it. The book was out a few years before that. I would be

And so it was on a rainy Saturday night in 1961 Norman and Freddy came into being. Going along to the scout hall while quietly singing an Adam Faith[162] hit I was a solo act. By the end of the night I was half of a double act. Life is a funny thing.

The night reminiscing took it out of Norman. He was pale and tired but seemed happy. I wheeled him to the bedroom, pulled his arms over my shoulders and got him to bed. While I was scratching him he fell asleep. As he lay there, withered, I felt the terrible truth about our past. It was as tired and wasted as my friend's body. The past is a dead thing and reliving it in memory akin to a séance: pointless and foolish. You're only dying when there is nothing planned for today or tomorrow. I dragged myself over to the couch. Although exhausted myself I ripped a page from one of my notebooks and made an itinerary for the next day. One thing was to get Norman in his wheelchair and out to the park for some fresh air. Stuck

---

surprised if he had read it. When I saw the film with the great Albert Finney I could imagine Norman being impressed with the character.

[162] Adam Faith looked a bit of a runt; post war, undernourished and underdeveloped. He made an extremely successful career in pop music in the late 50s, early 60s. His trademark sound was a hiccupping style that he lifted directly from Buddy Holly. Until The Beatles arrived he was never off the wireless or telly. Later, Adam would be embarrassed by the voice that made him a celebrity. As a result of this he reinvented himself as a *serious* actor. Though when I met him in the 1980s he sounded more like a property developer:

'Flats going for a song in Moscow. Invest, Freddy, invest.'

I really only got as far as enquiring why there was so many empty flats in Moscow.

'Not my business, cock.'

He was the poor boy made good, but made good three times over. First as a pop star, then as an actor, and then as a Financial Investments Advisor. The last of these would have been a surprise to many, but not to those who tuned into his 1962 Face To Face interview with John Freeman, where he came across as articulate, intelligent and very aware of his wealth. Adam died aged 62 from a heart attack in front of his 22-year-old lover. I met him a few times. A very likeable chap.

indoors every day couldn't be recuperative for any human being. But then recovery wasn't an option. *Degenerative.* Fresh air, though, could only be beneficial. I also wanted to follow up interest in our yet to be written story. Most people would know how to sell their mothers before how to sell an idea. I closed my eyes and slept.

29

2009

'*…I'm trying to create the truth.*'
Peter Mandelson

The flat was cold. The heating had been causing problems for some time. It made irregular bumping sounds and the radiators no longer heated up fully. A while ago Norman told me they needed bled. I had never *bled* a pipe. I was unsure what it even meant. Norman said something about a key and letting air out, but being careful before water came through.

And so I sat in the cold.

Plumber: I fix baths, guv'nor, not blood baths.

The grime and dirt of the flat – outwith blood smears – beggared belief. I got cleaning materials from under the sink – next to the soup pot gap – and scoured every nook and every cranny. All the while I was talking to the departed Norman about the South of France.

The sunshine, Norman. And the beautiful girls. Oh, you'll love that.

A loud knock on the door gripped my heart. I froze on my knees with a scrubbing brush in a yellow rubber-gloved hand, like some domestic petrification. Then silence. After a few moments I scrambled to my feet and got to the door and listened.

'Who is it? Who's there,' I said very quietly through the door. There was nothing. I opened it and looked out. It was the same sad empty landing. I took a few steps towards the door leading to the stairs.

'Anyone there?'

I waited.

Nothing.

'Anyone there?' I repeated.

Silence.

I pulled open the door and looked down the stairs. The fear left me. It had popped in for a visit, had a laugh, and then said its goodbyes.

'Come on, you little fuckers! Face an old man, you cunts. Face an old man with your hoodies and your scarves! You cowards! I'll stick you! I'll stick you, I will! Like pigs!' My voice echoed down the stairwell, falling dead on the ground below.

As I walked back the door opposite opened and the pale-faced girl emerged wearing what looked like a woman's housecoat. I became aware of my yellow rubber gloves and scrubbing brush. I relaxed:

'Kids. Trying to frighten people.'

She didn't speak, just closed her door again. I heard the bolts and chains go into place.

I was going to get the flat spotless.

The cleaning of the bathroom. The bath. Scrubbing away. Thinking and scrubbing. My dander had been got up. I found I was talking to myself. Mumbling. Threats. What I'd do. People don't know me. They thought they did. It's because the entertainer comes into your home. They sit with you for an evening. Laughing. Making you laugh. Shedding tears with you, having a bit of a sing song. They were your friends so you knew them. It was Ronnie and Millicent, Dickie – all the Dickie's – Hughie – *friends, friends* – Bernie, Lennie, Charlie – all the Charlie's – *Hello, my dahlings, me old flower* – Johnny, John, Colin – *thank you, please, around the room* – and Norman and Freddy in your room. And remember our exaggerated salute when we were coming off? Remember it? Yes, it made you feel good. *Hey dad, it's those guys that salute at the end!* You remember us now? Yes. Couldn't hear Norman though, could you? Under his breath, *thank-you and fuck you*. You couldn't hear because of the applause. We all came into your house – *mind the feet* – and sat down and stayed the night with you. In the box in the corner, unlimited company, plugging gaps in family chats until it just plugged family chat. You didn't have to entertain the kids any more, that magic box did it. It was supernatural, it was a shamanistic experience brought to you by the BBC, by ITV, London Weekend, Thames, Anglia, ATV. Was that a glass eye Hughie Green had? *Why's he look like that, mum?* Hughie was a fucking colossus! He was a fucking Cyclops! There he stood with a big giant-sized postcard and his *abracadabra* of *Teddington Lock, Middlesex.* Or Mike! Mike with his smile and his neat hair and he just couldn't be offensive. Mike was so safe and then he'd say *this is me* and you'd be goggle-eyed at the gogglebox. It was never ending, it poured out night after night, but the weekend, oh the weekend was the best with Charlie – how many times will he be thrown through that window? – and Freddie's sleeves slip down and touch the floor, and acrobats, and plate spinners, and tuxedoed magicians, contortionists, jugglers, and the beautiful assistants – *can you see her crack?* – Invite them all in. They're your friends. You know them. You know us. Norman and Freddy. You know all of us. We're in your living room most nights. You know them all. Benny and Ernie and Jimmy – and don't forget little Jimmy's halfwit brother, Danny, spluttering and falling and going into spasms on the carpet. And it didn't have to end, it just went on. When Jimmy died a schoolboy pensioner The Krankies could just plug the hole. And not just those people. What about the sounds? WAKEY WAKE!!!! It's Friday, it's five to five and it's…CRACKERJACK!!!! Or the trigger tunes that would sink you into the deepest of trances: Thames – *ba-ba-ba-ba-ba-baba-ba!* ATV – *ting-ting-ting-tong!* And these sounds would pick you up and keep you safe: *Comfort…warmth…escape.* It wasn't the real world, but you wished…if only…We knew that in this world Terry and June wouldn't get cancer,[163] Mike Yarwood would always be smiling[164]...Light entertainment, like a fairy cake, bite in: there's nothing there.[165] – *This is me* – All the words, the jokes, the sketches, forgotten, like they never existed – *thank-you please, around the room* – EXTREME CLOSE-UP! NOW! CHARLIE DRAKE, HIS PUCKERED LIPS, THE BABY CURLS, THE FACE LIKE FETAL ALCOHOL SYNDROME, SPEAK, TWIST THOSE WORDS OUT ...

HELLEW, MAHY DAHLINGS!!!!!

I'll get this bathroom clean enough to eat your dinner off. You don't know me. You only think you do. When I set my mind to something...those niggly threads of flesh stuck in the grouting, in the plug hole. I got them all, all the bits of Norman that wanted to cling on. Let the memories suffice, Norman. I can remember. Isn't that enough?

---

[163] 'I knew it would be better to give up the booze, fags and birds, but life would be so boring wouldn't it?' Terry Scott after being diagnosed with cancer.

[164] In 1989 Mike checked into the Priory clinic suffering from depression. I wished him well.

[165] The thing nobody asks, or people are too afraid to ask is, how has light entertainment flourished when it is plainly unfunny and un-entertaining?

30

Present

'You shouldn't make jokes if it makes you so unhappy.'
Alice to the Gnat, Alice In Wonderland.

Something happened during the first year of Norman's illness that had a big effect on Janice and me: we found ourselves staying in more, being there. Keeping him *positive*. But that was never really said. Janice and I spent a lot of nights playing cards. Poker, and Gin Rummy with pennies. We'd clear the table and dim the lights for the game. This was quite a big job as Janice every day bought a few pounds of fruit[166] and had it slap bang in the middle of the table. This she felt would allow Norman free and easy access to it. She had a notion in her head that if Norman caught up with all the fruit he had missed during his lifetime he would be back-flipping across the courtyard in no time. As if motor neurone disease was a vitamin deficiency. It wouldn't be until the cramps started that we found vitamin E[167] was beneficial to Norman. At that time, though, the idea that a banana and a Satsuma were going to help him spring back into life was quite ludicrous. Bit like Janice's argument about her breast later on.

I used to think the secret was to stay active and alert and show enthusiasm for the projects that came along. It is obviously patent nonsense. I have not been in a gym since my schooldays, but I do take life – well, I did – at a brisk trot. I was always moving and hopefully moving forward. Even when spokes stuck in the career I pushed onwards, and often upwards. But, of course, many do this and the only thanks

[166] She rarely ate it herself.
[167] Peanut butter sandwiches were a favourite.

they get are a cardiac arrest three score into their three score and ten. Some get a personal trainer and a nip and tuck waiting for that TV deal; only to find their chest tighten during their tenth ab crunch of the day. Life isn't a contract. It's just the cards you're dealt, by those who came before you. I was conceived in an air-raid shelter in the spring of 1940. The RMS Queen Elizabeth had just entered service as a troop ship a few yards away, my countrymen were interring Italians, and a stranger was entering my mum.

'I'll be honest, Freddy,' Mum had said. 'It was dark in those places. There was a lot of strange goings on. I got the feeling it was a young lad.'

I remember being devastated when she told me this. I wanted my father to have been a war hero – as I had been told often before.

'Why do you think he was young?'

'Well, I could smell Callard and Bowser off his breath. And he was quick.'

The fact that I might have been sired by a pubescent Zoot suited butter scotch eating swing kid was abhorrent to me.

'Did he force himself on you?' I asked hopefully.

'I wouldn't say that, son. We were holding each other because the bombs were so loud and the place was shaking. We got closer and I just felt the natural thing to do was open my legs.'

My mother died at sixty-four. My father might have had a very long life. As for me I can say that I have never enjoyed butter scotch since that conversation.

As far as I'm concerned there is nothing at all to be admired in the young. Apart from their years.[168] I do wish now I could have more years. Unlike Auden, I cannot look forward to death. I have enjoyed so much of my time on the planet. And I have always pushed onward regardless of age. When did

---

[168] Perhaps *envy* is the word I should use here.

Norman stop moving forward? It was long before his disease. Perhaps that moment in The Embassy Club when I couldn't listen to him properly?[169] I heard his voice but couldn't understand. One of the first times he had tried to communicate something to me and I ignored it. All those years of his inane chatter spilling out, everything ending with *birds and booze*. No wonder I was switched off. I didn't realise then that all Norman was doing was what everyone was doing: he was filling in time. Drink and sex was his choice.[170] I did it through parties and conversation. To be out there and to be seen was enough for me. Norman, though, was a private man in spite of all the gregariousness and wildness of his youth. As he grew older he preferred being out of the spotlight with small groups of people. The craving for applause that he had watching Ken Dodd receded over the years. If Arthur Haynes or Nervo and Knox had made an appearance things would have been different.

I missed young Norman, the main man, who wanted to be the one that girls flocked to. The man with a pocketful of stories about landladies and late-night service stations and one-night stands.

Here, Norman, tell us that story about the sheet music salesman and the magician's assistant.

And the story would get that bit longer on each telling. But they would listen. All those girls hanging on to his every word,

---

[169] There are some things that I cannot answer even now. I do not know what prompted my partner to open his heart at that moment. Perhaps it was a crisis of conscience; perhaps it was pre-midlife crisis; perhaps he looked in the stained mirror of the Embassy Club that evening and for a moment didn't like what he saw. Whatever it was it certainly took me by surprise, and I can say now that I didn't like that rare side of Norman on show. This is surprising because normally I would ask that people are open and honest with me. But when they do open up I would rather be somewhere else.
[170] This was perhaps at an age before sex became less of a joy and more of a confrontation.

his every nudge and wink and *oh dear* and *well you would, wouldn't you?* That's how Norman filled a lot of his time: being *on*. I was *on* too. It took me a long time to realise not in a better way.

Nearly a week had passed since I murdered my partner. I had very little push left; either onwards or upwards. It is still the case. Even now. But I shall tell our story. I shall get that done.

31

2006

'You can lead a horse to water but you can't teach him the breast stroke.'[171]
Norman and Freddy

There are things to do, I tell Norman. But every day he must get some fresh air. Luckily the stink of Victorian London would have been enough to make every fair lady or gentleman crave a cleaner living space, and so they produced *the park*. Civilisation indeed. One hundred years later parks can be dangerous places. One morning, though, I remember fondly. It was just after our first night of focussed reminiscence. We needed to clear our heads. Young mums and nannies were out with the prams, lovers were holding each other, and I was pushing Norman in his wheelchair. Feeding the ducks, I ruined the innocence of a school party by loudly informing Norman that ducks were the only creature in the bird kingdom that commit gang rape. The teachers gathered their charges and left for the swing park.

It was then down to the park café for tea[172] and a fruit scone.

We sat inside as there was a chill in the spring air. Some things had happened since we had first had the idea of a biography. I had called a few people[173] and as a result a film

---

[171] This is the first joke that I remember Norman telling me in the pub after our first meeting. He was drinking down a pint and went into a run of the feeblest gags I had heard. I told him this and he said that if I wanted funny that would cost.

[172] Decaffeinated as the caffeine would often cause painful cramps.

[173] I had approached publishers and film makers. One of the four publishers I wrote to replied with the kindest of words. They said that they would be happy to read a manuscript. By chance it was the very one Marc Taughton

company had got in touch with preliminary enquiries about a script possibility. Marc Taughton of Black Eye Films[174] told me that there was a process to go through but he didn't mind 'a wee chat'.[175] Later I found that the company had won a couple of prestigious awards, at the San Sebastian Film Festival and The Sundance Festivals. We did indeed have our 'wee' chat. We discussed how much the film, a biopic, might tell, how honest should we be? Should details be changed in order to see us in a better light? Taughton was all for a warts and all movie which would lift the lid on the British entertainment industry. In other words, a total hatchet job. And what of Norman's disease? He thought that framing the whole project around that might pull in audiences. I thought him presumptuous. I envisaged more a bigger picture: the laughs and tears but no incurable diseases. Who the fuck would want to sit through that? *Cathy Come Home* had been thirty years before. Audiences today wanted success stories, happy endings. I wanted to showcase the golden age of British comedy, tracing Norman and Freddy's successful return to British shores after a daring hiatus on a round the world cruise ship. The film could spark a new audience's interest in the old school comedians. It would be a fiction, of course, as our audience didn't give a flying fuck about who we really were. Maybe the latter stages of the film could touch on how motor neurone disease ended our career;[176] excuse our decline and justify opening our hearts and our lives in one last creative venture. The Yanks might take to that. Unlike the Brits they

---

would give me the card of. It is to them that I shall send this affair. One piece of advice I got was never ever have a prologue. Publishers don't want them, agents don't want them, and certainly readers don't want them.

[174] This meeting prompted me to actually sit down and get to actual work that night.

[175] He wasn't Scottish.

[176] It didn't, of course, but let's not let truth get in the way of a cracking story.

like guys who get up and fight against adversity. Should we
tell the story of Janice? Her DRUGS HELL!!!! Should I
mention my THIRTY-YEAR AFFAIR with her?[177] Probably
not. Although Norman was in no position to beat me to death
for it, I couldn't hurt him like that (unless of course, the
integrity of the work depended on it). After the chat, I
returned to Norman's. He was fast asleep in his wheelchair;
papers were scattered around him and a pen lay on the
floor.[178] Dare I say he looked positively sweet?

I cut Norman's scone and put butter, jam and cream on it.

'What's a treatment? Sure he wasn't a decorator?'

'You get your original proposal idea with a synopsis. Then
you start a more detailed scene by scene breakdown,'

'Tell him to fuck off. Why didn't you tell me this last night?'

'I thought you might tell me to tell him to fuck off.'

This was not the reason. I only ever told Norman as much
as he had to know about anything. I always slept on
information and considered if it was important enough to
share with him. The priority the night before had been to get
the computer set up[179] and make a general start on our story.
The fresh air of the morning filled me with positive thoughts.

---

[177] Affairs were nothing new in the entertainment world. They were a rule
rather than an exception. Most entertainers were *players*. The ones who were
invited into your house on a Saturday evening. The ones who were pictured
with their lovely wives. Les and Terry and Jim and Bernie and Tommy, *they
wouldn't do that to me,* saith your granny. *They wouldn't betray us like that, would
they?* But, of course, they would: *just like that.* Let's just clear this up right
now: you do not know them.

[178] He was finding it increasingly difficult to hold a pen and paper. I made a
note to get him a small whiteboard and a chunky black marker.

[179] How are writers expected to create with such nonsense? There was a
time anyone could write. They had us believe even Adam Faith as a novelist
in *What A Whopper*:

'How's the book going?'

'Still at the publishers.'

Now it appeared to me a writer needed a degree in computing science.

The fact that anyone was interested in anything we might do was worth sharing.

I took a card from my pocket and handed it to him.

'What's that?'

'I told the bloke about a book. He gave me that card. Said he was a film man, but that guy might be interested.'

Norman stared at the card.

'Robert O'Neil...Never heard of him.' He threw the card back at me.

Just then his knife clattered to the floor. The waitress was on it immediately, bending over beside Norman. His eyes opened wide.

'She's wet.'

Even by Norman's standards breaking the etiquette of tea and scones with a filthy comment was surprising. Luckily, I appeared to be the only one who had understood him. I smiled: 'And how would you know that?'

'I can smell it.'

The knife was returned to the table. The waitress made no offer to replace it with a clean one. I wiped it with a paper napkin.

'Listen, Norman,' I said, ignoring his comments, 'treatments are the way of that world now. Remember I had lunch with Colin Welland after he had won an Oscar? He told me that he was asked for a treatment for his next project. He told me it was insulting. But it's the way. Who knows? Maybe this will click with them.'[180]

Outside we watched some boys of no more than ten years old throwing stones at the ducks. From the swing park, some teachers shouted to them but they only got a finger gesture in response.

---

[180] I was wrong. They lost interest quickly. But I'm including this to show that there was something of an interest in Norman and Freddy at this late stage in their non-career. It came days too late. But more of that later.

'Norman,' I said, 'how come you didn't invite me up to your flat on our first meetings? How come we met in a café all the time?'

'I thought you were a poof.'

'Maybe you did, maybe you didn't. But that wouldn't have got in the way of your ambition.'

He made a grumbling sound and shifted his body around to look up at me. I walked around and crouched in front of him.

'My flat was a mess. It was pokey and damp. I was embarrassed by it. Although you were from Glasgow you sounded sophisticated.'

'You mutt,' I laughed. 'You absolute mutt.'

As we made our way home in silence I thought about that café all those years before. Norman lived in Plato Road just off Acre Lane. It was certainly nicer than my street by a mile. To get to the café we had to pass by the market on Atlantic Avenue. It was a Saturday morning when we met so the place was quite busy with shoppers. I liked the buzz of the market as it reminded me of the good times in Glasgow when my ma would take me up The Barras shopping. Norman and I would meet at Lyons Corner House and have a roll and soup followed by a cup of tea, then a cup of coffee.[181] It was there we truly forged our act. The jokes poured out of us and I'd take notes in a journal bought from Woolworths for

---

[181] I really did like the markets and I have a book worth of memories of them. One such memory was when I was poking around Berwick Street market one sunny April. I remember seeing a very pretty blonde girl and thinking she looked better than Norma Gladys Cappagli, the current Miss World. The markets were full of the most beautiful people. Why does that girl stay in my memory? And at Spitalfield Market, standing under cover of light rain at the corner of Greville Street, waiting for…? Who was I waiting for? Norman? Why at that corner? Why at that market? What importance do I put on these moments that they are brought up now? Leather Lane Market, a toothless red-faced man, laughing at an American: *It's not a market for leather, mate!* That time, that image, that voice, has stayed with me nearly half a century. Old man, you know nothing.

tuppence. One of us would say: 'I see a dog on the beach. It's eating an ice cream.' Then we would work backwards. The punchline would be 'the dog eating the ice cream.'

'That's not a punchline. That's a visual image.'

'Okay, it's a talking dog.'

'Right. The punchline would be *Well, if SHE don't want licked…*'

'No. Too filthy.'

'They left in such a hurry. Doesn't she like ice cream?'

'More like that.'

And so we would chase the joke. Start at the end. Work back. It went on like that until we had about an hour of funnies. But that was just gags. We hadn't built our relationship. One of the first that definitely worked was Norman telling me that he was leaving the act. All we did was script it like a married couple breaking up. The fact it was two men on stage would get them howling. We thought. In those days I was chipping in more of the gags and was getting more laughs. Later I would be defined as more of a straight man. I liked a lot of that very early stuff. Sometimes on the page it looked like Samuel Beckett had written it.

I remember saying to Norman that I wanted us to hit a target that no one else could see.

'Got to stand at the oche, lad, before you can throw your dart.'[182]

Our very first appearance as a double act was in the Angel Pub on Coldharbour Road. The show went down well with the few who listened. I thought we were electric together.

---

[182] I was reading Schopenhauer at the time – *The World as Will and Representation* – and was partly referencing his words. It was very typical of Norman to bring the erudition down, this time to a bar game. Our differences were particularly obvious even in those early days. My reading habits, acquired from my sick bed days and a lifetime of social climbing, never left me. I was as comfortable reading Bertrand Russell as I was Eddie Cantor's autobiography.

There was a real spark. At the end Norman ran over to the piano and belted out *They'll Be No New Tunes On This Old Piano*. Afterwards I approached his beer reddened face:

'That song at the end?'

'Ow ya gowin on then, Serri?'

'We didn't rehearse it.'

'I went with the flow, Freddy. Loosen up. We were a success.'

I wasn't happy that he took control, but I put it down to exuberance. What was it years later Robert Rennie would say? *That loose cannon of a partner.*

We were the resident double act there for the next couple of months. Word obviously spread that we were young, talented, and hungry, for there were no fewer than four bookers (not agents) in on our last night. Bernie Welsh, Paul Uzarewicz, John Hill and Grainne Mulhern,[183] (Grainne had the largest beehive in London. She protected it with a headscarf when outside or in). These people are now dead. Only Paul made it into his seventies. Showbiz is no soft option. The stress does for more of us than I care to think about. That night, though, we were the *Next Big Thing*. Norman and I listened to all four of them arguing over who was getting a piece of Norman and Freddy. Bookings would put them into the history books. They were surprised that we didn't have a manager or agent.

'I do the business side,' I piped up. Norman said nothing.

'Remember,' said Grainne, 'you can't ride two horses with one arse.'

'I think I'm on a winner here.'

Norman couldn't stay quiet: 'You're not fucking riding me,' he shrieked and laughed.

'Yes, dear. You just sit quietly and drink your beer.'

I was surprised Norman let Grainne speak to him like this until I glanced down and saw his leg between hers. She smiled.

---

[183] She would later refer to Norman as *The Mermaid*. He was always legless.

On the way home from the park. I asked him if he remembered that very first gig after The Angel Pub:

'Yes,' he smiled. 'It was Grainne Mulhern's.'

As I sit writing in the heat I remember that crisp day in the park, and that sweating night in the pub, thirty years apart, as though they were hand in hand; but they were more than thirty years apart. Memories and time, they play by different rules.

32

December 2006

'Someone slipping on a banana skin is no longer funny…unless it's an old lady.'
Bob Hope, Parkinson Show, December 1975.

I always liked to keep my private life private. Not that much was ever asked of me. Sure, little reminiscences, anecdotes of maybe meeting Max Bygraves or Dickie Henderson; how I ended up knowing so many famous people from all walks of life. I began to think that maybe as a double act we didn't really have a story. It was all about three individuals.
'My name is Janice Anne Calderwood. I was born on July 11ᵗʰ, 1944 in Stepney, London. Stepney was broken up a bit when I was born. Not the German bombs; it was the council. They wanted less people living there so they sent us packing. My dad said they were trying to split the working class up. My dad was always on about a man called Ted Bramley for years later. My mum wasn't of that mind, though. She thought the people deserved better. She wanted to bring her kids up in clean air somewhere modern. A lot of Stepney then looked dingy, she said. So we moved out to Crawley. My aunt Beryl stayed in Stepney.'[184]

There is so much I have not said about her, so much. Oh, my darling girl…We were sitting of an evening in the late 80s, all three of us, and we were watching a programme about a woman who had lost her son in a car crash. The programme was about grief and how, apparently, we handle it. Of course, we don't really *handle it*. But I remember Janice getting really

---

[184] This interview was used in a Granada television documentary about the changing face of London. It was narrated by the incomparable James Mason. Janice got to meet him. Neither Norman nor myself was asked to appear. If I had I'm sure Mr Mason and I would have got on as he was my sort: an individual; a gentleman; and well read.

animated. It was her third glass of red – a lovely Chianti that I had brought – and she was tipsy:

'Let me tell you; let me tell you both: you lose a husband or lover what you do is you try to find them. You go on the same holidays, stay in the same hotels, go to the same beaches, the towns, and such and so forth…But a child? Well, what do you do but sit down and cry for the rest of your life? That is a fact of life.'

And Norman, holding a beer glass and a cigarette in the same hand, just pointed at her.

'You're drunk, Mrs. We don't need a running commentary. Go to bed if you're going to yap.'

Janice stood up straight, and rather rigid, and marched into their bedroom, holding on to the glass.

'That was a bit harsh.'

'The last bus is at 11.27.'

The truth is she was given so little while alive. But back to us.

'That film might have been an idea if it had been a Norman Riddell biopic,' I said.

'You taking the piss?'[185]

'The film opens with a wide-eyed teenager sitting in the gods of the Nottingham Playhouse.'

'Me. A boy. Me mam and dad either side.'

'Down below, in the spot, a young Ken Dodd.'

'Difficult casting. There's prosthetics, I suppose.'

'Dissolve into title…Prick!'

'Very funny.'

'Right, what happened after those initial clubs?'

'We got a tour of Scotland.'

'The only reason you wanted to go was because Grainne

---

[185] It was a very rare occasion I got a chance to take the piss. Or maybe I had many chances but found it tiresome. Who knows what prompted me this time. All I had to do was imagine it was him speaking. He hated it, but for this moment he took the bait as I had done so often.

Mulhorn was getting clingy.'

'I was a young man sowing my wild oats. You always went about with a lemon under your tongue.'

We stopped bickering for a while and remembered the tour. Aberdeen, Inverness, Perth, Glasgow, Edinburgh, Dumfries. On the bill was Tommy Trinder,[186] Kathy Kirby and Cliff Bennett and The Rebel Rousers[187] Trinder was an old hand, a real pro. He didn't think much of Norman getting pissed before a show.

'You tell your partner that these people have travelled on a cold night and paid good money to see professionals.'

He was right, of course. After that Norman waited until after the show to get smashed. At least on that tour. I have always felt that we enter into a kind of bargain with an audience. We agree on a time and a venue and we prepare beforehand. There should be no lateness or tardiness. A few hours before, the audience would be getting ready. In the bath or in the shower cleaning off the grime of the real world, preparing themselves for a night of magic. Getting the suit out, the special one, the one maybe for weddings and funerals. The shoes would be polished; a bit of spit before the elbow grease. And then the jewellery, the cufflinks, tiepins, the rings, the bracelets, the necklaces, earrings; a night of sparkling things that would reflect the night ahead. And the hairspray and the Brylcreem, the aftershave, the deodorant, the perfume; the stinking paraphernalia the body needs to cover the smell of human. And the sharp words: *You ready yet?* A quick look for him – shit, the handkerchief for the breast pocket peeking out just so. *You ready yet?* A last look for her, turning, trying to see a full back view, head at an angle. Quick close up: the eyes, the lippie. *We'll miss the bus! I'm coming! I'm*

---

[186] Tommy called Norman *The Judge*, 'because you're always at the bar.'
[187] Norman kept asking how the Rebel Trousers were. They were not amused.

coming! And she totters quickly down the stairs. And they'll arrive early. Just in case.

There's one thing that people don't seem to understand about entertainers. I never believed that hoary old chestnut about this craving for love. Entertainers don't crave love any more than the next man. What they do crave is the applause. Now some might say that applause is the love: not Freddy Foster. Applause is like a slap on the back. The people are saying, *Well done. You've done your job.* That might come as a surprise to many but we are out to give, not to receive. The applause just tells them they've hit the bullseye. Of course, some comics do enter a place in the hearts of the public. Tommy Trinder understood that it was a job of work to be done to the best of your ability. Imagine you go to your dentist and he's three sheets to the wind? It's not on. And for an entertainer it's an insult to the audience. I might not have respected them but I did my best and therefore didn't insult them. Norman, though, positively despised them. He came from the school of comedy that says *If you don't like the jokes then fuck off.* There was a real anger in old Norman. There was a real anger in young Norman too. At first I thought that this anger must have come from his parents but he told me they were lovely people. No, I think that Norman's anger came from the fact that he never really liked himself.

'I was a twin. My brother was born dead. I murdered him in the womb. My umbilical cord wrapped tight around his neck.'

Was this true? Sometimes he would say things just for the effect. For all his passions in other areas he could be a cold man at heart. Perhaps that was our yin and yang. Did he see qualities in me that he missed in himself? More worryingly did I see qualities in Norman that I coveted? But I have known many cold men.[188] Norman was incapable of giving himself fully. To a friend, to a woman, to an audience, and maybe to

---

[188] Suddenly Hughie Green's face filled my mind.

himself.

In silences between writing and note taking these were my thoughts. At times it was a struggle to rein them in.

'Did anything unusual happen on the Scottish tour?'

'Yes, you bought a round.'

This might be our last shot at immortality and I expected something more than flippancy. Or maybe *expected* is the wrong word. I *wanted* more than flippancy. For many years writing together his attitude led to insults and arguments.[189]

Freddy: He didn't get much schooling. For years he thought parenthesis was a Greek God.

Norman: Too fucking clever.

Freddy: He didn't get much schooling. For years he thought parenthesis was a Greek mum or dad.

Norman: He didn't get much schooling. For years he thought brackets were caused by a poor diet.

Many years ago, there was a period where we had to write apart. I would write out a set of jokes or skits. I would then send them to Norman. He would go over the material, change some and send them back. I would go over the pages again and the process would be repeated until the act was 'as tight as a gnat's chuff'.[190] It was a way of speeding up the writing process and stopped us grinding to a halt until such times as we made up. Sometimes an envelope would arrive with the word *Corrections* scribbled on it, only to reveal, on closer inspection, that my work was untouched. Instead of working he would have been on a bender. Never mind *The Long Weekend*. This Ray Milland had long weeks. I occasionally faced him with it:

---

[189] I have always thought that the best things would surface and stay and the rest would be dross to fall away. I am, of course, paraphrasing Ezra Pound here.

[190] Obviously a quote from Norman. He had a turn of phrase that would make a docker blush.

'You have a problem.'

'You're not a problem, Freddy.'

'I mean your drinking.'

'That's no problem I can assure you, old man.'[191]

'I have saved and bought my flat. I had a goal. What's yours?'

'What?'

'What's yours?'

'A whisky and coke, thanks very much.'

I gave him a lecture about the business offering no guarantees:

'You could end up relying on the government to get you a roof over your head, to put food in your belly, to take care of you. For a few years we were a few shows short of poverty.'

'In Glasgow you went to see your mother.'

'What?'

'The Scottish tour. You went to see your mother when we were in Glasgow. You said you hadn't seen her for over a year. You asked me if I wanted to go.'

'Did you go?'

'No. I found a nice little bar in the West End. I tied one on. You said you'd come back.'

'And?'

'What?'

'Did I come back?'

'The next morning. You had a look on your face that told me you'd slept with her.'

'That is fucking disgusting. If you weren't dying I'd kill you.'

'Kill me, Freddy.'[192]

---

[191] When Norman felt threatened or when he was threatening he would often say 'old boy' or 'old man'.

[192] It seems right to mention that although all of this put a drain on our energies and humour, one doesn't spend one's life with a fellow quipster without latching onto the comic, even in the most grotesque of

33

Early 1960s

*What the mass media offer is not popular art, but entertainment which is
to be consumed like food, forgotten, and replaced by a new dish.'*
W.H Auden – The Dyer's Hand

I did indeed visit my mother when we played in Glasgow. It
took an unexpected turn when I sat down to watch a play by
Robert Muller[193] on the commercial channel. She was making
tea and wittering in the background. The single play series was
called Armchair Theatre, and as I watched it my thoughts
turned to writing my own. By the time we hit Dumfries I had
completed a rough draft. There was for a short while something
in the air that allowed people like me to consider such things.
ITV was not only in with the red brick yooni brigade, it had
ears for the non-U as well.[194] And so I wrote my one and only
television play. It was called R*emember Me*. It described –
accurately, I thought[195] – my visit home. When I got back to
London I tidied it up and sent it off to Sydney Newman at ABC.
Phillip Saville sent me the loveliest rejection, complementing its
real 'tenderness'. Since the script is still extant I offer it to you,
dear reader. It might give you the feel, if not the fact, of my

---

circumstances. At one point Norman had said to me that he wanted to
cascade into death. I was slightly surprised at the flowery language emanating
from such a brutal tongue. 'There will be no cascading while I'm in charge,
Sonny Jim,' I replied rather tartly. 'You'll have a slow death. Like the rest of
us.' At that we were both convulsed in laughter.

[193] Later to marry the wonderful Billie Whitelaw.

[194] This was, of course, only a perception. The BBC was spluttering about
the commercial channel bringing standards down.

[195] Well, with an element of dramatic licence, of course. People say that they
want a reflection of life, but of course that is nonsense. They want plot, and
life cares nothing of plot.

home and my mother.[196] A lot of what happened in my early days might be lying in the back court of my memory, not to be recalled; an impression warmed by the fire in my mother's front room.[197]

---

[196] I am finding it difficult writing this part of my story. The past can be a scary country.

[197] Sometimes of course memory can knock you for six. I have never been one for emotional scenes. In fact, I have been viewed, I know, as something of a cold fish. One incident that happened that I cannot really explain, and have little excuse for, occurred when I returned from a very short tour of the university campuses sometime in the late 80s or 90s. I was excited at seeing Norman and Janice and had bought them – well, Norman really – a small gift. It was one of those plastic slide projectors where you slip in a disc and click the images around. I had bought the thing in a junk shop in Nottingham. It had come with a plastic bag full of discs. I assumed – wrongly – that all the discs were like the one I tried in the shop: Scenes of Nottingham. I thought Norman would love this toy. And he did. He laughed all the way through, pointing out this site and that. The bag contained different discs and different cities. And there was Glasgow. There the High Street, the park, the buses. I crashed down into a seat at the kitchen table and bawled like a baby.

34

REMEMBER ME
A play for television
By
Frederick B. Foster

1. FADE UP *on still pictures of Glasgow life. The pictures dissolve into each other. The pictures should start with the elderly and move onto the young, settling on back court scenes of children. Throughout this opening a street song should be chanted by children.*

Gypsy, gypsy, Carol
Waashed her herr in V.P wine
V.P wine will make it shine
Gypsy, gypsy, Caroline.

DISSOLVE TO:
2. INT. BEDROOM. MORNING.
It is dark apart from a shard of light that cuts through the top of the curtains. MARY *lies in her double bed. Her eyes are open. Although in her early sixties she could quite easily pass for a decade older. A bedside table, busy with various medicines. A large, heavy wardrobe takes up most of the wall opposite the bed. One of the wardrobe doors is open and clothes have spilled out onto the floor.*

CUT TO:

3. INT. HALL. MORNING.
CLOSE-UP *of letterbox flapping open and post dropping through. The post lies on the floor. We can see envelopes of different sizes. One of them is stamped with British Army advertising.* MARY *appears in a dressing gown and picks up letters. She turns and walks into the* LIVING ROOM/KITCHEN.

CUT TO:

4. INT. LIVING ROOM/KITCHEN. MORNING.
MARY *enters carrying post. She puts it on the table then walks to sink. She fills the kettle and places it on the cooker hob. She picks up matches*

and lights a ring of the gas cooker. She goes over to gas fire and switches it on.

MARY
quietly
Heat this place up…

MARY *goes to table and picks up letters. She takes them back to easy chair by the fire and looks through them. The Army one she looks at for a moment then drops it with a pile of similar envelopes by the side of the chair. Another envelope she tears open. We can read it clearly. It is a hospital appointment. She puts the letter back in the envelope. Opening another we see that it is a birthday card.* HAPPY BIRTHDAY MAMMY FROM YOUR LOVING SON JOHNNY *is written on it. She doesn't look impressed as she looks at it. She stands and places the card by the clock on the mantelpiece. At the sink, she takes a cup from the cupboard and puts it on the kitchen table. Returning to the sink she takes an almost empty milk bottle and pours the last of it in the cup. She takes the bottle back to the sink and washes it out. She notices something out through the window and starts banging on it. 'No!' She rushes to the table, grabs a chair and takes it over to the sink. She climbs on it and then up onto sink. She takes a whistle that hangs by string to a nail hammered into the side of the window frame. She blows it three times, loudly:*

MARY
Aye, you're running now!
Quieter
Running now…like frightened rabbits
…yes…messing things up…
Shouting:
You hear? Go on! Go on now! Your parents
will know! Mark these words! Your parents
will be told!

176

She climbs down carefully.

MARY
Very quietly, to herself
Not that they care. Kick you out in
the morning see you at night. Dragged up.
Your necks not seen soap…

She is on the floor still holding the whistle. She looks at it then to the nail which she can't now reach. Disappointment. She takes the chair back to the table. A small teapot and a tea caddie sit on the table. She scoops two teaspoons of tea into the pot. The kettle starts to whistle loudly. She goes to the cooker and takes the kettle off the ring. She then fills the teapot with the boiling water.

MARY
What sort of life you got here, Mary? What sort of future?
Who even knows you're alive? No one, that's who. No
one. Well…good as…
She returns the kettle to the cooker. She returns to the table and stirs the tea in the pot. Picking up the pot she pours.

MARY
Might try and read the leaves. See what life has in store
today…A date with Elvis the Pelvis… *(She giggles to herself).*
A knock on the door might be a highlight. The war
brought people together. After…just drifted…aye…
Realisation
Here, what are you doing? Talking to yourself. What's that
about? They'll cart you away. To the loony bin with Mary
talking to herself. She's away with the fairies.
Sitting at table with tea. She pulls a ten pack of cigarettes from her dressing gown pocket and pulls one out.

What age was…what…?

She moves quickly to the chair and starts delving into the papers and envelopes. Success. She pulls out a Bible. She returns to table and pulls a gold coloured lighter from her dressing gown pocket. She lights and inhales deeply. She then starts turning pages frantically. Reading:

The days of our years are threescore years and ten; and if by the reason … Of strength they be fourscore years, yet is their strength labour and… Sorrow…How'd they do that? How'd they live so long? Without the medicines; without the modern conveniences? And what about…

Starts flicking through pages.

Here we are…Moses was one hundred and …one hundred and twenty years old when he died, yet …yet…

Holds book at arm's length.

…yet his eyes were not…his eyes were not weak nor his strength gone…Was it living in the desert?... Maybe the sun…Don't get much of that here…What about old Noah? Let's see…he lived a while too… *(flicking through Bible:)* Here we are: And all the days of Noah were nine hundred and fifty – what? – nine hundred and fifty? That can't be the sun…written by a fisherman no doubt…nine hundred and fifty years; and he died… *(Looks upwards:)* I'm doing my best but you don't make it easy.

(Takes out four bottles of pills from table drawer. Takes one pill from each bottle and lays them in single file on table.) One for the money… *(Takes a pill with a drink of tea.)* Two for the show… *(Takes second pill with drink of tea.)* Three to get ready… *(Takes third pill with a drink of tea.)* …now go cats go… *(Takes last pill with drink of tea. Inhales cigarette deeply.)* That was a good record. Four years ago…

She gets up and looks at herself in the mirror above the fire.

Oh, Mary…what a big four years…You're not looking well. Not well at all…Right, no point getting maudlin. Get changed. Those stairs won't wash themselves…

She goes to sink and pulls out a bucket…

FADE OUT:

5. INT. CLOSE. DAY

FADE UP *on* MARY *on her knees scrubbing the stairs. She is dressed in a floral apron and wearing a scarf. There is a bucket of disinfected water beside her.*

MARY

The things people traipse up these stairs with. All kinds of filth. And what about the fags? Stubbed out as you like. Bet they don't take their turns on the close. Well, Max and Jake I don't bother with because they're men. You wouldn't expect a man to get on his hunkers for this. Certainly not them. Not with their problem. The drink does it for so many. Who the hell invented it, that's what I'd like to know. Brought nothing but ill to everyone. Wonder if old Noah touched it? A wee dram to get him through the centuries. And if he did then he must have made it himself because everything was wiped out. I'll need to ask the minister that one.

A bang of a door.

She listens.

Silence.

Returns to cleaning the stairs.

I'll get these stairs finished and then get to the shops. Maggie always has bruised fruit before twelve. She's usually got bruised fruit after twelve as well, come to think about it. Buy some potatoes as well. Maybe a few carrots. Keep my health up. Although God knows what for. Seems like these days I'm just passing the time. Will he come for my birthday? He'll come because he wants to, not because I want him to. Never a truer word, Mary. I don't know what world he's in now. I'm not sure I know what world I'm in half the time. You get up. You clean. You shop. Sometimes hardly see a soul if you don't get to the shops. Nobody knocks the door. Nobody to speak to. Well, Maggie will have a gab, but she's got to serve people. Customers. She's got to make a living to keep that house in front of the park going. Never invited me up. Not that kind of relationship. I'm a customer. A good customer. In every day. Not the week's shop. The daily shop. Gets me out the house. Gets me in the air…And a gab. The talking has to be good. I'm an awful long time in silence these days. Was the time…I remember there was a lot more chat when I was a girl. There were a lot more people about. People I knew. Where the hell did they go? Where do people go? They just go away.

She continues scrubbing.

What's in these stairs? What do people traipse in on their feet? All the street ends up here. And the mopping isn't good enough. You need to get down on your knees. Like in the chapel. If God was there would people be here? I don't think so.

She stops and thinks about what she said.

Sorry God.

She continues scrubbing.

It's just I don't understand why the suffering. I mean there's Alice up the next close and her boys. Both of them driving her to an early grave. The drink and the fights. The boys in blue never away from her door. It always ended in tears. And it'll be more jail for the boys. Wonder if they put twins in the same cell?

She looks up at the gas mantle burning.

Still lit. That's a whole day.

A YOUNG WOMAN *and* MAN *pass. We see the feet but not the rest.* MARY *is startled.*

YOUNG WOMAN
That you talking to yourself again, Mary?
MARY
looking up
What? No, just taking my turn.
YOUNG WOMAN
Mind you don't wear out those knees.
YOUNG WOMAN *and* MAN *continue down the stairs, giggling.*

MARY
Well seen you don't get down cleaning. Might ruin your stockings.
Shouting:
You hear me? Might ruin your…
She splashes her brush into pail and starts scrubbing.
Still, she's young…This is for the old…Scrubbing…The hands…ruined…
She holds a hand out at arm's length and looks.
They were young…a long time ago…
MARY *looks down and lifts her hand. She looks at it for a moment. She splashes the brush in the pail and* continues *scrubbing the stairs. We see and hear a man's footsteps coming up the stairs. Cut between this and* MARY.
Can't see her cleaning the stairs. Not with those clothes…and the hands…mine were…soft…
The footsteps get closer and louder. MARY *listens, wary. The steps stop at* MARY *and her bucket. She looks up slowly, wide eyed.*
JOHNNY
Hello, ma.

FADE TO:

6. (a) INT. LIVING ROOM/KITCHEN   DAY

JOHNNY *sits on easy chair by the fire. He is looking at army brochures.* MARY *has her back to him, standing at the sink.*

MARY

I don't have coffee.

JOHNNY *slides the brochure down the side of the chair to the floor.*

JOHNNY

Tea's fine, ma. I see you got the card.

MARY

It's the only one.

She takes the kettle from the hob and carries it over to the table.

I don't bother with birthdays.

JOHNNY *stands at the mantelpiece. He picks up the card and looks at it.*

JOHNNY

I haven't had a chance to get you a present yet.

MARY

Oh, don't bother with that.

JOHNNY

It's just been so busy. The show and all. It's Shakespeare. King John. Cardinal Pandolf. Huge part. Huge importance. The play swings on it. I'm the lynchpin. The lynchpin.

MARY

One or two?

JOHNNY

What?

MARY

Sugars.

JOHNNY

Oh. Right. None.

MARY

You used to like your sugar.

JOHNNY

Got to watch my waistline. It's a physical role. Lots of…physical stuff…movement…Lots of movement about

the stage. It's … It's a main part. Shakespeare, you know?
Lots…

MARY *pours tea.*

MARY
I liked the variety shows.

JOHNNY
The variety shows?

MARY
The comedians and the magicians.

JOHNNY
There's no comedy in this. This isn't comedy. This is
history. Part of our culture.

MARY
I like a laugh. We need a laugh these days.

JOHNNY
That's as maybe, ma. But this isn't one of those shows. The
Bard did, of course, write comedy. Like…But that isn't what
we're doing. We're doing a serious play.

MARY
You know who I liked? That Jimmy Handley.
Handsome boy too.

JOHNNY *sits down.* MARY *gives him a cup of tea. She sits at the
table.*

JOHNNY
So, that's what I'm doing. Doing good, ma…

He sips at the tea.

Lynchpin…

He sips at tea.

MARY
It's hot.

JOHNNY
Aye.

He sips.

How have you been?

MARY

The hospital letter came.

JOHNNY

The tests?

MARY

I go in next week.

JOHNNY

Have you got anyone…?

MARY

Oh, I'm fine. Just tests.

JOHNNY

It's just…I'll be in …Well, wherever. Touring. You don't get time off. It's too big a part. Of course, normally…the understudy…but the budget…it's tight…

MARY

I'll be fine. Wouldn't expect you to. If you might drop me a line…

JOHNNY

A line? Of course.

MARY

I don't get letters.

JOHNNY

I send you postcards. Now and…A postcard…

MARY

But a letter. Maybe telling me what you're doing.

JOHNNY

I'm acting, ma. It's…I'm acting…

MARY

Oh, I know that. Sometimes a letter has more in it.

JOHNNY

It's the time, ma…It's so busy. My life is so busy.

MARY

I know that, son. You're making your way in the world. Carving a career. You said that. See, I remember.

JOHNNY

It's all so difficult...Time...I'm a...a lynchpin...but...there's people...

MARY

I've no biscuits.

JOHNNY

You've...? No, my waist and all that...I'll try ma. I'll try and drop you a line.

MARY

A letter.

JOHNNY

A letter, yes.

MARY *mantelpiece and looks at the birthday card.*

MARY

It's a nice card. Did you get it in...?

JOHNNY

Just a newsagent. A local newsagent. I just popped in...

MARY

There's no age on it. I prefer that.

JOHNNY

I couldn't remember if you were sixty-three or...

MARY

Oh, don't you bother about numbers.

JOHNNY

I like to get things right. I like to be exact.

He stands up and goes to the sink. He looks out through the back window.

Nothing changes.

MARY

Well, they're pulling down buildings. Leave them another few years they'll just fall down.

JOHNNY *picks up the whistle, looks at it and smiles.*

JOHNNY

The kids still bothering you?

MARY

They're so wild now. I don't know how that happened. I just blow the whistle. They think it's the police.

JOHNNY

No, ma, they think it's an old woman with a whistle.

MARY

They run.

JOHNNY

That's what children do.

PAUSE

What has the hospital said?

MARY

They said that there's no reason to jump to conclusions.

JOHNNY

Are you in pain?

MARY

Pain? I'm not sure.

JOHNNY

You're either in pain or you're not.

MARY

They give me pills, so they might be covering it up.

JOHNNY

You were washing the stairs.

MARY

The world doesn't stop, Johnny.

JOHNNY

No.

JOHNNY *suddenly turns, full of life, enthusiastic.*

Why don't I get you something? Why don't I buy you something? Something big. A television?

MARY

Some people have one. I have the wireless. You

can listen and do things. But with a picture how would I see it if I'm making my tea. I'd have to keep turning my head around. And my eyes. They're not too good.

JOHNNY

But a television, ma. It's the future. Everyone will have one.

MARY

Will it make it good if everyone has one?

JOHNNY

It is good. There's programmes for all tastes. There's quality from the BBC. And there's the other channel for more…for different tastes. There's a revolution happening.

MARY

I don't think I can cope with a revolution. It's all I can do to wash the stairs.

JOHNNY

I'll get you a television. Once I get on my feet. Money wise. I'll get you the best.

MARY

Are you short, son?

JOHNNY

No. ma, not…not short. You see it's how it works this acting game. You have to build. You have to build up a…You build up a repertoire. That's what you call it, a repertoire. That's where you get the phrase *repertory company*. You see, ma? It's built up over time. You start…You start in the smaller roles. These are small roles but they're…they're important. Important roles because…Laurence Olivier spoke about this. You know Laurence Olivier?

MARY

The film actor?

JOHNNY

Yes. But he's a man of the stage. The best. He's doing modern things on the stage. What a man.

                         MARY
                  Will he see you okay?
                        JOHNNY
    Who? Laurence Olivier? No, you don't understand. I don't
know him. I don't know him yet. But I read about what he
said about smaller roles. You can be the lynchpin of the play.
But…Of course you must start, you must struggle at first.
Nothing is handed to you on a plate in this game. So the
money is…

MARY *rises and goes towards the sideboard.*
                         MARY
                    I've got a bit…
                        JOHNNY
                Oh, ma, you don't have to…
                         MARY
                    Don't be daft.
*She takes a tin from one of the cupboards and opens it. We can see
there are a few notes.* JOHNNY *watches her. She stops. Thinks.*
            What am I thinking? This is my rent. But listen…
She leaves the tin on the sideboard top. She exits.
                    Wait a bit…

CUT TO:

6. (b) INT. BEDROOM. DAY

MARY *enters. She gets on her knees and pulls a suitcase from under the
bed. She opens it and pulls from a pocket a £5 note. She closes the
suitcase and returns it under the bed.*
She exits bedroom.

CUT TO:
6. (c) INT. KITCHEN/LIVING ROOM. DAY
JOHNNY *is sitting drinking his tea.* MARY *comes up to him.*

MARY

I had this put away for…

JOHNNY *looks at the money.*

JOHNNY

Ma, listen, if this is going to leave you short…

MARY

If you can't help your own son…

JOHNNY

You're the best ma in the world.

MARY

Oh, I'm sure every son says that. And means it.

JOHNNY *takes the £5 and takes out his wallet. He opens the wallet slowly to show how empty it is.*

JOHNNY

That'll look just fine in here, ma.

MARY *looks pleased. She sits at table.*

MARY

I'm sure you're just finding your feet.

JOHNNY

I am. That's the nature of showbusiness. Finding your feet and getting the breaks are all important.

He stands at the mantelpiece and looks again at the card.

Just one good break and your life can change. Maybe next year I can get you that television.

MARY

A letter now and again would be fine.

JOHNNY

I see you've been sending off for the army brochures again?

MARY

Oh, they don't mean anything. I just like to hear the postman.

JOHNNY

Not thinking of signing up?

MARY

(*laughing*)

Bit old for that.

JOHNNY

Listen, ma, you know this was a flying visit? I'm supposed to meet some of the others. The cast. It's to discuss some last-minute details. I hardly get a minute to myself these days. But next time I promise I'll stay longer. In fact, next time why don't I stay over? How would that be? I could stay over, and we could listen to the radio. We could listen to Jimmy Handley. Just the two of us.

He stands up.

What about this hospital? Now, I don't want you worrying. You hear? Things will be fine. It's just procedures. They're going through procedures. They have to. It's the law. You're going to be fine. I'll send you a card.

MARY

A letter.

JOHNNY

I'll send you the longest letter.

He moves quickly towards the door. MARY *follows him. They exit.*

MARY

You make sure you're wrapped up.

JOHNNY

You're a fusspot! Take care ma!

MARY

Bye, son.

We hear the door closing. MARY *enters. She goes over to the chair and picks up the cup. She puts the cup down and picks up the hospital letter. She leans it against the birthday card and picks up the cup again. She goes over to the sink. She looks out the window and looks agitated. She bangs on the window.*

No! You stop that! The police are coming!
She picks up the whistle and blows it.
Go on! Run!
She goes over and brings the chair over to the sink. She climbs up on it and onto the sink area. She hangs the whistle up on a nail. Stops. Looks shocked. Looks down at the tin on top of the sideboard. Scurries down to the floor and across to the sideboard. She opens tin. It is empty. She crosses to chair at sink and slumps into it still holding tin. She stares ahead.
As we fade to black children's voices can be heard:

Gypsy, gypsy, Caroline
Waashed her herr in V.P wine
V.P wine will make it shine
Gypsy, gypsy, Caroline.

FADE TO BLACK

3

35

Present

'Dogs are only smart in comparison to other dogs. When was the last time you saw a dog open a bottle of wine?'
                                                        Freddy Foster

I remember it all too clearly, my younger years. I remember my clothes. I remember a photograph; the shorts hitched up to chest height, with the large buttons, the straps over my shoulders – and over a woollen jersey! My knee has a bandage wrapped around. The bandage was made from a pillow slip torn into strips. I was three or four years old. The backdrop was a desolate no man's land, buildings broken in half, a diseased back court. I stared at the camera, again, a fleeting moment, Freddy frozen in time. This memory frightens me more than most that I have related. I think it is because I still remember that boy.

'Qu'est-ce qu'il y a?'

'I'm fine,' I reply.

 I have been shaken into the present. I want to say something else. I want to tell him about the years that have gone, the life wasted. But I haven't got enough of the language, or really the inclination, to speak of things he wouldn't understand. The distance travelled in miles and memory, the terrible reality of life. Who are you, Freddy Foster? I ask myself again. Is this all about you? Are these words trying to give shape and substance to your own existence? Trimming the excesses of daily routine. Maybe that was my great pull towards the artistic in our society. All art is biography. A Henry Moore sculpture tells me more than a book ever could. If my art was the jokes and the sketches am I revealed in those? At the time, I thought I was re-inventing myself, I thought that I was hiding the past. The things Freddy Foster has learned way too late…

Memory is, of course, a curse and a blessing. We revisit something that we can no longer hold, no longer truly experience. It brings me some kind of exquisite pain to be once again drinking tea with Norman, to be stumbling down narrow stairs in a small Greek street, to be creating our act, and yes, to be holding Janice. Oh, the wonderful times. But not to truly have them is one of life's cruellest gifts. The rain can never be as it was on the night of our first meeting, the sun never the same as the afternoon of our first Palladium rehearsal, the snow never as fresh as on our first tour. Nothing can ever be truly revisited. We are given a glimpse of what was and are whisked back to the reality of what is. Why suicide is not the common coin of living escapes me.

Kill me, Freddy.

36

Janice passed away on July 8th, 2006. I find it too difficult to write at the moment. She was buried in London. She left us. What had we left in this world?

37

2009

> *Norman: It's true. As sure as my name's Norman N.*
> *Riddell*
> *Freddy: What's the 'N' for?*
> *Norman: Nothing.*
> *Freddy: I walked into that one, didn't I?*
> *Norman: Rack 'em up, lad, rack 'em up![198]*
> *The Good Old Days, BBC1 Thursday 25th March 1976.*

There's a sure sign that you're in the domain of the older generation: linoleum. It stretches wall to wall from the runner of the doorframe of the kitchen to the sink and the cooker. It's the colour of a cheap blonde rinse. Years of steam and grease and cigarette smoke and shod feet and unshod feet leaves it looking tired and old, like the people who laid it. It will eventually crack and unfurl at the corners. You can tack it down but the material will tear. And then it just lies there collecting scraps of dropped food, crumbs, mouse droppings, and every bit of shit you can think of. It will be ground into it; it will catch the scuffs and scrapes and smudges in the windowlight. But you don't tear it up. That's the thing about linoleum: you don't tear it up. That's something for the new people to do. When you move out. Or are carted out. When they move in. When they look at the crack den and think holy fuck what sort of animal lived in this stinking slop bucket? It's

---

[198] This was 1976. We weren't getting a lot of work but it was a popular show and it was 9.25 on a Thursday night. We had appeared higher up the bill years before but post-cruise things were more sporadic. We accepted the billing and had a good night. Norman complained to Larry Grayson about having to wear Edwardian 'clobber'. He replied that he was' sweating like Everard in a Chinese chippie.'

the first thing I thought of when my eyes opened. And yet only the day before I had cleaned it. One can do so much with a sow's ear and I wasn't in the market for a silk purse.

I usually like mornings. The older that I get I'm glad I'm allowed to wake at all. On this one I awoke with my joints totally seized up.[199] Probably it is not advisable for a pensioner to fall asleep on the hall floor. It took me several minutes to move my legs at all. I rubbed them vigorously to get my cold blood moving. Getting to the kitchen I stuck on the kettle and made myself tea. I had to plan my day. Freddy Foster was a busy boy. Norman had been dead about three or four days. I was trying my best to get my flat sold to gather as much cash as possible. It was while I was sitting at the table drinking the tea that the phone rang. It rang sharp through the silence.[200] This was the only intrusion I had had during my grim task and it revealed how removed I was from the world around me.

'Yes?' Even the sound of my voice seemed like an intrusion in the room's silence.

'Norman?'

'It's Freddy.'

'Freddy?'

'His partner.'

'I know who you are, you fuck. It's me. It's Gordon Tait at Channel 7. I've been trying to contact you.'

'This is Norman's number.'

---

[199] There were frequent wake ups at this time when I didn't appear to have been sleeping. I shall have to call them *senior moments* – no doubt brought on by my horrifying and catastrophic recent actions. I even emerged in that present slapping out a short jazz tap routine in a puddle of Norman's blood. My dreadful murderous performance obviously had consequences on my mental well-being. I doubt that my lovely partner ever considered this when he proposed his assisted death.

[200] I was going to type deathly silence! What a sad old slap Freddy can be! Forever looking for the humour; the line; the quip; the story. Now I can smile at all of this. It is astounding what a few weeks can do.

'I know, but I've been calling your flat all yesterday.'

'I wasn't in.'

'I know you weren't in.'

'I was out.'[201]

'Listen, I got a proposition.'

'I'm listening.' It came naturally to me to offer such a reply. I had done so many times before.

'How's Norman?'

'He's had better days.' A gross and foul understatement, but the reply came out naturally. Sometimes my tongue is too sharp for its own good.

'We're all gob-smacked at his illness.'

'It's been a few years now.'

'We were gob-smacked.' There was a slight pause before he followed up with: 'He got all of his faculties?'

'Faculties?'

'I mean is he clear in his thinking? Does the disease muddle his mind? I'm asking for a reason.'

'One of the tragedies of MND is that the mind is fine.' I knew from the silence that Gordon Tait hadn't a clue about Norman's tragedy. 'What is it you have in mind, Gordon?'

'Lunch. We'll talk over lunch, Freddy.'

'Look, Gordon, it's not a great time. We haven't had a great time these last few years. Norman's illness, the work dried up. There was the passing of Janice. Life sort of knocked the puff out of me.'

'Listen to something, Freddy. I'm not a charitable institution. I don't do charity unless it's going to boost ratings. The fact that you were buddies with my dad doesn't cut ice either. I'm not into the nepotism stuff. I just think the time is right to have a proper blast of the past. I have some ideas.

---

[201] My flat had been on the market a matter of days. I'd told the estate agent a quick sale was a priority. I had pretty much been living at Norman's the best part of a year.

We'll do lunch. How about tomorrow at Amaya?'

'Somewhere I know, Gordon. Somewhere an old man knows. A pub would do me. But a classy pub.'

'Harewood Arms, Fulham. One fifteen?'

I agreed and hung up. The phone sits like an antique for two years and then you murder your sidekick and it kicks into life. It's the nature of the beast.

Bunny Tait left the British Army in 1946. He was 26 years old and a fighting veteran. He fought in the Battle of France in 1940. The British lost 100,000 men, the Germans too lost as many. The French tally was 350,000. Bunny Tait went into that battle an innocent, he left feeling 'corrupted'. But that wasn't the end of it. There were five years of war left. Afterwards there was the chance to go to Oxford, but Bunny took the BBC route and rose from floor manager to producer in a few years. On the way he met and married Anne Shore and produced one child, Gordon. It was by all accounts a bitter, unhappy marriage, each silently blaming the other for their daily tragedy. Bunny got through it all with the help of a few pathetic affairs; Anne got through it tending her garden and swallowing diet pills. They often had garden parties where they would put on the bravest of faces and *entertain* the entertainers. She once made a pass at me:

'Freddy, are you a homosexual?'

'No, Anne, I'm a Mason.'

She walked over to me and closed her eyes:

'You can touch me if you like.'

I returned to the garden. I was having none of it.

Bunny always took a while getting to the business of the business. It was well after eleven, when we were drinking brandy and smoking cigars in the conservatory, when he told me about his new quiz show: *Six Of The Best*. It would involve six contestants each week fighting through five rounds to reach the headmaster's room where they had the chance to be *top of the class* and win £1000. What was unusual at the time was that he had a guaranteed one hour slot on a Saturday evening. He wanted us. *You boys have earned the respect. The public know that. The whole damn business knows it.* This was prime entertainment and could have made Norman and Freddy huge, if it had been a success. It wasn't.

'Should have got Jimmy Edwards,' Bunny said rather uncharitably later.

We did one episode and whoever chose the contestants should have been horsewhipped. The British public are not cretins, but some can test the boundaries:

Norman: What did Harold get in his eye?

I ran up the aisle whipping up the audience.

Contestant (Nan from Stoke): Was it mud?

That was the very first question. The second was met with equal stupidity:

Norman: Julius Caesar's last words?

Contestant (John from Essex): I know that.

Norman: You must have heard this from your English master.

Contestant (John from Essex): Yes, that was it. At school.

Norman: When Brutus did that dirty deed.

Contestant (John from Essex) Yes. What?

Norman: Brutus, John.

John from Essex looked panic stricken.

Norman: Take your time. Here, Freddy let's enact it. Might help John.

And we did. We mimed the assassination with me as Julius and Norman as an assailant. There was a trickle of applause. For such a piece of impro we would have expected loud cheers and thunderous applause. But they lost. I could smell failure. It descended on the set like a corpse. John from Essex stood like a rabbit caught in headlights.

Me: Come on, John. People have homes to go to.

Norman: Julius Caesar's last words.
Contestant (John from Essex): I…
Me: You'll understand, ladies and gentlemen, why this programme is an hour long.
Contestant (John from Essex): I…
For a moment I thought his heart had stopped. Norman turned his back and walked upstage shaking his head in anger and disbelief. If he had been miked up the programme would have been taken off the air at that moment because I could hear him quite clearly cursing. When he walked back downstage his face was red and sweating.
Norman: Julius Caesar, John. His last words. Before he died. When he was assassinated by Brutus and his cohorts. What did he say, John?
Contestant (John from Essex): Was it…Forgive them, father, for they know not what they do?
  We often hear the expression that a jaw drops. That evening the nation became a single plummeting mandible. They felt ashamed to be British.
Me: No, John, that was…somebody else. But a good guess. A round of applause for John who, sadly, goes away empty handed.
I should have added empty headed. In my eagerness to get the fool off the stage I forgot to read the answer. This was brought up at the autopsy in the boardroom on Sunday morning. But Bunny was quite philosophical about it.[202]
  'You win some, you lose some.'
He understood that Norman and Freddy were consummate pros. We flogged a dead horse and came up with plums. That's show biz, folks.

---

[202] Apart from mentioning Jimmy Edwards. Edwards was a well-loved British figure who made the move from radio to television seamlessly. Much of his humour derived from the threat or actual beating of boys' backsides with a cane.

Gordon Tait was Bunny's son. He was a chip off the old block. When I looked at him, I could be staring at his father. But there was something flashier and – dare I say it? – trivial about his son. For all of his eagerness and enthusiasm there was something superficial about young Gordon that I couldn't seem to get my head around. If I'm totally honest here I feel that about most of the current crop. There's a sheen of ignorance beneath the namedropping. Today, though, his flattery was on the money. 'I admire you boys,' he said. 'I admire your tenacity. I don't have to talk to you about fame and its fickle nature. It's a cunt. I don't have to talk to you about what makes the great *special*. You know, the Brucies, the fucking Tarbucks. But fame has been brought down to what now? Fame for doing nothing? Sweet Fanny Adams? Okay, I'll throw a bone to Ant and Dec. But, in general, the more people become famous then the more fame becomes worthless. What was the golden age of Hollywood? It was Gable and Lombard, it was Bogie and Bacall, it was Chaplin and Brando and Cagney and Sinatra, Niven and Taylor, Hope and Bing*aroony*. These people were special because it was a rare thing. It was fucking celebrity. They were untouchable. Unreachable. Stars. Real fucking stars sparkling in the firmament. And I make no apology for mentioning Bruce Forsyth and Jimmy Tarbuck in that company. Fucking stars. They walked those boards. They learned their craft. Like you boys. You are pros. You and Norman. I know that. You were a rare breed. It was the rarity that made stars. Freddy, the easier fame becomes the more it becomes devalued. Mark my words, Freddy…'

'You said,' I interrupted.

'Don't make stardom easily available otherwise it becomes the common coin. And who wants the common coin?'

This was true, of course, but the devaluation had set in long before Gordon began his impersonation of his dad. It was

Mandy Rice Davies; it was Christine Keeler, the girls who didn't have a talent other than being in all the right places on the arms of the right men. It didn't matter if that man was Douglas Fairbanks Jnr or Peter Rachman. (a pair of dodgy characters as ever was.) They made it seem easy to the discarded souls who haunted the late-night chemists in Chelsea. It blew up in some of their faces, though. I met a young man outside the boutique *Granny Takes A Trip* in late '67. He was leaning on the Dodge Saloon that smashed out of its front.

'It's just dust, man,' he kept repeating. 'It's just dust.' He was possibly the unhappiest man I had met in Swinging London. His haunted face stayed in my mind a very long time, and his voice gave lie to the myth of the 60s. It was a warning salvo fired somewhere in the recesses of my memory. For every celebrity, there were a thousand of those young men taken prisoner in the Fame Game. Bunny understood this better than his son. He understood that you should have something to give in order to earn that fame. He knew that if the bubble burst on rarity, then anything would go and everything would be going cheap. But this was not Bunny sitting in front of me with a G&T in his hand, it was Gordon, clutching a Jura, a facsimile of his father. His speech could have been the one Bunny gave to Norman and me immediately prior to *Six of the Best*.

'I want to bring something to the public with longevity. You boys have earned your stripes. The public know that. The pros know it. I know it.'

'You sound like just your old man, Gordon.'

Maybe he'd heard this too often. He prickled at the words.

'I'm my own man, Freddy. What my dad did is what my dad did. That was a while ago. I'm proud of what he achieved but this is a different world to the one he walked. What have you been doing? You and Norman?'

203

'We've been working on a film script, Gordon. Off and on.'[203]

'Where do you get the energy? You are working. Still knocking on that door.'

'We started knocking over fifty years ago. Once you decide on this business there's no turning back. You give it every breath. Norman's very ill. He'll not walk again. His speech has all but gone…' I tailed off here. There was a tightness. At this, Gordon reached over the table and placed, to my discomfort, his hand on top of mine. He said in hushed tones:

'Nothing is funnier than unhappiness.'

I understand inappropriate behaviour. Christ, I'd worked with Norman for over fifty years. I'd just cut up his body. I know inappropriate. These words of Gordon's were not appropriate. My lip curled slightly into what I presume must have looked like a snarl, and my eyes clouded.

'Samuel Beckett,' he said.

'I don't care if it's Thomas a Becket, or Margaret Beckett. Are you suggesting that there might be humour to be found in Motor Neurone Disease?' I watched him sit back and take a drink of his whisky.

'Don't be daft, Freddy. What I'm saying is that we deal with tragedy on a day to day basis. Comedy is often a way of dealing with the unfairness of life.'

'There is no fairness or unfairness. Life is just as it is. Why should Norman Riddell be any more exempt from disease and illness than the next man? I've come to realise something, Gordon, time marches on. You don't get in its way, I don't get in its way, the bloody Queen doesn't get in its way. I used to think that with a little luck, this and that. Luck has nothing

---

[203] I forgot to add that we were off and on until I caved in his chest, dismembered his body and distributed bits of him about several London postal codes. I smile now at the thought of Gordon's face if I had just told him.

to do with your price, Gordon. People find you funny or they don't. It's to do with the gags and the personality. This has nothing to do with luck. We never became great for the simple reason that we weren't good enough. We weren't Morecambe and Wise, we weren't Ken Dodd, we weren't Jimmy fucking Tarbuck.'

'I think now you're being too hard on yourself. You have a place in the British public's heart.'

'What place?' It's all about them. When they see us they remember where they were then. They remember when the future held promise. And then they realise that they are fucked. We are what could have been. We are a reminder of decay.'

He picked up the menu and stared at it. He couldn't look me in the eye. I felt bad for him.

'Let's eat,' he said.

'Are we having a starter?'

Gordon looked up at me and smiled.

'Of course we are. It's all expenses paid.'

I started with the rabbit and prune faggots followed by Berkshire roe deer and Douglas Fir sausage. To finish I ordered poached English quince with mead and raison ice cream.[204] Gordon ordered a chocolate structure for desert. I wasn't sure if he was going to eat it or climb it. I imagined my mother sitting opposite me sniffing at each course.

There's nothing the matter with plain food.'

'I didn't say there was.'

'Pass the lard.'

While the coffee was being poured I asked Gordon what his ideas were. It was dreadful. He explained that he wanted to do a pilot with three acts from the past. Each would get a ten minutes live stand-up slot. The only stipulation being that the

---

[204] I once returned to a hotel room with a warm quiche. Norman saw it and raised his eyes heavenwards.

jokes shouldn't be *dated*. I was under no illusions; Norman and Freddy were interesting because they were failures. There would be a five minute *Where Are They Now* profile. It's the losers who tell the best stories. *How I climbed To The Top And Fell*. Not, *How I Climbed To The Top And Kept Going*.

'What's it called?' I asked.

'Opportunity Always Knocks Twice. I've approached Ant and Dec.[205]

I pushed my ice cream around the bowl with my spoon.

'You know that Janice died?'

'Freddy, the public remember you as a comic double act. Janice didn't join you until you went on that mad cruise ship thing. What the hell was that about? My dad thought you were going to jump ship in Australia and try to break there.'

'I never harboured any illusions, Gordon. We were like Venus crossing the sun. In transit Norman and Freddy, passing over showbusiness, insignificant and rarely seen.'

Gordon laughed.

'You boys were not insignificant. How is Norman, physically?'

'Norman isn't mobile.' I had a flash of where I'd left his legs.

'He was a terrible man for the sauce.'

'Crushed he was when he first tried winegums.'

There was a short silence while Gordon looked away and busied himself with his glass.

'So, not mobile? Can't he use sticks?'

'Sticks? Gordon, he's dying.'

'How about Freddy Foster? Just Freddy. We can show pictures of you both at the start. Then a short film of Norman just now. Human interest. The heartbreak of the disease. How

---

[205] My heart sank.

it broke up the act.'[206]

'I'm not sure about that. Some things are too personal. Like stirring a man's tea. It didn't break up the act anyhow. Norman had quit before that happened. He was tired of it.'

'But you're still working together. On the script?'

'Yes. Off and on.'

'There. The public – your public – will love that.'

It struck me that we are forever trying to recapture the past. When Janice died Norman was no different. A month after her funeral he suggested we take a trip to Greece. We could see the haunts of years before. I sat beside him and held his hand.

'She's gone, Norman,' I said. 'We'll never get her back.'

And he cried and let his head fall onto my shoulder. I held him while he moaned. My poor, dear friend.

'I'm not sure we have a public anymore, Gordon. Most of them are dead, probably. Cancer, dementia, or a thousand and one diseases we are prone to.'

'But you're alive and kicking, Freddy.'

'Is that what you think?'

---

[206] This was reality television he was pitching. I shivered at the thought. I wanted to cut to pieces everyone who worked for that vulgar, humiliating genre. I wanted to kill all of their audiences; all those who graze on it like dumb beasts of the field.

38

2009

'Old age ain't no place for sissies.'
Bette Davis.

In the hall all was quiet but for the aural blur of Saturday night screens behind the doors, or should I say behind the grilles? In these troubled times we make prisoners of ourselves. We no longer dare confront. Noises freeze our blood. Imaginings – sometimes true – of killers lurking in the shadows, of death hanging around our doorsteps. Fear. It looks like a young boy with his hand up like a gun. Maybe another time he'll have a scarf covering his face; or will stick a gun hard into our bellies; it seems like fear has knocked our door, hungry for company. But we don't want to make it a guest, so we stay inside hoping he'll pass by and chap another. But we know deep down that one night it's coming home to stay. Saturday night in with Norman and Freddy. The scuffles outside; the animals; the knocks.

Just before Norman's diagnosis he'd become increasingly nervous behind the wheel. It came to a head when he drove into a bollard half a block from his house. He was shaking and kept asking me to take over. When we got out of the car to switch places a group of youths standing at the bus stop opposite were jeering and passing around a bottle.

'You want some of this, mister?' one of them shouted.

And then one grabbed his crotch and stepped pantomime like forward: 'How about some of this?'

'Let's go, Freddy. Get moving. I'm scared. I'm really scared.'

He kept grabbing at my sleeve with shaking hands. I took his head in my hands. 'No, Norman! No! Stop it!' I got back out of the car and told them all to clear off. Surprisingly they did, laughing as they went. I told him that everything was all right.

I would soon be chauffeur and taxi service. And it was the end of something for Norman, a loss of control, the first of many to come. It was just as difficult to watch, particularly because I knew the man he had been. At the start, he often fell down. The walking stick and leg braces he was given made getting up all that more difficult. In pubs, on buses, in the street, in the lift, in the flat, he fell. People's reaction to a frail man in his sixties falling was curious. In the street they often walked past him, thinking him drunk – the irony! In restaurants I cut up his food.

'What is it you feel?'

'My hands are like boxing gloves. Fingers numb.'

When you're part of a double act you have someone to rely on, someone to help you through the bad nights – and by Christ, let me tell you this, there were bad nights. One night in the early 80s we were playing in a large bar in Sunderland when a glass came flying out of the dark. It hit me full on the chest and splattered down my tuxedo. It had contained a cocktail of some sort and stained my suit badly.

'Hey,' countered Norman. 'Good shot! If you want to stand there throwing glasses at Freddy I could maybe take your girlfriend around the back. She looks like she hasn't had any meat in a while.'

'Here we go,' a voice called out. 'The same old tired jokes.'

And Norman continued: 'We're tired old men.'

'Should be *re*tired.'

'Did you say retard?'

'Bet you're not so big without a mike.'

'As the actress said to Bernie.'

'You're not funny.'

'Well, I can't argue with that, lad. We just take the bookings, the applause and the fee.'

'You get paid for this shit?'

'Of course. Don't you?'

'How would you like a punch in the mouth?'

'No one ever tell you that in a relationship there's only room for one cunt? I can't quite see your face. It's not Max Bygraves, is it?'

Norman clenched his fists.

I butted in:

'Now please, no fisticuffs. Look sir, have a drink on the house and let the rest of the people enjoy the show.'

'Nobody likes it.'

'We'll let the audience decide on that.'

From the dark, through the spot, a hundred glittering colours as glasses were hurled towards the stage. I exited, stage left, without bear. Looking back, I saw Norman take off his jacket and roll up his sleeves. 'Come on, you fuckers,' he screamed into the dark bar. 'Come on! I'm here. I'm standing here!' Bottles and glasses rained down on my partner, and shattered on his hands, face and head. Blood followed.[207] The stage manager/mc, Terry, ran onstage with an opened umbrella and pulled Norman to the wings.

'Freddy,' Norman said, 'I think we need new material.'

And that's the man Norman. But once the fear gets you, it's there for keeps.

It was crisp outside. The night sky was sheathed in blue. A soft grey cloud drifted idly across the moon. Were it not for the situation it would have been the perfect evening. I drew my coat collar tighter, and I pulled at the strap of the bag that sat heavily on my shoulder. Norman could never wrap up warm again. This thought caused me great distress. The idea

---

[207] I was so concerned for Norman's safety that I didn't feel a sliver of glass pierce my skin between the middle and index finger. The small scar remained with me for the rest of my life.

that I would never clap eyes on my dear partner again was too distressing to contemplate. In some curious and perverse manner, I was brought even closer to him by the act of dismemberment. There was something almost holy about my actions and the manner of them, like the Holy Mother cleansing her dead Son. Damn, I thought. I forgot to clean him. Just walked out with his legs in a bag. And here they were. I did not clean him. Me, of all people.

Are you a keen golfer? Maybe I was an Old Boy coming back from a day's golfing. Tired after trailing my bag to the 19th hole. *Are you a keen golfer?* But I just didn't look like an Old Boy. Then again, I didn't look like a killer, although I certainly was. How much did this bag cost me, Norman? Forty quid? Fifty? What with that and the name printed on the side. But I didn't mind, Norman. Money wasn't an issue with me. Straight down the middle, old son. *Are you a keen golfer?* Straight down the middle. That's what I wanted. I was never in this game for the money. This was a good thing considering the career we had. It was much more fundamental than that. All performers are lacking in something. They seek out recognition, just something to legitimise their place in this world. I always felt alone. Even with someone beside me, even with an audience in front. It was something that pushed me on. I wanted to feel complete. I wanted not to feel as I did. I felt as though somehow I stood not in a world inhabited with others, but a man who stood cold and alone. That was maybe the secret of my comic voice. I was forever rattling around in a black universe. That night I felt more lost and alone than ever.

Not unlike, perhaps, the pasty-faced little toe rag who suddenly appeared before me. I was about to be mugged for a golf bag and an incomplete set of human remains. I grabbed the back of his head with both hands and pulled his face towards my mouth. In an instant, his nose was between my teeth. I bit down and threw my head back. He staggered back too shocked to scream. I spat his blood onto the pavement as he fell to the ground. My shirt front was soaked with it. I pulled my coat together before rushing away. My jaw hurt. I wanted to be around people so wiped my face with the golf towel that I'd stuffed in my coat pocket and crossed to the pub. Someone noticed the blood on the shirt. A nose bleed, I said. I felt like a ghost as I stood there clutching a half pint of beer, apart from the merriment emanating from the younger set. It was something I really hadn't felt a part of in a very long time. Don't get me wrong, I did try, for so long, to stay connected to each generation. But it's impossible to stay there. If your looks don't let you down then your conversation most certainly will. There is something in the desperation of the old trying to keep up with the young. The best they can hope for is an element of respect, but even that has a taint of pity.[208]

And so, clutching my half pint, I stared ahead at some distant past. When I came back to the here and now I saw an old fellow looking at me. The shock that it was me in a mirror made me splash my beer down my coat. As one gets older the skin loses its fit. It hangs there rumpled and creased as though

---

[208] Pity! Ha! Even pity could be in short supply with a generation that seemed to have *entitlement* tattooed on their foreheads. I remember sometime in the late 80s playing a student bar alone. Norman had been somewhere else. He couldn't really do those gigs and I had to apologise for his absence. Was it the last time I played as a solo act? No, that's not possible. I'm getting confused now. It is strange that I can remember what was said that night but not my last. It was a horrendous student club and they were all drunk, baying for my blood and throwing the filthiest of insults. There wasn't a whiff of gentlemanly conduct in the place.
Yowr a farking cunt!
There was desperation in my voice that night. And there was no pity in return.
Yower boat looks like a bucket of smashed crabs, mate!
For something more of that night please turn to Appendix 3.

something has been removed. Escaping youth, perhaps, leaving one deflated.

I wasn't the only senior there. In the corner, a few old men sat talking and not talking. That was always the way. They get trapped in a memory and they disappear for a while. The moment isn't always the best time. I knew that well. One bloke was staring down into his pint like he was staring into the bowels of hell. I could understand that. The real old guard. One of the gang has to be the last man standing and he'd drawn the short straw. No doubt he was poking around the long cold embers of his past. With only the future staring back. If that didn't strike fear into his soul then nothing would. I felt a pain again somewhere in my mouth. My fingers searched and found a wobbling bit of tooth. Getting old and the teeth just snap in your head if you bite too hard. I pulled it out with ease and slipped the premolar in my coat pocket.

'There is but one truly philosophical problem, and that is suicide.' And so starts *The Myth of Sisyphus* by that great French goalkeeper and philosopher, Albert Camus. He tends to go on a bit afterwards but this little existential nugget is the start of the essay and not the end. I have often contemplated these words but perhaps never more so than that night. I confess that I was drained of the force of life. If I could have plucked myself from this sorry state then I would have shown myself mercy. The last years had disintegrated in a flurry. It was Norman's disintegration. From that day we left the hospital things had grown steadily worse. Hopes would be raised, after tests, or misdiagnosis. But each hope was dashed. Our hearts sank like stones in water. In my stupid ignorance I argued with the doctors after the first blood tests. They found a rise in creatine kinase.[209] This did not point certainly towards

---

[209] By this time I had done the research. I had listened to the side effects, the names of the drugs. I was becoming the right little Doctor Foster, or perhaps Dr Faustus. But I still confess to knowing virtually nothing.

motor neurone disease and indeed was not always found in those sufferers. I argued that it was a pointless test and brought more stress to bear on my friend. But I was foolish, and had to end up apologising. I knew almost nothing of this terrible illness. Norman knew less than me and for a while held onto the mistaken belief that there would be a cure. This is something that is difficult to comprehend. Nothing could be done. Bit by awful bit the body would break down. To make things worse, I thought, the patient, faculties intact, would be able to contemplate the nightmare descending upon his body. At the time of diagnostic tests Norman, Janice and I spent a lot of our days in hospitals. How at times like those I went over our life together. I would think of the wasted days and the hours we spent chatting over afternoon drinks. But the more I thought the more I understood that those days were golden and the very stuff of life. We never grasped that the priceless gems of life were so fragile and fleeting and could never be relived. Had we been aware of this would the time have been treasured more? In the hospital waiting rooms I thought so and berated my younger self, but now I think not. Why should thoughts of mortality spoil our moments of cakes and ale?

I finished my half pint and left. Outside, I realised with shock that I didn't have the golf bag. I rushed back to the door until it came to me that I hadn't carried it there in the first place. I traced myself back to the moment when I bit the boy. I remembered the bag had slid off my shoulder to the ground. I looked across the road. The boy and the bag had gone.

There was nothing to be done. I returned to Norman's flat as though entering the Promised Land. I felt at home there, as always. But this homecoming was different. I felt as though I was … safe. Is that why the criminal returns to the scene of

his crime?[210] The crime scene becomes a church offering
sanctuary. And that's what I needed. I needed more than that,
of course. I needed succour and warmth. I needed someone
to hold me. Bathsheba? Janice? Or even Lianna, dearest
reader. How remiss that Freddy has not –

Inside the door, I slid down the wall until my knees cracked.
I settled on the floor and hugged them to me. There, Freddy,
on your own. Needing no one, the great Freddy Foster. I
thought I might weep quietly, but only a low animal sound
escaped from me; the tears had dried up.

---

[210] A dog also returns to its vomit.

39

Past, present

M.J:[211] *When things dry up for an entertainer,*
when the telephone stops ringing, how
does one feel?
Freddy: Like piffy on a rock bun.
From 'Can You Hear Me, Mother?' a review in Campus Voice,
October 1987.

It seems to me that opposites really do attract. Now some people might have thought – could it be so? – that the only reason that Norman and Freddy stayed together was the act. There might be a smidgeon of truth in that; the act and we were bound as one. At the Brittle Bone Society dance I felt that Norman and I had formed an immediate and true friendship. To many we might have been seen as an odd couple.[212] But we did put in the innings. A lot didn't. There

---

[211] This was how it appeared in the student magazine.

[212] I pitched the idea to Bernard Delfont many years ago about Norman and Freddie doing the Neil Simon play *The Odd Couple*. The idea was refused, foolishly, I thought. Norman was not enthusiastic either.
'I can't lad; I'd fuck it up.'
'You fuck up so much anyway. What's the difference?'
As it was. Lord Delfont – who was a fan – told us that stand up was our game. It was a game though that was tiring us more and more as the years progressed. I felt that it would have been good for us to spread our wings a little and put more into that entertainers' bag of tricks. We had to be more of the all-round entertainers. Brucie was that, and Des. Fuck me if Des didn't collapse on stage at the old Glasgow Empire. The punters thought it was an act – the fall down clown – and laughed. He came round to applause and a dance and a song with that sweet voice. He had strings to his bow. The more strings, the more chances. And Lonnie Donegan, although principally a skiffle boy, could produce the neatest soft shoe shuffles. We could dance a little, but a bit of the old thesps would have been a career changer.

were a lot of casualties of the boards. One of them was Jimmy Davies. Jimmy didn't make any sort of a name for himself as a performer. We met him in the mid-seventies. He had an act that looked towards the deadpan genius of Chic Murray. Unfortunately, Jimmy couldn't get a joke right. He was almost always off the bullseye with a punchline. For a while people actually thought it was deliberate and he was confused by the laughs and the applause. The joke was always there but it was rarely the one that Jimmy would deliver. That, though, is not the point. The point is that Jimmy wrote the most moving article for *The Guardian* titled *No Pension For Top Bananas*, pointing out just how financially precarious our business was.[213] The article was read widely by those in the biz, and hit hard those at the starting post. It seemed to touch a raw nerve about the profession. I thought that it should have been compulsory reading for anyone who ever thought of being a comic. Norman, though, phoned Jimmy up to inform him he was a 'whinging prick.'

No Pension For The Top Banana had a profound impact on me at that time. I had been thinking along those lines off and on for some years, but Jimmy expressed it so well. There were a lot of sacrifices in showbusiness with, for most, little reward. Statistically, the business gave a very poor yield for the effort. To create a character, then become your creation, then have doubts about it was a costly occupation. I formed the persona Freddy Foster, comedian, from Freddy Bartholomew Foster, sickly Glasgow boy, inspired by several readings of *The Great Gatsby*. If Gatsby could create another human being then so could I. Like the young Jay I also wrote my weekly incomings and outgoings:

Tap dancing – 2/8d

---

[213] It was not unusual to find your car being parked at the BBC by a seasoned music hall performer of a few years before. A cruel, cruel business.

Elocution – 4/6d
Library – Free
Theatre – 5 shillings
Clothes – 2/6d per week (Provie man)

And where did a sickly boy like me get this cash? I took a delivery job in the local butchers.[214] It was no job for a sensitive and aspiring young man like myself but I had just left school with no qualifications. Certainly, I could have hung around Glasgow and no doubt have eventually joined that showbiz mafia,[215] but my dreams were bigger. London was my goal. I thought that my life didn't have to be lived in black and white with a ration card in my pocket. Did I sense that the country was about to change so rapidly within a few years? I think many young men and women across the nation, victims of post war authority, had the same thoughts at the same time. The party was about to begin. I wanted to be a part of it all. No doubt Norman felt the same when he made his way from Nottingham Victoria to London.

I was quietly singing a Max Bygraves hit as I popped Norman's hands into a brown paper bag, walked along the River Brent, and dropped them ever so casually into the water just before the river joined the Tideway stretch of the Thames.

---

[214] Those skills in butchery had stayed with me and helped with the cutting up of the body. The butcher, Tom Smith, taught me how to cut up pieces of meat. He thought I would be following in his footsteps. I felt sick even delivering the stuff, but this apprenticeship served me well.
[215] A small group of entertainers who sewed up the clootie dumpling cloth some years before.

40

1992/1968

'Believe only half of what you see, and nothing that you hear.'
Edgar Allan Poe

The first time you give someone a bath can be a somewhat gross experience, as our transatlantic cousins might say. To be perfectly frank, the part that I found most distasteful was not the arse wiping or the ball sac lifting; nor was it between the hard-skinned toes (not that I didn't flinch at those tasks!). The one part of Norman's body that gave me the *willies* was the washing of his hair. I would let the sponge soak up the bath water until it was heavy in my hand. Holding the back of his head and neck with one hand I would squeeze the sponge and let the water cover his hair and red face. A sharp intake of breath usually reassured me that he was still alive. I would turn the bottle of shampoo upside down and a glob of orange liquid would fall onto his crown like random birdshit. My face distorted in disgust. I was not aiming for sainthood but my daily life required a good deal of heroic virtue. The hair had changed over the years. The thick and golden mop now reminded me of seaweed stuck to a shelving wall. Although not green, illness and ageing had conspired to remove the melanin from the strands. This gave his head a dirty grey coastal appearance; that called to mind softened driftwood and suppurating algae. Occasionally, the thought did skip across my mind that a trim might benefit Norman's general appearance. A second skip convinced me that my cutting skills were not up to the job. Clumps of varying length hung like offshoots from an octopus's garden. As I gathered the shampoo and hair on my partner's noggin the texture in my hand was akin to sweeping up a jellyfish.

'Did you ever have any connection with the sea?' I asked him.

'I told you before; I grew up in a mining community.' My constant attendance on him at this time helped my understanding of the slurred consonants and vowels. As the shampoo was massaged in I tried to protect his eyes from the Quatermass of foam,[216] and I must confess that I was a bit of a big girl's blouse about this procedure. It was as though motor neurone disease could be spread like some skin disease; something that could be transmitted by contact alone. All the more credit towards my beatification. After the bathing I would get him dried, into a dressing gown and onto the couch. Then there was a matter of the oxygen mask that he was wearing more often as the disease progressed. We must have looked a proper sight sitting in that room in front of the television, Norman in his blue bath robe and mask, me in my slacks, brown mules, yellow button-down shirt and cashmere cardie.

People have often asked me what it was like having a partner in show business for so long. I can only liken it to a marriage – although I must confess that I never did enter into that wonderful institution. This lack of a lady on a permanent basis in my life did lead at time to some salacious gossip regarding my sexuality. People in the business know me well enough: discretion is my motto. But let me tell you now I have had several experiences and one of those I'm still a little confused about. This was Lianna. Aah, Lianna. *Lee…ann…aaah.* It is a soft breath. Just like *Lo-li-ta.* A pale faced, fragile blonde, with breasts like alabaster peaches. Her voice was little more than a whisper. Which meant that you had to lean close in order to catch her soft words. It was a trick to lure the foolish and the gullible.

---

[216] I am not good with illness, I never have been.

From the 1968 Entertainment Awards in Grosvenor Square I whisked her away before the purple-faced legion of comedy pulled a train in the hotel toilets. So enamoured was I with my sweet Lianna we left before the Best Comedy Entertainer was announced. I had harboured some hope it would be Norman and Freddy. Instead it went to Marty Feldman. A fine comedian, no doubt, but fuck me backwards, this could have made the difference between Scunthorpe and Shaftesbury Avenue.

Marty Feldman could have got the thing the following year. I believed, and still believe, that a debt was owed to the likes of Norman and Freddy. It wasn't just our peers that owed us, but British society in general. I mean, Max Wall was dug up and given kudos through Beckett and a renewed interest in music hall. He stalked the stage like a refugee from German expressionism. In the last couple of years he looked as though he travelled with a defibrillator. Those years, the very late 60s, were really our last chance. And the public let us down. Why? You may ask. Well, look at whom they were championing. Norman fucking 'swinging dodgy' Vaughn and Ted Rodgers. Cunts.[217]

Just what was it about the 60s that London held sway over the other great capitals? It was simple; you didn't have to have a particular talent to experience its best. An attitude was enough. Knowing where the right doors were – open or closed – was enough. In this I was very much a man of the times. Norman was very much a man of the previous decade. I was at least tolerated at the right parties. It seemed to be enough. I've been side-tracked again. Back to Lianna.

I headed towards the exit of Grosvenor House.

It was noticed by quite a few of our family viewing

---

[217] More often than not I tend to see things through rose-tinted glasses. This is because the world can be an ugly place. Even with hindsight some people really still get my goat up.

favourites that I was making a hasty exit with the delightful Lianna.

'Hey, Freddy,' shouted Hughie Green. 'You not staying for your award?'

'Business, Hughie,' I shouted.

'Enjoy! More than a handful there,' he shot back and laughed loudly. And he gave me a look. I can see it now. Something in that look.

Everybody knew the score and mum was the word. This sort of calling out really wasn't appropriate or appreciated by anyone. Most of them had wives or long- term lovers, or both. Hughie knew this well.[218] Discreet silence had always been the order of the day. As far as I'm concerned it's all about dignity and manners. It was always about courtesy and a degree of respect: dare I say *gentlemanly behaviour*? It wasn't all breeding as many, if not all, of the success stories here tonight came from abject poverty. These were not the Oxbridge boys with their sneering comments. We were the non-U grafters, and in general we took care of each other.[219] So, the comment was vulgar at best and vicious at worst. Lianna blushed and let her head dip. What an absolute lady, I thought. I was blazing, and if we hadn't been where we were I would have chinned him. One golden rule of showbusiness: keep your dignity at all times. If for no other reason, there's always a hack around ready to stick it to you.

Having said that I do tend to look for the goodness in people and try not to dwell on the ugly side of this *sullied*

---

[218] Hughie once button-holed me at a shindig. He insisted talking about aeroplanes, about which he knew a lot. While he droned on my thoughts drifted to stabbing him in the eye with my cocktail stick.

[219] No, this is how I wanted it to be. It was not all like this. Some would walk past, oh so friendly, the nod of recognition, the quiet cough or laugh, the turn of the head, the whispers. People I admired and people for whom I cared nothing. I would like to say that none of it bothered me, but that would be a lie.

flesh.[220] Beauty is all that we should aspire to.

On the way out I bumped into Norman coming out of a gent's toilet. He was busy zipping himself up.

'Norman, I told you time and again: do that before you leave the toilet.'

'Girls love it, Freddy,' he replied. 'Gets their minds on the meat!'

I just kept walking, guiding Lianna towards the glass door exit. The doorman raised his hand in one of those subservient working-class half salutes and said:

'Have a good night, Mister Foster.'

I couldn't be sure that he wasn't trying to take the piss, so I told him to fuck off anyway.

In a cab with my companion, sweet rich perfume filling the air, it was impossible not to get excited. The driver, Henry Carr, was a clever, if ill-judged, commentator on our times. He was concerned about the 'black boys' moving into his area. He had memorised and was reciting a fair chunk of Enoch Powell's *rivers of blood* speech; Des O'Connor was 1-2-3 O'Leary-ing it on the wireless. I personally had no axe to grind on that front. I had met and genuinely liked that fantastic coloured singer and comedian Kenny Lynch.[221] He was a

---

[220] We did a Hamlet sketch once where I was Polonius, Janice was Ophelia, and Norman was the Prince. Norman was worse for drink but surprisingly good. But for the fates he could have ended up at the Old Vic. The sketch was picked up in Larry Pringle's column: *Messrs Riddell and Foster tried to entertain with a comedy interlude that would have had the Bard fairly birling in his grave. There was an unexpected weight of tragedy to Mr Riddell's short performance. But Mr Gielgud need not worry.*

[221] I arrived in London at a great time, a time of change. The party was about to start. There seemed to be the tail end of the ugly, though, as one morning I passed some older teddy boys who were talking loudly of going 'nigger hunting'. This was alien to me. I had never mixed with the Glasgow Teds. I was always searching out the finer things in life. Of course, I spoke to people who were around the Notting Hill race riots before I arrived.

decent bloke and an extremely talented performer. His quiet demeanour covered up a tough upbringing.[222] A man, though, should be given the freedom to express his inner thoughts; otherwise it leads to searing resentment, which can't be good for any society. That's what I call good old British democracy

The driver, Henry Carr, got a small tip and a big pat on the back before Lianna and I went into my apartment block. The next morning this taxi ride would be described in detail in Larry Pringle's column. Maybe the tip wasn't enough.

They said there was no one from Notting Hill involved; all the racists came in on buses and on the tube. That was a common feeling at the time.
[222] Ron Kray told me that Kenny was brought up just down the road from him and his brothers and had popped in a few times. I'll let you, dear reader, mull over criminals being the product of their environment. Kenny was a gentleman.

41

1968/1972

'It is the greatest fanaticism is on him, and it is coming to no end.'
Nora, speaking of James Joyce

Romance is something that I think the younger generation are
missing. They do not understand the etiquette of making a girl
feel like a princess. It also increases your chances of getting
your hole. My flat was a girl's dream. It was immaculate, and
on the coffee table I always had a bottle of red wine – maybe
Chianti – and two crystal wine glasses. The cushions on the
couch were arranged with the tips touching the seat giving a
rather attractive diamond shape, which I believe set the tone
perfectly. Before taking Lianna's faux fur wrap I switched on
all four bars of my *Newheat* electric fire. She sat herself down
while I searched my small but beautifully eclectic record
collection. The radiogram had perhaps seen better days, but
with the soft and intimate lighting it wouldn't have been
noticed. If Lianna had been a scrubber I would have shoved
on The Kinks' wonderful *Sunny Afternoon* long player on the
Music For Pleasure record label, or indeed one of those *Top of
the Pops* discs with the hot covers. Lianna seemed to me like a
classier bird. I flicked past *George Mitchell's Black and White
Minstrel Show*[223] (compilation of musical hits from those
halcyon days) and opted for the man who was indeed the
Chairman of the Board, Mister Frank Sinatra. That just-flat
voice was the key to making a woman feel *open*. Who cares if
the man had to shake hands with gangsters? Few people in my

---

[223] We appeared on the show a couple of times. Norman called it spoon
feeding the self-loathing: *Cosy, safe, middle class shit.* When asked how he was
fine about The Cilla Black Show he replied, *Cilla does not black up.* This was
indeed true; I never witnessed Cilla in *blackface*.

line of business had been untouched by those paws themselves.[224]

While I put the record on Lianna went to the bathroom to *freshen up*. I was happy about this as it gave me the chance to adjust myself. Unless she was blind, I thought, she could not have failed to notice that I was more than a little excited. I have known men who have been embarrassed by this perfectly natural physiological occurrence. I, though, have always prided myself on the old meat and two veg. Surely no woman could interpret it as less than a compliment to their femaleness?

While I was standing in front of the mirror removing my constricting dickey-bow and undoing the top button of my shirt, Lianna entered.

'Freddy,' she whispered.

I turned to face her.

I have always thought that to slap someone is always more deeply painful – physically and psychologically – than to punch them. A slap adds the humiliation factor to the assault. I mention this because when I turned from the mirror I felt that same humiliation, and not a little disgrace.

Lianna was standing just inside the room framed by the bathroom doorway, unclothed apart from a black see-through lace bodice, black ten denier stockings, and a pair of red patent leather high heeled shoes.

Pouting out of her top was a pair of the ripe firm small breasts, budding with pink still surprisingly soft nipples. All of

---

[224] Many years later I had the great honour of seeing Sinatra at Ibrox Stadium in Glasgow. A bad time since I was there for my mother's funeral. But Francis Albert certainly took my mind off grieving for a few hours. 'My kind of town, Glasgow is…' he sang. It was a great tribute to my city. Norman was by my side. He agreed. He did add, though, that it would not have been a hit if that had been the lyric.

the body, and its clothing, framed an engorged cock that stuck out like a flagpole and defiled and interrupted my moment of joy and pleasure. I picked up my glass of wine from the table and threw it down my throat in one movement. I replaced the glass, picked up his/hers and threw that down also. *Witchcraft* was playing loudly somewhere in my head. I picked up the bottle and filled the glass again.

'Don't be angry,' she said. It was the same whisper, but now it seemed more helpless and pleading and, dare I say *masculine*? 'I'm on a waiting list.'

I sipped from my glass. A waiting list, I thought? Was this a joke? Everyone I have known has had a joke. A new double act, with me as the straight man. But Lianna had nothing funny to say.

I stood with an empty glass in my hand. My reaction had felled his/her stinger. After a while I heard my voice speak, more tenderly than either of us expected.

'Go into the bedroom and lie face down.' I followed him/her in, stripped, and whacked off over his girl-arse.

And that was where the stories about my sexuality originated. As I'd left the Grosvenor that night in 1968 half the audience must have known. They must have laughed loudly the next morning when taxi driver, Henry Carr, told Larry Pringle that Freddy Foster was 'canoodling with a Danny la Rue,' in the back of his cab. Fuck them all, I think now. Now it doesn't matter, any of it. I just wish I could have been that strong then. I could have handled it all better. Instead, I threatened the paper with legal action. I got a letter back from their firm of solicitors warning me about the dangers of such action since I would surely lose. The beautiful Lianna would do a fucking Garbo in court and Norman and Freddy would be bollixed. Larry Pringle, the newspaper columnist, did send me a sympathetic letter saying that it was best to drop the whole defamation thing. In return, he had convinced his editor to drop a story with James Thomas Smith aka Lianna Ferrier. I wouldn't meet Pringle face to face until a year later. That was the night in The Colony Rooms. I thought that this was the sign of a true gentleman, though.

In 1972 I was sitting in a small bar in Mexico City[225] a young man came in with some news. Larry Pringle, famous newspaper columnist, had been found face down in a swimming pool, much like one of my fictional mentors, Jay Gatsby. He had enough drugs in him to open a chemist: heroin, cocaine, and the obligatory *wacky baccy*. There were also traces of DNP, phentermine and fenfluramine, in addition to whisky and wine, in his belly. This was perhaps not so like Jay Gatsby. (So much for the gentleman Larry Pringle, I thought.) His broken dentures were found beside his flip-flops. The couple of years that had passed had lessened my truck with him. I took no pleasure from his fall. The waste. My dear God, the waste.[226]

---

[225] Norman, Janice and I had some time off from the cruise ship which was harboured in Mazatlan on Mexico's Gold Coast. We took a short flight to DF for no other reason than we could.

[226] I thought that if we were given the power to see our own death that power would be a curse. When, many years ago, Pringle had loudly related stories of Francis Bacon, who would have guessed his end? Well, many, actually. But why take your own life when you have passed your four score and ten? Surely nature would soon take its natural course? Perhaps we shall never know. I found it rather ironic the picture that accompanied the story he had grown to bear a remarkable resemblance to one of the Screaming Popes. And again, I have gone back to add this piece two weeks later. Larry left a suicide note which apparently got boring half way through.

42

2009

*'…a couple of gleaming things that everyone remembers while they've
forgotten the dross.'*
                                              Michael Palin.

It had been a dreadful night. There are many things that I
might have seen myself becoming when I was lying in my
slum bed,[227] but a ghoul was not one of them. I felt drained
and not a little sickened at my recent nocturnal activities.
Slipping a receptacle into the lapping Thames water's edge
was one thing – rather decent, if I do say so myself – but
poking around in a loved one's last resting place at midnight
was perhaps pushing the barriers of taste to a less respectable
boundary.

As I entered the courtyard to Norman's flats I looked out
for the *homeboys*, but no doubt it was bath night. The light of
the vestibule was imbued with an eerie yellow hue, which
seemed to match the mood of my recent gruesome
shenanigans. A couple of hours before I had struggled to get
the torso in the wheelie case. It was a tight fit. The arms were
wrapped in a copy of a local paper. There were apparently
twenty-three gangs in Norman's area alone: OTT,
Shakespeare Youts, Willesden Green Boys caught my eye as I
wrapped the limbs tightly and pushed them into the front
pocket elasticated netting. Returning, I no longer had the

---

[227] Those were the days when I had hoped my life ahead, my life to be lived,
would be an ocean of joy. When I sat with Norman outside a café with our
teas or coffees on a crisp morning the joy was certainly there to be savoured
in the future. It was there in our laughter, in our breath, in our hopes, in our
fresh youthful dreams. But, of course, I only saw that many years later. It is
one of life's tragedies we rarely see the moments of joy.

baggage. I was not afraid, but I was certainly wary as I waited on the lift. The sound of its arrival demolished the silence as it descended like some prehistoric beast. Both my eyes and my heart were as heavy as at any time since Norman's demise. I did think at that moment, dear readers, that it would have been much easier to wander in to the local scuffers' shop and tell them *It's a fair cop, guv.* Inside the lift I stabbed the button to the fourth floor. It seemed to take an eternity before they *shoogled* shut.

The lights to the lift had been smashed so my short ascent was in pitch black. Perhaps if my night's deeds had not been even darker I would have experienced the grip of fear; but creeping amongst the dead at night was no doubt adequate preparation for any unnerving situation.

I had been wearing my Gannex raincoat[228] when I left. I'd had it for some years. It obviously did not strike me at the time that a light-coloured coat was probably not the best cover for the nefarious activity to come. When I set off on my journey one hand was thrust deep into a pocket while the other trailed the wheeled case. The whole journey *atatatatatatatrrrrrrrrrrrrrrratatatatatatatatatrrrrrrrrrrrrrrrrrrrr (The wheels of the case go round and round…) atatatatatatatrrrrrrrrrrrrrrrrhrrrrrrrrrrrrrhrrrrrrrrrrrr (…round and round…) rrrrrrrrrrrratatataatarrrrrrrrrrrratatatatata.* It crossed my mind as I crossed the road that perhaps this was not the best

---

[228] Much like the one that Harold Wilson became associated with many years before. I forsook the pipe. Actually, that pipe was more of a prop; he was more a smoker of cigars and cigarettes. Wilson was always popping up at entertainment parties. I truly believe he was a frustrated performer as much as a frustrated Premier. He once – I met him several times – asked me if I was a charlatan! I'm not sure what was going on in his life but his secretary, Marcia Williams, was making a beeline for him through mingled guests. I gave her the sharpest of looks before replying, 'But, sir, aren't we all charlatans?' He nodded before being ushered away. It's all I'll say on the matter: I liked Harold.

receptacle for inconspicuous travel through the late-night streets of London. *Hrrrrrrrrrratatatata*…Hardly the quietest of luggage, I will grant you. But a snug fit. Ample storage on the move *atatatatatatata*. The convenience and security of the double decker zip fastening *atatatatatatatahrrrrrrratatata*. The telescopic handle high enough that I didn't have to bend in any fashion or hold its padded handle grips *atatatatatatatatata*. I was wise enough to go to the graveyard as prepared as any badged Scout. In fact, the shovel that I'd brought along had been purchased in a Scout shop at John Lewis in Brent Cross.[229] It was a small item and fitted snugly in the netted side pocket of the case.[230] I dug to just under two feet deep before planting and covering the case. My intention was to get down to Janice's coffin, but there was little chance of me excavating down the three or four feet of normal burial depth.[231]

It was the most foul of nights and the memory of it will be etched on my face for as long as I have left on this earth. The walk back was Shakespearean. Harrow Road onto Wellington Road. There was no one at the bus stop I passed and I kept heading on, fighting my way against the wind and rain, carrying the shovel. For some inexplicable reason I had not thrown it away. Perhaps I thought I might be seen doing so, or perhaps I thought it might come in useful some other day; and so I walked, while clutching it to my chest like a shield. It was a sharp right on to Regent Street, narrow and unlit by a solitary streetlight. Still on and into Kilburn Lane, past the club on the corner and into more driving rain. My eyes were

---

[229] It was upsetting walking into this shop as it brought to mind my first meeting with Norman at the scout hall in Tooting 46 years before. The coincidences, or Karma, in life never fail to surprise me.
[230] I really was impressed by these wheeled doo-dah's. A traveller's, or indeed, a murderer's needs were well catered for.
[231] The bubonic plague's six foot under must have been back breaking work for the *fossors* of the time.

stinging and my face felt like a death mask. There were some revelers up ahead who seemed unconcerned by the weather. I crossed to the opposite side of the road feeling that my face might give away my guilt,[232] less a death mask and more a wanted poster. Another right and more Kilburn Lane. It seemed to be never-ending. At last there was a turn left that took me to Carlton Vale. I remember cursing under my breath and thinking that if I never saw Kilburn Lane again it would be too soon. It was Carlton Hill next then on to Abbey Road. Before turning off the hill the weather had quietened, and I felt a warmth cover my body that seemed to revive my brain. In Abbey Avenue, just off Abbey Road, I disposed of the dirt encrusted shovel in a lone skip.

I am not surprised that I can name those streets still. But you, dearest reader, can you? Do you really know that evening? Can any description be as accurate as the moment? What of the things I have left out? The puddle water that got in my shoe and soaked the heel of my sock; the growing pain from a bout of osteoarthritic inflammation in my big toe; the rain drips caught on the back of my collar, fallen from a hanging row of hornbeams planted along one of the roads mentioned; the window that I chanced to look at that stirred up another memory not noted; the moment – what moment? – a woman closed her curtains and our eyes locked in a strangers' recognition? She had short, red hair and doe eyes, or hair that was long and black with small eyes, or any combination therein, bar blonde and short or long and blonde. I can ask my reader to fill in the details. So, what worth is this memory? Is it me or time that dictates what comes to mind? Recreating the past in the present. I ask again, what worth is this memory?

The past is gone.

---

[232] However impossible. Guilt and a moral conscience: two things I am beginning to doubt I have ever really possessed. Or indeed anyone else.

I have failed before I begin.

I remember nothing of the rest of my journey back to Norman's. Only from my arrival at his block of flats.

The lift jolted to a stop and the doors shook open. The lights had been all but destroyed on the landing but I could just make out the crouching figure of a man by Norman's door. At that moment I could have easily pressed the descend button, but the truth is I could never walk away in life. Instead, I rushed forward and threw my whole body on the figure. As I did so my teeth clenched as I spat out the words:

'So you think I like golf, you little bastard?'

My body weight has always registered below eleven stone, so the mountain that it landed on shook me off easily as it rose up. I went over it head first and landed on my back totally winded. The shadowed figure stood swaying over me:

'Freddy? What the fuck are you doing?'

'Gordon?'

I had just jumped on the back of the man who wanted to return me to television. Might I advise all budding entertainers this is not a recommended career move? Being something of a gentleman he helped me to my feet.

'Where's Norman? I was passing. Thought I'd drop in. It's bloody dark here.'

'Norman will be sleeping, Gordon. He gets his head down early.' An image flashed up behind my eyeballs of Norman's head under the Thames in a soup pot. Gordon pressed a switch on his watch that made it glow a phosphorescent green. He staggered slightly before leaning against the wall. The smell of whisky and cigarettes suddenly hit me. Gordon had obviously been out on the batter. He burped as he brought the watch close to his eyes:

'Bloody Christ in a manger, it's after one. I passed a pumpkin outside. Must've been Cinderella.'

'Gordon, you have to go. Come on, I'll help you down.

We'll hail a taxi.'

I was expecting some drunken belligerence in return, but not every drunk was like Norman. While we waited on the lift Gordon asked,

'Hey, Freddy, why are your hands so filthy? You been moonlighting as a miner?'

In my concern about getting Gordon away from Norman's flat I forgot that my hands bore the evidence of a night's digging. On the way to Norman's I had been picking at the dirt on my hands that were stuffed in my coat pocket. Gordon was obviously more observant:

'This weather, Gordon. I slipped in the park. Be building an ark soon.'

'This is Tuesday, isn't it?'

It seemed the most curious of statements at this time. He was also wrong, as the hands of the clock had well and truly slipped into Wednesday.

'Fuck, what time is it?'

'After one. Remember the pumpkin?'

'What...?' He obviously had no recollection of the conversation from minutes before. He then informed me that he had a meeting with someone about the *phone-in scandal* and The British Comedy Awards. 'Fuck all to do with me...' At this Gordon pulled me close in bear hug camaraderie. I disappeared into his bulk.

'Look,' he said. 'I like to talk about my old man. You know? When I'm drunk? Seeing you the other day...Well, you knew him. I just wanted to know him a bit more. Maybe you had stories...I mean like ones I haven't heard...' The ones he hadn't heard were the very ones he wouldn't want to hear. Should I tell him about his father's regret in marrying a pill-popping drunken slut? Or maybe his forays into some of the strangest parties? Like the Diana Dors sex parties where he was filmed having unsuccessful sex with two Rank Charm

School failures? While we waited on a cab to stop – no mean feat in these parts – I told him what he wanted to hear. As one drew to a halt, he said to me:

'You see, you're part of it, Freddy. You're part of my past. You're part of all our pasts. And we can't let you go.'

I smiled and just before I closed the door behind him, informed him that it was the coach, not Cinders, that was transformed back into a pumpkin. I heard his noisy laughter through the glass.

As I walked across the forecourt a boy shouted from a balcony, *Hey, Mister! Hey! Mister! Hey!* I didn't know if it was a cry for help or the start of a threat. Either way, I didn't give a fuck.

43

1970 – 2007

'Who speaks is not who writes, and who writes is not who is.'
Roland Barthes

Yes, having a partner for so many years was indeed like a marriage, and ours was stronger than most in the business. What cemented our relationship, I felt, was the cruise ship. Okay, we'd been together for nine years before, but there was something of the war zone about the whole thing; fighting for a way of life. We weren't below the parapet in this one; we were in the front line: Norman, Freddy, and Janice. It was up and at 'em. Seven nights a week while at sea, two hour shows a time. Soul destroying, for quite a while. I got through it with alcohol, Norman with sex, and Janice with an assortment of drugs. All of us smoked like hell and argued with each other a lot. Norman seemed to be on a mission to fuck every female on board. I did overhear a funny tale about this:

DANCER 1: You're the only girl in the dance troupe that Norman hasn't slept with.

DANCER 2: How dare he!

I think I suffered most in all of this. It was my ego, I suppose. Although I could put on a cheery face most of the time the whole fucking experience was a nightmare. I felt that I was running away from my country, the gossip, like Byron on his *grand tour*. The stories true and the stories embellished amounted to the same thing. I had told people we wanted to travel, to broaden our horizons; old Byron had told everyone he was going to fight for Greek independence. Both excuses now appear absurd. Our horizons, though, were broadened and we pulled some pretty poses.[233]

At first Norman saw it as a holiday that he never had growing up. He wasn't interested in the history or culture, wherever we might dock: the Nile, Easter Island, or Santiago de Compostela. But he did meet a lot of people in bars.

Norman and Janice, the Silver Princess, 1971

'They're all a shower of drunks. You should fit in,' I said.

'You said meet the locals. Only people I see you meeting are other tourists. You ought to get out, lad. Alcohol breaks down a lot of barriers. It's the great leveller.'

The great leveller? I watched him stagger out of many bistros and tavernas and I can assure you, dearest reader, there was nothing level about that gait. But Norman was a better

---

[233] I speak of this because the ship made a brief port stop in Missolonghi. Janice took a very funny picture of me with a towel around my head. Like many mementos they were lost over time. As a joke I had written *She walks in beauty*…on the back of the picture. Norman shook his head when he read that. He wouldn't have known Byron from Vasco de Balboa or even Bach. He could be annoyingly proud of his philistinism: *I've learned nothing from a book.*

man than me. I resisted seeing what was in front of me. I rarely acknowledged the complex light and shade of any person I met. I accepted them on the most surface of levels. I know now that this was a great flaw in my nature. Norman could say *He's a nice guy but…* I only saw the nice guy. Perhaps that's why I needed Norman so much. For all my reading, there was no real understanding of what made me function, my centre, that without which, I was nothing. Despite having an instinctive, almost primitive understanding of his place in the world, Norman was light years ahead of me as a human being. I could only lurch at ever increasing speed towards oblivion.

The time on the ship, though, was perhaps our happiest as a unit, but there were other points in our lives that brought us closer.

Tragedy is the great leveller; it can destroy petty jealousies and full-blown hatreds. Tragedy can heal long term feuds and cement everlasting love.

If Norman's disease were not enough to strike us down, a second illness took us to our knees and had us reeling from the randomness of life. Janice was diagnosed with breast cancer in December 2004. This was a mere eleven months after Norman's certain diagnosis of MND. If there was a God, then he was testing us to the limit. Janice believed; Norman and I did not.

'What sort of God would inflect this on us?' Norman would say. I would say nothing.

Of course, nothing prepares us for tragic events. Long nights of paranoid imaginings cannot prepare us for the reality. This is a cold fact of life. It took me years to arrive at that conclusion. It also took me many years to come to the understanding that people are often driven by motives they themselves might not fully understand at the time. It is later on they might realise that they were driven by ego, or fear, or misplaced loyalty. I think Norman and Freddy were not unique; every life, I believe, is a kind of failure because every life will eventually lose its ability to be itself. I've often heard about someone being *their own man*, but I really don't think I've met such a person. Norman perhaps got close, but even he was hiding something away, using alcohol as cover. Whatever, it was he, during those months, who was strong for her, despite his own illness.

After the removal of her breast we collected her from the hospital. I waited in the car while Norman went inside. His walking was stable at this time, apart from the occasional dropfoot. The decision to leave me outside seemed to have been taken between Norman and her before. I had no argument. After my experience with Norman's results months before I didn't relish my return visit. I waited in the car part of the time listening to Radio 2: Abba, The Walker Brothers and Fat Boy Slim. After a while I decided to wait inside the building. I had hardly taken two steps through the entrance when they appeared. Janice was not as I expected. Without make-up her face had a cartonnage death mask look about it. I thought, for the first time ever, that she looked like an old lady. Norman had an arm around her and he held her close. Perhaps it was the gesture, perhaps the light of the day, but they appeared to be emerging in an old grey and grainy film. For a split second I had a flash of Janice skipping around a fountain in Trafalgar Square it was July 1967. She was wearing a flower print mini dress, yellow tights, and red shoes. In her hand she held a floppy, wide-brimmed, cream coloured hat. Her dark hair had been cut short with a fringe, but which swung as she skipped. How inopportune and cruel memory can be. As they got closer, I could see that he was saying something to her but she was pushing ahead. In the car they were both silent.

Norman and Freddy had a marriage, certainly; but it was nothing compared to Norman and Janice. Nothing.

44

2007

Marty Feldman: What's it like keeping Norman away from the booze?
Freddy: Like herding cats.

i

From the window of Norman's flat, I looked down below and saw a young man with a brown windcheater jacket. Standing some yards from him groups of young people moved about like caged animals. There seemed to be no point to any of their movements unless it was to intimidate anyone looking. I know that when I was a young man in a post-war slum in Glasgow I never walked like that. This place and people were not always so. When Norman moved in the Divine Margaret – as Norman St John Stevens called her – was yet to take her place in the parliamentary arena and make her mark on the world stage. Jim Callaghan occupied Number 10 and was most certainly drowning, but not waving. The miners and the unions would sink him and themselves in the coming years. It was, though, in those early years before post-war Britain took a proper step into late capitalism, that Norman got his council house.[234] The night he found out where he's been allocated he told me that he was getting too old to be driving up and down the motorways of Britain at all hours. He was worried that he didn't have a pension. I had to laugh:

---

[234] This was early1979, just before Thatcher won the May election. The flat was on the east side of Wembley park across from Neasden and the sacred waters of the River Brent. It didn't look too bad and seemed to settle him. Norman was only 40 years old. As the few records will show, he worked on for another nearly twenty years, albeit to a much-diminished timetable as me. I would often work solo towards the end. My act was very different from our double act.

'Pension? You're a stand-up; you're a comedian. This business isn't work like other jobs are work. You become a comedian because you don't want to get your hands dirty. If you were looking for a proper job you could have followed your old man down the pits. And you could have died like him too.'

'I'm fucking tired. I'm tired, Freddy,' he repeated. 'I'm tired of the touring and I'm tired of the shit digs, the shit food and the shit wages. I'm also sick of how people look at us.'

I was hurt by it, this criticism of everything I had lived for.

'How do you mean *look at us*? How do they look at us? You bastard,' I shouted. 'You fucking bastard!'

I don't think, as I look back, that I glamorise anything. What I say is how it was for me. For a few brief years I think that there was an openness of spirit in those earlier days; a sense in the air of the times that you could achieve anything if you really tried. Norman and I failed, but that's not the point. There was a hope that golden things were just around the corner. For Norman and Freddy that corner may never have been turned but it was there, it was a tangible thing. If the human condition is simply *being there*[235] then we were there. I can drag up the past but my present gives it no more substance than a held snowflake. We reached out for the stars, for the toppermost, for that state of supreme nirvana. And we were close. It just didn't work. And that's the worst and cruellest of blows that fate dealt us two boys: we could see our promised land but were never allowed to enter. It was a bitter pill that Norman swallowed with a lot of drink. It drove him to occasional bouts of violence and deep depression.

I had a forgiving nature, and I forgave a lot, but that night I

---

[235] I am, of course, referring to Heidegger's sense of *there*. My wide reading meant I could easily flit between the weighty questions of being and the life story of Freddy *Parrotface* Davies. I saw neither as being more valid than the other.

stormed off and had no communication with him for nearly six months. It was one of the worst periods of my life. At the end of that huff my ego had settled down somewhat and I put out the hand of friendship. How could I have done otherwise? We still had some hope left then. Not just us, but people in general. Norman had moved into the flat. The area was still a community back then. It really was alright.[236]

In the soulless concrete courtyard below one of the kids was looking up at me. He raised a hand as if holding a pistol, then pointed it downwards. Then he smiled. I moved as quickly as I could from the window and squatted down below the sink. I felt like a soldier cowering in a shell hole. When Norman first arrived no kid would have dared.

Norman's flats were built in the 1920s but by the 70s and 80s had a bad reputation.[237] The old dears who were here in the 50s and 60s told me that the flats were in an immaculate state and everything in their metaphorical gardens was very rosy indeed. What happened, they asked? Well, what happened indeed? All I can say is that it must have been the sons and daughters of that idyllic community that wreaked havoc upon it. Isn't it just like the little tykes to shit on Eden? In the beginning there was a grassy area on the concourse. One could stop and smell the flowers. There were bright swings. There were also communal bin areas and off-street parking for around twelve cars. The flats were one, two and three-bedroomed. Each had a bath and shower. A few years before they would have been called *luxury*. (Only when comparing them to the Victorian slums that occupied the

---

[236] It was during this break that I voted in Margaret Thatcher and the Conservative Party. Later, when I told Norman he called me a 'jumped up arsepiece.' It was the only time I saw a political action move him. Not to vote, but just to insult me.

[237] Not the high-rise nonsense. As Norman said to the council at the time: 'I'll wait until I'm dead before I live in the sky.'

space before.) Still, they were certainly better than what I was born into. Glasgow, following the war, really was in a class of its own.

Times change, though, and what's one generation's haven might be another's nightmare. Then, as I looked down on the square – for I had sidled back slowly lest the young hoodlum saw me – I saw swings – probably where the original ones had been – but the seats were broken and graffitied and looped over the crossbar. The buildings that faced me were strewn with slogans describing quite unbelievable – even with my experiences – sexual encounters. Strange gaudy words were daubed on walls, on the ground, on the bus shelter just beyond. Wherever paint could be put then paint was there: what would darling Francis Bacon say to that? Who could have guessed that Warhol's philosophy would come so terribly true? Territorial trainers hung by their laces over telephone cables. Stains, like sweat patches spread on the walls of the buildings opposite.

As a young boy in my bedroom I would dream of what lay in store for me. What had life to offer. As I lay, dreaming, my mother's weeping moans would seep into my thoughts from the other room. I only asked her once why she cried. I stood in the doorway in my blue and white striped pyjamas which were tied with cotton cord at the waist. She raised her head from the table.

'But what choice do I have?' she said. And that was it.

Some years later it would be my turn to cry. I had received a phone call from Glasgow in the middle of the night. After the call I lay awake until sunrise. I showered and drove round to Norman and Janice's.

'I have to go to Glasgow. My mother…'

Janice reached out and held my arms that hung dead by my side.

'Oh, my love,' she said.

With no thought or poesy, or Wordsworth, I replied:
'The worm is on her cheek.'

The news of death touches us like nothing else. Janice organised train tickets and sorted out a suit for each of us. She was a hero at that time.

The day in Glasgow was as funereal as it could be. The sun was hidden by a wrap of grey cloud that settled just above the black slate roofs; the air – such as it was – had a weight to it that seemed to hinder breathing.

Norman sat in the kitchen with my Uncle John while I watched a tear that had dropped from my eyes fall on my mother's lips. That, if anything, must bring her to life again. But, of course not. No, of course not.[238] If she could not live a moment longer then life for her was gone. She had her days. She lived a life that suddenly for me seemed like another age. And she did it all without a man to drag her down. How many women like that? Where did she get that strength? I never asked.

I'll tell you now, my lovely son. It was from you and for you. That's why you were a sickly boy. Mammy sucked all the health from you. It was for your own good.

Everything was for me. Few crumbs for mammy. I was her baby, her shining star. Was she happy to see me go?

No mother wants to see her child leave.

She wanted me to have a life better than hers. Going away was part of it.

You could have visited more. You could have written, Freddy. A phone

---

[238] I have something of the smell of my mother on me still: lioness and cub, always, and through death. I remember as a child, waking, my eyes stuck tight with gound. I heard her spit softly on a handkerchief and felt the moist warmth as she drew it across the lids. My eyes opened to find her sitting on the edge of the bed ready for work; the blue raincoat and brown bag; the bag that was almost always empty, but always carried.

'You just stay in bed, son. Mammy will see your teacher.'

With a cooling hand she swept the hair back off my forehead.

call even. You could have shown her only son was there.

But the truth is I was never really there. And then I upped roots and sticks and was gone forever.

From the funeral car the city looked like a Lionel Wendt brometched photograph.[239] My auntie Mary sat opposite me. She had been crying in the house, keeping watch over her dead sister; she had been crying in the street going into the car; and now she was crying inside the car. I leaned over several times and said *There, there*, while patting her fat knees. *Oh, Freddy*, she kept repeating. *Oh Freddy*. It crossed my mind that as sisters they were as close as strangers.

It should be noted that everything did not go according to plan. As the car turned a corner approaching the crematorium there was some kind of palaver up ahead, and smoke could be seen billowing from the building: the crematorium was ablaze. We left the car and joined the staring others.

'It's a sign,' Auntie Mary said.

'Of what?' Norman asked. It sounded rude, and very like him, but he told me later that it was a genuine enquiry. I didn't believe it for a moment.

While the fire was doused we waited in another building some yards away which was untouched by the flames. Every half hour another funeral party would join us until the service was hastily rescheduled two hours later at another crematorium on the south side. Auntie Mary cried for those hours.

We went to the purvey before it. There was a good spread, even if the sandwiches had turned in slightly at the corners. Let us now and forever give thanks to the Co-Op. To corner a market in death, bread and milk is no mean feat. In my mind, I would forever see the teardrop hit those dead lips. It was a sign indeed. I wanted away from it all. I saw nothing of my relations after that day ever again. There would be no

---

[239] I had a few prints.

returning. And the sigh that was mistaken for grief was relief, but the next day I saw Sinatra.

Freddie Foster? Hang your head in shame.

One thing in my head seems to run into another. Me in my bedroom, my mother crying, my mother dead, Frank Sinatra. Maybe it is not so unnatural. This is not just about Norman; it's about me and it's about everyone I have ever known, for they have all brought me to this moment. I understand that now.

Before I left home for fame and fortune, I killed my mother. It was a slow death, brought on by worry about her one and only. Anxiety was heaped upon anxiety over many years; stress stretched out before her, offering no reprieve, the weight of guilt upon her. And she would have taken upon herself a weight of guilt that would have edged her ever closer to the grave. I brought that to her. I was to be the son who brought about his mother's destruction, like most sons, from Orestes onwards, by confusing the womb with the house of Atreus. And so I left her. I repaid a lifetime of love by jumping on a morning train to Euston.

Her death devastated me. A burial in a gawping grave would have been better.

The boy who stood in the courtyard below lit a cigarette as a girl approached him. They exchanged some words before he put his arm around her shoulders, and they both walked away.

45

2007

ii

'She was a boozy girl with much to offer in extracurricular entertainment.'
Freddy comments on the death of a British comedienne.

Look, let's get this straight, I'm a very simple man; a man who was poorly educated and suffered much at the hands of others. Growing up I always felt that I was at the mill of slaves, blinded to many opportunities in my life purely because of my humble origins. I learned my love of story through my mother reading a passage from the Bible every single night. I was such a sensitive boy in many ways and brutalised by my environment. That much is clear to me now. Two things rescued me and perhaps redeemed me: comedy, and a battered copy of Francis Scott Fitzgerald's *The Great Gatsby*. I once said this to a major political figure of the 70s and he laughed and said, 'It's just F. Scott'. I had to remind him that Francis was his name and since it was then I would use it. He continued to laugh.

'It's the kind of person I am,' I told him. 'I learned his name, so I use it.'

He kept on laughing and slapping me on the shoulder.

'You're a queer fish, Freddy. Where did you get that voice? Where do you come from?'

That rang in my head a long time: *Where did you get that voice? Where do you come from? Now don't you be rising above your station, little man.* But, like Jay Gatsby, I had decided a long time before that I would change who I was. I would use any money that I earned to break from the Gaza that I was born to.[240] I would recreate myself. In my bedroom in 1958 in Glasgow I sat and made a list of areas that needed attention. The voice was certainly the first. and I ended up working with voice coach Norah Cooper at The Royal Scottish Academy of Music and Drama twice a week for two years. Other things came during that time: suits, shoes, and haircuts.

I had to get out of Norman's kitchen and breathe some comparatively fresh air. What else was there to dispose of? The body parts were gone. I opened the kitchen cupboards and started emptying perishables into a plastic bag. They were all so Norman.

What's this?
Potatoes.
In a tin? In a tin? Potatoes in a tin?
They're tinned potatoes.
Who would buy potatoes in a tin?
They cut out a lot of fuss.
Do they taste of potato?
I wouldn't say that.

Every packet and tin was a memory. At the rate I was going, the task would never be done, so I began to sweep them all in the bag without care or contemplation. I wanted not just the cupboards bare, but the flat emptied. The bathroom was getting there in bits, when I could stomach it, but splashes of blood in the grout were proving difficult to remove. *Ajax foams as it cleans.* I made a mental note to get some scourers.[241]

---

[240] I refer, of course, to the Gaza of myth. Today's troubled region was once again the fault of old Blighty. We seemed to gift to one what belonged to another. Running an empire led us into madness.
[241] When I had dragged him from the bed and laid him out I had stepped around the fresh cadaver as though at any moment a hand would reach out and grip my foot.

No Chapter

2006

I tried this before and failed. I cannot write of the day.
Janice died.
We had the funeral.
We played one of her favourite songs:
Frank Sinatra
What A Funny Girl (You Used To Be).
We wept.
Lost.

46

2009/Present

'Once we learned to lie the world became prone to fiction.'
One line in an ill-judged spot at Cardiff University, Nov. 2000[242]

I was obsessed with cleanliness. Always washing. I was prone to sitting on my hands. I never liked shaking hands if mine were damp and clammy. That's why I hated a lot of the clubs. There were no shower facilities. Was it Bernard Manning's place that didn't have a sink? Not that it mattered to Norman. The cruise was a nightmare when it came to personal hygiene.

'Norman,' I said, 'could you perhaps wash a bit more? You're honestly beginning to pong a bit.'

'It's the lights, Freddy, I sweat under the lights.'

'It's not sweat, Norman, it's stale sperm. Unless the floods and Fresnel's are making you come in your pants just wash a bit more. It's not pleasant to work with. Doesn't Janice say anything? She's trapped in a cabin with you.'

'Oh, she'd notice, wouldn't she?'

'She probably notices a lot more than you think.' I had to stick up for Janice because I noticed that the more he shagged his way around the ship the more insulting and dismissive he was towards her.

'Most days her eyes are like pin-pricks. You not fucking noticed? I'm not talking fucking dexies this time.'

What is it that drives people to behave in a way that is quite clearly harmful to them? Before we arrived on *The Silver*

---

[242] My solo act was spinning out of control. I was offering my thoughts on life rather than gags. I had obviously confused myself that night with the Dalai Lama. I had been on the road without Norman for many years by that time. I cajoled him out on stage several times though. He was always my partner.

Princess I knew that Janice had been reliant on amphetamines of various sorts. A year before we had left Britain I had, purely by chance, gone into her handbag for a cigarette and found at the bottom two purple hearts.[243] They were also known as dexies and they were as widely available in showbiz circles as dickie bows and dinner suits. It is a fallacy that drugs were exclusive to pop stars. Pills were passed around everywhere like Smarties at a kids' party. Although not everyone indulged, everyone knew about them. The rule of the day was: if you value your squeaky-clean image don't talk about drugs – even if you weren't doing them. Unless you were Paul McCartney or Mick Jagger. Then you could do it on television and articulate a culture. And increase your record sales into the bargain. If anyone had found out about Janice she would have fallen, hard. And she would have taken Norman and Freddy with her. As it was the worst of it all was contained within that cruise ship and on far off lands

Before she left she was pregnant, and before she was pregnant she had become addicted to heroin. Whether it was the imminent arrival that made her sit up and take a good look at herself I don't know, but quit she did. There seemed to be no wrestling with personal demons; she just stopped. The loss of the baby was devastating and sent her running back to her protector: drugs. She did not return immediately to heroin on the ship; her drug of choice seemed to be cocaine. She had been told it was a great weight loss tool. There was a heavy price to pay for all of this, though. Her body fell prey to so many illnesses and her mind fell prey to such desperation and anxiety. This showed in her inability to concentrate or sleep. She wittered on constantly about anything, everything, or nothing. She developed a curious habit of finishing people's sentences for them.

---

[243] They weren't purple and they weren't heart shaped. They were triangular and blue.

Janice blew apart a theory that I had regarding age and the use of legs. I always believed that people who were on their feet all day – walking or whatever – would live longer. She hadn't used drugs for years. I assumed that she would die *the grande dame*, clutching a telegram from the Queen. This, though, was not to be. She died some days before her sixty-second birthday on July 11th, 2006. Norman and I had a table booked for her birthday at Gordon Ramsay at 68 Royal Hospital Road. I had sold some personal mementos to cover this. For Janice, I would happily have sold my soul. As it was Norman and I dined alone and in silence.[244]

I won't lie: I never fully recovered from her death. It was not only unexpected it was grossly unfair in the general scheme of things. She was the nurse, the mother, the lover: she was our best friend. Her absence left gaps that could never be filled. When something like that happens to someone that you care about so much, life loses its gilt. This does not mean that you too want to die; it just means that life will never again be so important. As it was for me so it was doubly for Norman. Her tireless nursing in the first year of his illness could only be explained by true love. If only someone had loved me as much I'm sure I could have conquered the world. Throughout everything she loved Norman; pure and simple. Truth[245] be told Janice only *cared* for me. These crumbs I took gratefully. I didn't blame Norman for any of it.

The Ajax was doing sterling work in the bathroom. For anyone who

---

[244] We weren't going to go but decided it's what Janice would have wanted. Strangely, it was as though she were with us. She would have been over the moon. The darling girl would have been over the moon.

[245] This word is beginning to stick in my craw. We might ask is anything true. Is Norman dead? Did he even exist? I tell you such and so and so, but did you meet him? Do I exist? All of this could be a yarn spun by some omniscient god for all you know. This is a fine how do you do. I am now starting to question my own existence. This was never an intention. The history that we agree upon shall become the history of a time.

kills and dismembers a loved one at home, I really do give it my full recommendation. It is not only stronger than dirt, it is stronger than blood.

47

2009

'The only heckle that ever really hurts is the one you suspect might be true.'
Steve Punt

With Norman's lifeless body somewhere beneath me I was lifted up, my whole being sharply pulled from the floor. An electric shock of realisation at the act committed shot through my every nerve; an electric impulse blasted through every axon, every neuron, every vein and every membrane. It sent me spinning in irregular motion, first flung forward, the head dipping as the legs swung up behind me, and then back and Catherine wheeled to the side. My thoughts were being tossed with images flicked before my eyes – YOU – The word came at me as real and clear as though shouted in my ear – YOU – again, but this time faster and more high-pitched. The word was gaining momentum and drilling into me, somewhere deep in my belly causing a rising nausea. And a high-pitched whistle Eeeeeeeeeee! I couldn't get any sense of myself, where I was – YOU – again and again and again and again, repeated. But then everything stopped and the tumbling blocks of my past collapsed before me. Eeeeeeeee! Words and pictures. Janice, you'll save me, Janice. If I hold onto your voice and your image you'll save me, pick me up from this, cradle me in your arms – Bang me, Freddy! Bang me! But now it's you, Janice, holding on, wanting saved, desperate. I can't do that, girl! I can't do that! – What's Bill's mother's? Norman's laughter. What's Bill mother's? I try to ask this calmly, a respite in a raging storm. But Norman's laughter drowns out the words. Loud and fragmented as though laughter from different times were edited together. Eeeeeeee! Where did you get that voice, Freddy? That voice – My name is Janice Anne Calderwood – Truths and lies, mister. We had moments shared. An audio flicker book of voices rushed through my ears. Where are you Freddy? I asked. Get a grip, old son. Where are you? Find an anchor, find the root. But at that moment there seemed nothing to hold on to. There was nothing to hold on to. My life, constantly trying to find something to give it – what? Purpose? Reason? Something to…hold onto? FREDDY! It was Norman's voice as sure as ever. FREDDY! Norman, coming to save me, to tell me what to do. FREDDY! And the sound Eeeeeeee! Hastily slowed down, it's tone more human – FREDDY! Eeeeeeee! Hear it, Freddy? Cling on to it! Eeeeeeeee! And like a man who has found his star I am guided towards a truth too horrible, too foul to contemplate. And everything came to a dead stop. I was standing over Norman's bed, the sound coming from somewhere inside him – Eeeeeeeeh…The pyjama jacket torn open, revealing a chest smeared with blood, the skin bearing the marks of a laptops edge brought down again and again and again and again…the body more broken than before…but that sound continued – Eeeeeeeee…But it was not from him because his body was lifeless. His breath had gone. His sweet breath had gone. The sound was coming from me. What is the stuff of life that can take over and make you a foreign country to yourself? Eeeeeeee! And I thought of Bernie Winters at The Empire, poking his stupid, gormless head through the curtain – Eeeeeeee! And the voices. Fucking hell, there's two of them! There are always two of them…the classic act. The sound emanating from the stranger I had become of myself made me think of Mike and Bernie. However inappropriate that might be it was accepted at that moment as a normal connection. I was returning to myself and the sound slowed – Eeeee…eeee….eeee. I was breathing more regularly – Eeeeee…eee,,, I suddenly felt chilled to the bone, cold as only truth can be. I started to shiver – Eeeeee…eee…eeeee….And I had to stop it so I spoke:

Norman…Norman…What have we done?

48

The past/the present

'Life is a moderately good play with a badly written third act.'
Truman Capote

In the latter part of your life you look back at the first part.
You remember what you can and no doubt the memories are
shaped by the life you have lived between. They are all echoes.
And what use pictures? Who can seriously look at any pictures
of themselves and say, that is me? I mean, it just isn't. Ever. I
have memories that cannot be all true but as I remember, then
they are.[246] Freddy Foster need not exist for all that anyone
cares. The same goes for Norman Riddell's time on this earth.
People often pass through life without causing ripples in
others' lives. As far as I am concerned the memories I relate
might as well be a fiction[247] for all anyone will truly care.
Everything must ultimately come to nought.

As a child I sat in bed all day, every day: and that's how I
remember it. Ill I was, or so I must have been. I was not, I
truly believe, the *malingerer* that the visiting school inspector
described. I was a special case, too sensitive for the world into
which I was thrown. As such I had no friends and spent so
little time outside, that I gathered no enemies either. Apart
from, of course, my mother, who became both friend and
enemy. *Enemy* when she returned from a shop without a
desired comic or book. *Couldn't you see I had been waiting an
eternity for your return?* She did not see this at all. She came in
talking about the lives of those she had met, as though I
would be interested. All I wanted to know was what *Bill*

---

[246] Might I say – if any readers haven't already noticed – you will find no
profundity in this life story, or indeed any significance.
[247] If only.

Sampson, The Wolf of Kabul was up to. Or maybe *Wilson the Wonder Athlete – Go on, William!* Like the young Marcel awaiting a kiss! Comics or kisses, what did it matter? The waiting was interminable and quite ridiculous. The shops were really no more than fifty feet from my bed, but she'd be discussing affairs of the day with Mrs MacLeod, or Mrs Lindsay, or Mrs Barbour, or Terry in the newsagents, or Maggie who sold the bruised fruit. And that would be an hour more of waiting.

But she was my only friend also. When I cried at night in the rattling windowed dark afraid that the *man with the horns* would steal me away for ever she would hold me to her bosom and sing a soft song: maybe *I'll Tell Me Ma* or *Too-Ra-Loo-Ra-Loo.* She had never seen Ireland but remembered the songs her mother taught her. At times like that I'd fall into sleep as though tumbling into a great warm ocean. And the next morning we would play the old game:

I'm too no' well for school.

Well, you do look a bit peely-wally.

Once I got up in the morning and turned white as a ghost and fell to the floor.

That's it, no school for you.

And then she'd tuck me in and go off to her cleaning job. *Bring me back a comic!* I'd shout. Or later, a book, like *The Egg Tree,* or *Dick Whittington*[248] or much later *As I Lay Dying,* or *The Great Gatsby,* or *Homer* or *Plato* from the library. I would eventually venture out to get the books myself. Rather than borrow them I bought them with saved pocket money. When I officially left school my mother had a word with Jackie Annett, the local butcher, and got me a job delivering and clearing up. Watching the dismemberment of carcasses certainly stood me in good stead for my future murderous

---

[248] I truly believe we underestimate how influential that story has been in youngsters heading to London.

actions. The job provided something of an income and so I could begin to change – or perhaps start – my life. Books taught me that life had to be lived. Mother dear[249] did help me in my aspirations to better myself in that she did not criticize or mock. But there is a darker side to all of this that I am loathe to go into but, in the interests of truth and openness, I shall.

Mother dear did in some way damage her *little Freddy*. She did not prepare me for the monster that was the outside world. Not everything could be learned from books – nor, might I add, should everything be learned from books. Mother dear made me different, or encouraged me to be different, to be unlike the common herd. She told me several times that I was not like other boys and had a very different future waiting for me. The truth was that she should have whipped me and tossed me out of the flat and into school. *Was it love that made you cling to me, mother? Or was it your fear of being alone? Your Freddy actually needed others. He always needed others. I set off to London to find them, to lose you. But as I sit now writing these words, with you many, many years dead, you are as close as ever: my breath, your breath; my blood, your blood; my heartbeat, your heartbeat. I would tear the world to shreds to hear again your soft voice singing, while my head rests on your pillowed bosom.* A man's life cannot be a tragedy of what is or what will be, but of what was and can never be again.

I catch my sad flesh in the mirror and look away immediately. I dress slowly. Red boxer shorts, red socks; my cream coloured Chinos;[250] a white, freshly ironed short sleeved shirt is pulled from a hanger; brown loafers; a crumpled linen jacket

---

[249] This was an affectionate term and not a real affectation.
[250] Flying in the face of prostate induced dribble I threw caution to the wind and purchased the trousers at the airport on the way out. I would of course check for any damp staining before leaving any toilet.

that matches the trousers. And then I pull from the back of a wicker chair a cravat. It is slate blue with a small grey diamond pattern.

That's it, Freddy. Over the knot, not through like a tie.

I learned that skill before I had left Glasgow. I was preparing myself for all eventualities in the entertainment business.

I have to return to the mirror. The whole ensemble is topped off with a hat in the style of Panama, and a silver plated, knob handle cane walking stick. I look at the face again, the fallen, the eyes that I can only relate to a fishmonger's slab. If I do not know the person who stares back, how can you, reader, know me? The conscience creates the prison. The freedom myth. I have to tilt the ego to a jaunty angle, straighten it just so, and brush it with a flick of my hand. I am ready for the day.

I pick up the laptop before leaving, letting the door click to a close behind me.

And now I walk, somewhat unsteadily. My arm for some reason wants to rest in front of me and my hand involuntarily shakes like some *hep cat* in the throes of a Cab Calloway number. For those reasons the cane was purchased: it steadies my gait and occupies my hand. The steady hand clutches the laptop bag by my side.

Outside I start my daily routine, walking towards the café where I sit for most of the day writing these words. I am losing the power of conversation, disappearing into silence. Words in the present no longer hold the magic for me. My only conversation is with the handsome and charming waiter, Etienne. He is by no means a clever boy, but I forgive him that in a way I could never have years before. *Frederique*, he will say, *What you are write?* And I always reply with: *A letter home*. He is my last contact with an outside world that I have grown to have little enthusiasm for. I'm growing so much older. When did it all fall away?

I never thought of dying in another country; a country that was not mine. To return…But sometimes we cannot do that…Sometimes we…Again…I am dying here. I do not belong. I am not from here. Not. I write, I delete. Again. Start the paragraph again.

I can now count my days, unfettered by aspiration. Let me play it all out, day by day, by hour and by minute, by seconds. I pass this time not only writing and remembering, but my life is also pleasurable and mundane. I count the tables – there are ten in this outdoor section – and there are ashtrays stacked on a table just inside the door. Of these there are about twenty, at the moment. To the right of ashtrays there is a stack of newspapers and magazines, solely for use by patrons. There are no chairs around this table. To walk from my table – which is number 8 – to the door is seven average steps. If I were asked to describe my table position I would guess at the North East side. There are three other tables around me, with six at the opposite side. I am sitting in a chair. I am still, apart from my fingers passing like shadows across the keyboard. There is more than a normal distance between my eyes and the screen. If I move forward there is a slight blurring of the words. I possibly/probably need spectacles, but I do without. My head does not move, the appearance of the black letters on the screen being the only movement. Beyond this screen, the waiter moves slowly around a table, picking up dishes from a recently departed customer. He is in no hurry. Beyond him, a motorcycle travels away from me down a narrow and shaded street. And above that white clouds move as though part of Etienne's task. Etienne slowly moving the clouds, tidying the sky. No one and nothing is in a hurry here. These must be the quietest times I have ever spent – outside those spent in my sick bed waiting on my mother to return from her work or her shopping. Then, also, I could see clouds pass slowly in the same sky. Etienne carries the dishes indoors.

I am thinking: What if I had no name? If the name Freddie Foster had not existed? If my past and the relationships within it had not existed? If I had no history? But that's not what I want of course. Why else would I be writing this? It's to fix my position in the world forever.[251]

A plate appears before me:

'Des tomates farcies? Frederique, for you? Et vino?'

A tomato stuffed with ground meat, garlic and breadcrumbs and a dry rosé are put out on the table.

'But I…'

'I give to you.' He smiled a broad smile that spread across his face and lit up his eyes. My eyes well up.

'Oh, you are too kind…Thank you…thank you…'

Unlike Blanche DuBois, I did not rely on the kindness of strangers, but his kindness touches me deeply. Etienne returns indoors while I dab my tears. What silly old fools we can become.

---

[251] I must also confess that I am obviously the first reader of this work thus far and I am not too impressed. I am little impressed by the writing or by most of the lives of those being portrayed. Having lived through all of the events it seems to me a less than accurate account. I feel that some supplementary reading is required in order to fully appreciate the times. This might reflect dismally on me as a memoirist, and perhaps even as a biographer. I will not suggest particular titles, but I am sure your lecturer or local library can offer guidance.

49

Present/Past Nov. 1963

'It's time to grow up and sell out.'
Lenny Bruce

I think I saw a youth across the forecourt sporting a plaster over his nose. He was part of a group. The same group, I presume, that were always there. They watched me constantly. I don't know why they never approached, although if they did I would have high tailed it, no doubt. Or ambled off with my tail between my legs? *(Oh, you are nothing new, boys. My greatness also didn't get a chance to flicker; it too fell into the running gutter of a broken youth. Like most. Snuffed out before the flame caught, before any fire was allowed to blaze. I was a victim of circumstance. Like most. I was a victim of poverty. Like most. I was condemned before that mewling scream announced another drain on resources. Like most. My card was marked, the game complete, before my first move. Another pawn to know his place. Like most).*

If it was indeed the youth whose nose I had bitten when I was carrying the golf bag I would assume revenge might have been the dish of the day. But they did not approach. They stared. They followed my comings and goings, but that was it. If they were waiting for an opportune time to pounce I couldn't fathom when that time might be. I sometimes heard them making whooping sounds, or let rip the occasional scream or yelp. The lack of action, though, did indeed trouble me. Perhaps that was all part of the intimidation.

I wondered what the boy had done with the golf bag. There was little doubt in my mind that he would have shared such scandal with his cohorts. I refuse to believe that the stealing of human remains is yet a common occurrence of estate life. I was of the mind that the story had indeed been shared, but that it was heavily edited. Perhaps the character of the *victim* had dropped several decades in age. It could not have been anything other than humiliating to have been beaten by a pensioner. The young lad's street credibility would no doubt have suffered something of a dent. Whatever the story, as I crossed near them, I was thankful that it was stares that I was subjected to and not boots or knives. These *corner boys* perhaps still had something to learn from the *Teddy Boys* of their grandfathers' youth.

But these boys, what was going on in their minds? If they are truly as empty headed as those I grew up with then very little. But regardless, I could not bring myself to hate them. I could think them foolish and misguided; I could pity their almost certainly bleak future. I could sympathise with their frustrations; I could be irritated by their lack of understanding of life. But hate was not on my agenda. It was the waste of youth that got me most of all. Strangely, I felt the same towards the *Teddy Boys* fifty years before. The language and the clothes had changed; the hair styles had changed; but the sneers were pretty much as I remembered; the emptiness remained the same.

I decided at a young age it wasn't for me. So I made plans for *the big smoke*. By the time I returned I was already a foreigner in my home city. It was during a tour in November 1963 that I first felt this. I couldn't have cared less about the death of John Kennedy, nor indeed the first episode of Doctor Who – which were the same week.[252] No, on my mind was the time Norman and Freddy met Janice. We were playing the King's Theatre. Not, of course, top of the bill, but after a year of little, these slots on tour were a godsend. It was on these tours that we honed our craft. We stayed in digs and were paid a wage. It wasn't much but we saw ourselves as proper

---

[252] A conspiracy theory if ever there was one! I jest.

entertainers, professionals. Wasn't that what we had both dreamed of?

The show had played to packed houses around Scotland, but none were livelier than the two Glasgow shows. The dancers were high kickers – much like *The Tiller Girls* – and opened the show with the warmth and pzazz that one associates with classic variety.

On that first night I started chatting to a tall blonde. She was always in the dead centre of the kicking line. I'd watched her on each show as we'd travelled around Scotland, but only now did I have the chance of speaking alone with her: lookers were often surrounded by admirers. The conversation was a non-starter. Her one word answer to any of my questions seemed to pull the shutters down on romance. Instead I moved in on her shorter friend whom I did not recognise as part of the troupe.[253] In an unlit lane around the corner from the old theatre our passions got the better of us.

'Turn around,' I gasped. She looked confused but turned unsteadily in her Cha-Cha shoes and bent over. I mounted her like a dog.

'Edinburgh next,' she said.

'Yes…'

'Dumfries.'

'Yes…'

'I like your act.'

'Yes…'

'Your act…your act…'

'Yes…'

'You and your partner…'

'Yes…'

'He's quiet…'

'Not when…oh god…not when he's drunk…he's on a warning…'

---

[253] She was, though, quite forgettable.

'What's his name?'

'Norman…'

'Norman…So you're Freddy…'

'Yeeeee…sss…I'm…Freddy…Oh, fuck…' I pulled out and came over the back of her legs. 'Sorry, Jane.' I wiped the mess with a left breast pocket handkerchief.

As she pulled up her knickers and smoothed down her dress she asked if I wanted to go with some of the others to a bar in Sauchiehall Street. The thought of the tall blonde friend made me consider for a moment but as I'd shot my load I decided against it.

'I'm staying with my mother. She lives here. I don't want to turn up smelling of drink. She's very Presbyterian.' I also wanted to show Norman the west end of the city and let him explore the nicer pubs down from the university.

'Hey, you can maybe introduce your partner to the rest of the girls tomorrow.'

'I shall. Look, Jane, I hope you don't mind but I have to rush.[254]

'That's all right. So do I.'

There was some awkwardness in the parting.

'So,' she said. 'I'll see you tomorrow?'

'Of course.'

'I'm the one third from the left. And my name's Janice.' She then laughed at my apology and embarrassment.

'Ta-ta,' she said as she walked away.

The boy with the plaster over his nose, did he have dreams? Did he have aspirations for the future?[255] Did he even have any sense of a future? It seemed to me sometimes that the Baby Boomers had bred monsters. All the great dreams that

---

[254] This is not the sort of behaviour acceptable to most, but theatre dancers tended to be a bit more relaxed when it came to sexual etiquette.
[255] Even of a snatched fuck with a dancer down a lane.

were held of a better society after the break down of The Good Old Days seemed to have come to nought. Is this what the old guard had felt when the red flag was nailed to the NAAFI wall? Or the frustrated youth had ripped up cinema seats? Or when the Lady Chatterley case fell for a few fucks and cunts?[256] Or when the Mods and Rockers fought on Brighton Beach? Or when a punk rock group swore ten years after that? And so it goes on, what is à la mode, and what monsters disturb the older generation. There seems only to be one certainty: the young shall always view the old as foolish.

When I left Glasgow on a cold, snowy January in 1961 I'd had enough of the old and the dying. London offered the chance of a life. I could leave that Freddy behind. I could wipe him out like he'd never existed. That is truly how I felt. I could have stayed, yes, and stayed quiet, but my hat was meant for the ring of life. On the train down south my heart was bursting in my chest. I could have wept with the joy. I had £10 in my pocket, but I would just have happily left with nothing. Did those lads on the forecourt even begin to understand that?

Between that youthful escape and the here and now there was a point that I seemed to lose a grip on life, something of my old confidence fell away.[257]

Failure is not something that one courts, but once it gains entry into your world it hangs about like an unwelcome guest. Returning to Britain in 1972 after so long away was fraught with professional danger. We were either starting again with a totally different act, a total re-invention or were continuing in

---

[256] Mervyn Griffith-Jones may have been mocked for asking if it was the kind of book 'you would let wish your wife or servants to read?' but I would most certainly never have let it fall into the hands of my wee mammy.

[257] Would that happen to the boys outside? But of course. No one escapes this. The aggression will fall away as they weaken, the arrogance melt into understanding. One day they'll wake up and think, *We're all going the same place. We're all food for the worms. We're all fucked.*

the rut that we had been stuck in before we had left. Two
people who had a great influence in the decision taken wanted
to carry on *as was*. One was Norman and the other was Janice.
The fact was when it came to career decisions I had the final
say. This was, in Janice's case, because she trusted my
judgement. In Norman's, it was the fact that he was bone-idle
and had to have his arse kicked at every turn. I couldn't let
him know that, of course. I had to cajole him or let him think
that it was his idea in the first place. I carried a heavy burden
for a lot of years. It was my lot in life and I did it out of love. I
think that they both understood that: I hope that they both
understood that.

Fame is not a disease. It doesn't spread through the
drinking of dirty water. Fame is sought out. It is tracked
down. People who achieve it are thirsty. Really thirsty. They
need to satisfy that thirst. That can only be done through
constant attention at parties, at dinner tables, in restaurants
and in bars. The famous are the loudest, the most talkative,
and the boors. The stories they have repeated so often will get
yet another airing. Repeat upon repeat, oblivious of the rictus
grin of their audience. The famous are arch snobs determined
to keep the division between them and the common herd.
They will be noticed and they will complain about it. They will
shout about being pointed at in the street. But, as Norman
often said: *Fuck them, that's what they signed up for.* This is the
golden prize. They start to believe that fame has magical
properties, that can shield them from all. But that has never
been the case. It is less than nothing. Norman understood this
more than most. He never lost the common touch. Brutal and
brash he could be, but on every level no more so than the
man in the street. He hated pretension, which is why no doubt
he goaded me so much. He saw my faults and my foolishness
and always pointed them out. As years moved on I think I
discovered what Norman always knew about me. It's a long

journey to get to the start.

There is a real lack of tenderness today. I don't know when it started. The 80s? Is it too easy to blame the free market economy and free market emotions? Before that I sensed an anger growing in the country. It was everywhere. And it seemed to be fuelled by the red tops that were mixing facts and fluff in much the same way as a propaganda unit might do during wartime, making a sort of celebrity soup. Mick Jagger and Reggie Kray are on the same page. Myra Hindley has as much to do with The Beatles as she does with Rose West. I have attended parties where the great and the good rub shoulders with gangsters and whores. Christine Keeler floated easily between Yevgeny Ivanov and John Profumo.[258] and mingled at Lord Astor's parties, just as easily as Stephen Ward cricked the backs of Churchill, Sinatra and Liz Taylor during the day while pimping for the aristocracy in the evening.[259] I tried to attach myself more permanently to it all. One night I tried to wangle a trip to Mustique from Lord Glenconner, but he was too busy talking about his newly discovered son. Eventually I blurted out:

---

[258] I visited The Pinstripe Club, where they met, once. They were not, of course, there. Although I wasn't taken with the place it later became the Bag o' Nails and attracted a much younger music loving set. I went there several times with various people to see the latest chart-toppers either playing or being seen. I was always recognised by the musicians and they never failed to say a hello, but, if truth be told, I was thought of as square and old by 1966, although I was in my mid-twenties. Some of the much younger, ill-educated, little shits saw me as the butt of their humour. This I could have done without.

[259] I am, of course, referring to public perceptions. The truth of the matter is a lot more unsavoury, particularly in the matter of the British judicial system. I met Mr Ward briefly in 1963 and thought he had given up. If dead men could walk then I would say Stephen Ward was a dead man. Some days later he was. The cause of death was given as an overdose of pills, although Michael Bentine told me he thought Ward had been murdered. Thinking of it all now I still feel sick to the stomach.

'Some nights Francis haemorrhages money!' It was almost shouted and the talk stopped with Glenconner looking at me slowly and saying quietly:

'A good eye, though.[260]

Celebrity is incestuous and also cannibalistic in its behaviour. To become part of that family is to give up something of yourself to the feast. Not everyone can survive it, but people are willing to sell their grandmothers for a slice of it. I was no different. Norman did not sell himself for that. The truth is all Norman wanted to do was entertain, go home and drink and fuck. The famous held no sway with him. He was not a man easily impressed.

Richard Harris?

A cunt.

Beatles?

Cunts.

Bruce Forsyth?

A cunt.

Adam Faith?

A whippet cunt.

Ken Dodd?

Now, careful, lad…

Celebrity, though, is not a bubble. It is far reaching, uncontained, a Quatermass like monster spilling into corners never before considered worthy of attention. It is being sold to the people and all it wants in payment in their lives. Don't worry that you have nothing to offer, just be. The media will create you. It doesn't even have to lie anymore. Are you talentless? That can be dealt with. I sometimes asked myself was I shaped by and created by others? Am I a fiction? Freddy appearing at the parties, the TV spots. Is that me? But I held back. I didn't give everything. It was me in a bed in a Glasgow

---

[260] The son discovered was to the mother of Bacon's muse Henrietta Moraes.

tenement in the 1950s that created Freddy Bartholomew Foster. The middle name would be dropped. Just like Eric dropped his in favour of Morecambe.[261] No, Freddy Foster was in control at all times. Maybe if I had handed him over to someone else things would have been better. But who wants to give themselves up? The great unread only see the lights. They are dazzled, each an unwitting Faust.

---

[261] I considered a name change like Eric's. Just take a holiday destination and it would contain traces of good times, of freedom, of belonging to something: Freddy Irvine, Freddy Carradale, Freddy Kingussie. But none of them sounded right. So, I just cut it down, dropped the middle name, made the first name less class-ridden. Our names are our lives; they define who we are. I have met many over the years who have tried to escape their name in an effort to become invisible.

'... Etienne slowly moving the clouds, tidying the sky...'

50

March 25ᵗʰ 2004/Present

Reporter: Is Janice an integral part of the act now?
Freddy: Her fou rire is refreshing.
                    Brent and Kilburn Times.

My elbow rests on the table. The upper arm at a 45-degree angle, the forearm tilted to complete a V shape. My liver-spotted hand has turned brown in the South of France summer. The blue veins and length of thin bones stretch out like chicken feet below that loose brown skin. My fingers are long but have lost some of their languid movement of youth. Mild arthritis has put paid to that. There is stiffness to the fingers now that reflect a mind that is tense and troubled. I cannot undo that now. I cannot reel history back, only memory. The anxiety planted from my green youth and nurtured throughout my days cannot be shaken off with a few Freudian facts. It is better to recognise at this late stage that one is totally fucked and move on. But the stiffness bears witness to the fact that I have not moved in any direction whatsoever. Between the distal phalanx and the index and middle fingers a cigarette playfully burned. The ribbons of smoke that sail skyward hold Etienne in a dreamscape. There he is, turning, smiling, with the dark trousers, the burgundy short jacket, and the white shirt. He is a smart and handsome boy and I hope life is good to him before time comes stamping in as it does to all. I look at the computer screen only finding moments later that I have been staring at Etienne for another while. My time passes in shadows, as though measured by some ancient Egyptian clock or obelisk. I notice these shadows, from my vantage point of café table and café seat, jut from a building across the courtyard. Its edge casts a shard that shifts midday grey to a late day gloom over me. This suits me well as I am not as enamoured of the heat as I once was. We change so much throughout life that the former selves might as well be another. We try to recapture feelings but only capture memories of action scattered across various locations. And we analyse these actions with newer feelings garnered throughout the intervening years. What has that to do with what you felt then? You can only guess. But you will be well out on that guess. Sometimes you have a moment – unconscious as it is in its recall – that will stop you in your tracks. It will be a moment that is so light in its touch, like smell or taste that will fling the past so much into your present you will be chilled to the bone. For me, it is the movements that recall the moments. I let my arm lower to bring the cigarette nearer the ash tray and am reminded of Norman's arm exercises. He was finding it increasingly difficult to hold a cup – or indeed anything – and I would lift his forearm up and down in a passive exercise routine. He would, of course, do the best he could without my aid, but I began to enjoy helping him in these small ways. We hoped it would slow up the march of decline.[262] But the disease did indeed march on. When a universal cuff arrived for him his face lit up. I strapped it on and stuck a fork in it and presented him with a plate of baked beans. What a joyous mess! My partner was as happy as I'd ever seen him. And so it's the memory of ever-decreasing movements. My arm drops, so Norman's arm drops. It is the way of the mind. I looked down at the laptop on the table in front of me and the fingers punched out the words *That day*.

---

[262] Did these exercises actually help? I like to think so but I am not certain. What I am certain of is that we believed at the time they were beneficial. Was it just that the contact was just as important? Truthfully, I would have held him all day long if that was what was required.

That day the hospital was busy when we entered. There were three waiting areas full of people. Outside the sun was bright and the temperature was in the high eighties. For some inexplicable reason the heating was on full belt. Children were running about screaming and fighting. Janice did the speaking at the reception. She was holding onto her man's sleeve, partly out of care and partly to stop him walking out. I stood behind them both. I was there to support and to drive them to and fro.

We were shown to Area C and then Norman and Janice were taken into a room to have our lives changed.

Aye…that's right…we knew there was something.

While Blair spoke on the TV someone turned the sound off the mute, but I just blocked out his voice. The children in the waiting area were still making a racket.

After about forty minutes the door opened and my partner came out, his face emotional embers, red-blotched but ashen. His head was shaking to and fro, partly in disbelief, partly some spasmodic twitch. He was like some great dumb beast. I stood up as Janice came through the door next. She was wiping her tearful fat face and repeating again and again *Thank-you doctor, thank-you doctor.* Thank you for what? Emotions are strange things. I wanted at that moment to hold Janice and kiss her. She turned to close the door as Norman passed me. As he did so he stared into my eyes.

'I'm fucked. He told me, Freddy, I'm fucked. He told me,' he said.

Unless the NHS had undergone a drastic review of doctor/patient dialogue, I assumed that more had been said. Is it cancer, Norman. I lowered my voice as my mother did when uttering the C word. He moved towards the drinking water sink and pushed a young girl of about ten years out of the way.

'My ticket's been punched today.'

Bending down to drink the water his top set slipped out and clattered into the sink: *I'm phuuukked, I'm phuuukked*, he spluttered toothless, while slurping up the water.[263] Collecting his teeth and wiping them on his trousers he made towards the automatic doors. The girl lost her thirst and walked away. I put my arm around Janice's shoulder. On the way to the car she told me that Norman had Motor Neurone Disease and that it was an incurable degenerative disease. I thought nothing was incurable.

Nothing could be the same again. Ever. The journey home was spent in silence, apart from Janice's sobbing.

I had written a very flowery letter to the council informing them that my name was Norman Riddell and I was giving up my tenancy of the flat. I told them that I was going to live abroad so my name could be removed from the council list. The letter was typed out on the murder weapon, which worked remarkably well after I let it dry out and spent some time with a cotton bud cleaning blood from between the keys.

My own flat had sold. A quite ridiculous price for a one bedroom flat anywhere. I wasn't complaining. I had made a tidy profit from someone who obviously had the money to splash out on the extortionate asking price. (Thank-you, Mrs. Thatcher). Funnily enough, it made me think hard about where I had come from. The lazy comedian's jibe about the mean Scot got the audiences laughing, but I never got it. We had nothing. The joke was about people being poor,[264] and

---

[263] Norman had lost his teeth when he was 56. He had an infection of the gums and it was a proper surgical procedure. He was devastated. To lose one's keys is an inconvenience; to lose one's hair is a worry; but the loss of teeth is tragedy on a grand scale.

[264] Somehow, over the years the working class, so iconic in the 60s and 70s, began to slip back into its place, became erased from the agenda.

poverty really wasn't so funny as far as I could see. Only Billy Connolly could carry it off. When my ma and me had no food, the neighbours would sometimes come around with some potatoes or some bread. I never really knew poor people to be stingy. Ever. It wasn't until I came to London and met people with lots of stuff, that I encountered the mean and the stingy. I soon learned that jokes could be expressions of power, told to keep people like mother dear and me in our place. Norman and Freddy learned early to rise above that. Apart from that one time at our first meeting Norman never said anything about the mean Jock.

'Why didn't you?'

'You put me right on that in the pub once. Regardless of what you think of me, I'm not a total arsehole.'

Often when her wages didn't stretch to the rent, or food, you would see the gaunt figures of a mother and her son heading westward along the railway track of a morning, heads bowed, coats pulled tight, an empty shopping bag in her hand. I would try and walk along the rail, which would slow her down:

'C'mon. We don't want seen.' And she would charge ahead.

'Ma!' I would shout. 'Ma! Wait fur me!'

And we'd go down at the hill where the fencing had been pulled away and onto the back streets. Along one block and then onto the main road. I'd see it ahead. It was a game to me, but it was a game I knew never to speak of.

Pawnbroking as a business is older than most religions and is certainly of more practical use. If we were lucky there would be no other customers, but that was never a guarantee. There were four heavy doors each with a small opaque window. The place smelled of polish and wood. There were no pictures on the walls, just a framed certificate proving that the broker had the right to trade. I would have to help ma pull the door open on its heavy hinge. Inside was cramped, like a confessional box. The man behind the desk was always pale and dark eyed; old, to me, but now I realise much younger than I am now.

'I've got a few things,' she'd say while pulling at the three rings on her fingers. 'Just need a bit for the boy. Just for the week.' And, of course, it would be for the week. We would make the same journey and redeem her rings time after time after time…until one week she couldn't. And they were lost forever. That day she didn't wait until she got home before she started crying. The reality of poverty has a thousand stories, each in its own way destructive. For many years I hid from that truth. Now I harbour not a little shame at my behaviour.

Don't let money and the lights blind you to what's important, lad.
You knew, Norman, you knew…

51

2009

'We're a couple of guys
Just swinging by…'
From Norman and Freddy's theme song, A Couple of Guys.

A knot is being undone. Not by dexterous fingers, but by the
blade of a sword coming down upon it. The past is being cut
into the open wound it is. I have caressed and comforted you
with *dear reader* and tales of the most tender and private
moments to which Freddy's life has been party. Yet the truth
is that it is not you, dearest reader, but me that these words
serve. Now I must stand or fall before my own truths. I take
responsibility for it all. All this life, this waste of time. If I
have recalled these past incidents as though through a dirty
window, and darkly, then this must be the nature of memory:
the stains of the past return in a different form and obscure
our histories. No matter how we tell of the surroundings, or
people or objects, there is a lie in our lines. The past crumbles
as we try to grasp it. My recollections are tainted by the
expediency of times present and an awareness of the futility of
trying to recreate times past. Still, this is what we do on a daily
basis. Memory encroaches as we walk along the street, drive
our cars, drink a coffee, or read a book. A flashing glimpse of
something not lost but hidden so deeply that ten thousand
years of digging could not reveal. This might be Janice as I
recall her now, but ten seconds of that time would capture
more of her than all my memory could. Is Norman really the
man that I speak about now? Or just some character created
from fragments of distant pasts? I first thought this a few
weeks ago while making good my escape. I felt that I was
recreating Norman from selective memories. His smile

remembered from here, his hands from there, moving
Norman around like Theseus's ship. Other memories and it
would be another Norman.[265] What I came up with is the
Norman I needed to let me flee Britain forever. At one time, I
thought that we could only really speak of ourselves, but the
truth is that none of us can even do that. I should become a
dumb, immobile body, for nothing I say is of any
consequence.[266] The world should be quieter. It needn't be
overnight, but a gradual silence, that stills the nonsense. And
that is how I left my country: silently.[267]

There is an emotional weight at any airport. It is that of
excitement and of expectation. This weight cannot be placed
on the scales and it does not go into the hold. When Leif
Ericsson set off on his travels at the start of the second
millennium, or when, 500 years later, Columbus set sail; or
indeed when any explorer got ready to set foot on new lands

---

[265] And now this just sounds silly. I was leaving. That's all. I was leaving
before I was captured, of course. But as far as I'm aware no one was even
looking for me. And at this moment they still are not. But, of course, my
exile – my second – is nothing compared to death's exile. Grief lies
across you like cold earth. It offers no hope. Norman's death was no
perfect ending, it was an ill-fitting grief that I carried with me.
Geographical banishment always left hope of some return. There would
be no letters asking for a reprieve. I cared not a jot about it. Not a jot. No.
[266] Perhaps the greatest gift would be the capacity not to think.
[267] There were few regrets about leaving the land I had loved. The love
had all but turned sour. My opening for one of my last slots I sang a
corrupted verse of Dibdin's *The Tight Little Island*: 'Oh! What a smug
little island; a right little, tight little island.' True to form it was the wrong
audience for such satire. The boo boys at the front were wearing flaming
torch printed tee shirts of the Conservative Party. This was immediately
before the oak tree symbol was ushered in to make party and policy more
palatable. But I felt there was something rather poisonous and small
about my land. And as for television it was all clutter and noise as far as I
could tell. I truly could not think worse of everything should my life
depend upon it. Which in many ways it did.

in the 19th century, the feeling could not have been much different from a man who sits with a milk weakened tea in the departure lounge of Heathrow Airport. Well, this man.

When I was asked if there was anything to declare there was no ache to confess my awful crime. I did, though, carry the contraband of guilt and memory through customs. Only a fool would think that these things are not visible; anyone who has read of the perverse relationship between Raskolnikov and Ilya Petrovitch can vouch for this. At any moment I expected to be approached by airport security, if not Scotland Yard. It was not the first time I had run away, but it was my first at a pace slowed down by my arthritic toes and a troublesome prostrate. Let us then say that I was literally taking flight. Foreign fields were certainly my destination, and Nice in particular. What attracted me to the South of France was that it was close enough to Africa[268] that I could high tail it should Interpol ever come sniffing.

In the departure lounge, I had different pictures in my head of Norman, and my mind could not settle on one. It also struck me that I had different *types* of Norman in my mind. He was the *I don't give a fuck* sort, then the *Take care of this hopeless drunk*, Norman, and then he was the *Vulnerable and broken man*. This lack of clarity about the man that I knew for so long continued for days after I arrived at L'Hotel Suisse. So, if the scuffers had indeed arrived and asked me about him, I would have said *Which Norman?*

To kill and to disappear seemed totally impossible in this age of the internet. I was by no stretch of the imagination a first-class criminal mastermind. If anyone questions this, may I refer them to the pages in which I describe the disappearance of Norman's legs. But I had taken care of all of my partner's societal connections, which did put my mind at ease. It actually struck me that it would be of a great benefit to many

---

[268] The warmth and splendour!

if the old just died quickly and with as little fuss as possible. Perhaps one day a disease will be introduced that would cull us before we start to be a burden? Cancer cannot be relied upon, and MND affects too few. Possibly while I type these words there are laboratories around the globe working on this very thing. Politicians have a habit of making the most unpalatable of suggestions into modest proposals.

The flight was noisy and warm and cramped, and reminiscent of the hospital, but luckily those few hours went quickly as I reviewed the recent horrors. What in the end drove me to commit such an act? *Kill me, Freddy*? Could I have refrained and gathered enough calm to walk out the door? Could I have soothed my savage breast with a Theatreland walk? *Kill me, Freddy!* I kept telling myself that it didn't really matter a jot as the deed was done. Nevertheless, what if?

Strange things had started to happen before I left. Things that, perhaps due to my heightened state of anxiety, I placed more importance on than they warranted. Since the last meeting with Gordon Tait I had been rather concerned about him turning up again and causing some fuss. But it was not a visit, rather a chance meeting that got me. In order to get cash together for the great escape I had been around a few shops flogging some nice and not so nice pieces of jewellery I'd accumulated over the years. None of it was of great sentimental value[269] so selling was no great wrench. Bentley

---

[269] Let me say now that objects do not really interest me. I am not a collector of sentimental pieces. When I first arrived in London I was fascinated by the cards and such in phone boxes advertising sexual favours. These were called *walk ups* and I had a nice little collection in my Goldham Road flat, and indeed my Fulham and Soho flats. By the time I had enough dosh for Chelsea, my way of life had changed. I dumped the cards and went for sophistication. The jewellery I had were things that I wore to make an impression. These included rings, bracelets, tiepins, and cufflinks. My flat was testament to a life that was in its own way austere. I had three small paintings on the walls, of little value, a very large Satsuma vase as you

and Skinner's in Mayfair was my last port of call. I had just read about it in connection with Damien Hurst's diamond skull *For The Love Of God*. The attraction of such a store to me was obvious, but had I known that Gordon Tait would be sniffing about trying to purchase a brooch for his young mistress, I would have jumped a fast black down to Camden Market instead. He looked as surprised to see me as I him:

'Good Lord, Freddy Foster!' He smiled like the curtain rising at The Gielgud.[270] He was swinging a cane like an assegai[271] and jabbing it at me.

'Gordon! What brings you here?'

'The baubles, man, the baubles. Got to keep the girlies happy. He nodded towards a young woman's back at the counter.

I rubbed my hands thinking that I might have blood on them. I didn't, of course. Lady Macbeth's spot never made more sense than at that moment.

'Indeed.'

'What about you? Not your usual neck of the woods.'

'Oh you know me, Gordon, London is my neck of the woods. I'm just looking for some pensioner bling.' He laughed

---

entered the hallway, a pink ground Japanese Wireless Cloisonne Egret vase on one end of the mantelpiece with a lovely Chinese Qing Moon vase with phoenix birds at the other end. In the centre sat a 19th century French gilt bronze mantel clock.

[270] I met old Johnny on a number of occasions. Possibly the most bizarre was the time he asked me about pornographic films. He was writing one. I told him about the time I lived beside a prostitute called Bathsheba. Johnny was a wonderful, charming, and funny man.

[271] I have not used, or indeed known, that word before last night. I was reading a Colin MacInness novel and came across it. Such synchronicity. I thought I would give him the credit. Giving a fellow writer a compliment like this is probably not the done thing in a scribbler's world these days. Although I must confess I would have no interest in writing a novel: I shall leave its blanched bones for others. I prefer to be a witness. Of all the arts, it is perhaps the most bourgeois and vulgar.

at this, as intended. My own verbal leap across the generation gap.

'It's just I went around to Norman's place again the other day.'

'I told you, Gordon, phone first. The boy isn't well. He wouldn't appreciate surprise visits.'

He moved his head close to mine and lowered his voice:

'Well, I can understand that, eh?' He nodded towards his *squeeze*, who was busying herself looking at necklaces which she would never truly own. 'But no,' he continued. 'It wasn't that. Who was the young boy leaving the flat?' My body tensed and I stared at him for a second more than was natural.

'Boy?'

'Ill-fitting clothes and a beanie. Looked like any other kid.'

I took a deep breath and started to button up my coat. I needed to be doing something other than looking at him when replying.

'Oh, you'd have to ask Norman.'

'Well, I will do, if I ever see him. The boy closed the door and walked off. I knocked but there was no answer.'

I was rapidly running out of buttons.

'You sure you got the right door?'

'Must be honest, not even sure I got the right floor, Freddy. Have you spoken to him about the offer?'

'I told you he's enjoying his retirement. As much as possible.' If I didn't leave soon I would have to go onto my laces.

'Norman Riddell, living the quiet life?'

Quieter than you can imagine, Gordon.

'Oh, you wouldn't recognise him now.' I hung my head over my turned wrist and said:

'Bugger me, is that the time?'

At this moment the gods seemed to want some sport, for the shop door opened and in walked Monica Tait, Gordon's wife. If he had looked surprised when he saw me some moments ago, he now looked as though the firing squad were just about to empty their chambers, and he his bowels.

'Oops,' Gordon said in mock tones. 'I've been caught bang to rights.'

'What are you doing here?' She looked suspicious in the way only a woman who has often been cheated on can.

'Bumped into old Freddy.'

Monica marched up to the young woman Gordon had entered with.

'What are you looking at?'

'Wot?'

'I've seen you before.'

'Don't fink so, missus.'

'What are you doing?'

'Just looking at stuff. It's a free country.'

'I don't know where you heard that. Look, just fuck off.'

It was quite obvious the girl was out of her depth. She floundered in words, as though drowning.

'Well, I never…'

'Of course you bloody have. Now bugger off before you get a Stuart Weitzman heel in your fucking eye.'

The girl looked to Gordon, then to me. No help was being offered. Monica went over to the door and opened it wide.

'Go on. Get.'

The girl held her shoulder bag close to her chest with as much dignity as she could muster – which was none – and left the shop. As she brushed past Monica she was greeted with a parting shot: 'Back to the estate.'

Gordon held out his arms in a gesture of surrender, but one which he must have mistaken for innocence.

'I was talking to Freddy.'

She slammed the door shut.

'Freddy?' she said, eyeing me up and down. 'I thought you

were dead.'

'The brave man dies but once, the coward –'

'Oh, shut up. And you,' she said, pointing at her husband. 'You'll be buying me something expensive.'

This was a scenario that in some form had been played out before, judging by Gordon's acquiescence:

'Of course, Monica, my love.'

I made my excuses and told him that Norman and I were going away for a while. I told him I would call him when we returned. It even sounded like a lie to me.

'Goodbye, Gordon.'

'Bye, Freddy.'

At the door I turned and called back to him.

'Your dad was a legend in television entertainment! A legend!' A few crumbs cost nothing, and on this occasion, it wasn't a lie. Gordon half-smiled.

I could not say for certain that no one had been in Norman's flat. It hadn't been broken into and nothing appeared to have been disturbed. The whole thing worried me though, so I hired a house clearance company to uplift and dispose of everything the next day. I had already handed Norman's clothes into a charity shop. Janice's three scrapbooks were wrapped up and put in my case. They would be essential research tools. All the writing I had on the murder weapon was transferred. I had quickly become very adept at this technology. I bought a top of the range laptop computer and a pen drive. The young man in the store said that there was many a silver surfer. I told him I would only be using the machine to write. Once I had transferred the files the old laptop went the way of Norman's head: into the Thames at midnight.

During the flight, in the taxi at Nice, to the hotel, these are the things that occupied my mind. I didn't realise how many times I would go over them in the next few weeks.

52

Past and present

Freddy: We have to create ourselves.
Norman: We don't exist?
Freddy: No.
London, 1961.

Some of the comedy of Norman and Freddy came from Norman's quick wit. Often banter would be written down verbatim. I thought long and hard about jokes, but my partner was more spontaneous. If I was going to be the butt of this verbal sparring, I thought it might as well be used in the act. But Norman didn't always see the joke. Or rather he said he didn't see it. This was not, of course, always the case. Sometimes, though, his words sounded just bitter. This was the case more often towards the end. I once told him that Thomas Edison said that he failed his way to success. When Norman replied that that was a bit like me I fell for it again:

Freddy: Oh, do you think so? Thank you, Norman.

Norman: Except you succeeded your way to failure.

It got to the point I just ignored him. Sometimes an argument just wouldn't be worth it.[272] I mumbled something of this while sitting at the café the other day. This is the most strange and worrying thing. I am starting to articulate my thoughts verbally. How long before I become one of those loud care in the community sorts that hang around train stations, carrying on arguments from twenty years before in full earshot of the commuters?

Etienne overheard me and thought I was addressing him. 'I was just thinking of something foolish that an old friend

---

[272] The provocation was most certainly there, though. How can one not argue with a man who states that chlamydia was a daughter of Clytemnestra?

said to me. He was being foolish.'

Etienne made circular gestures with a finger to his head and said, 'Loco?'

'Loco? No…although…Maybe we all are a bit. It takes a true idiot not to be disappointed by life.'

He looked at me for a moment obviously not understanding what I said. But he shrugged politely and moved to serve what looked like a mother and daughter at another table. I people-watched for a while but did not write immediately. The afternoon heat and haze sucked from me any thought of typing. Instead, I had a few slow Sauvignon Blancs.

Later in the afternoon, when the sun had dipped, I thought of taking the lift up to Parc du Chateau. There, gently holding a flute of Alfred Gratien, I could watch the dying of the day. Occasionally, when my joints are up to it, I eschew the lift and take the back route from Rue de la Providence or Rue Rossetti. These days Freddy Foster is in no hurry. My afternoons are, in general, slow, and filled with memory. And it is that which has carried me through my entire story. Thus far.

Etienne is the only waiter at the café; but there are two waitresses, Agace and Doriane. They look like sisters but are not related. It took me a while to realise their lack of service to me was to do with table numbers, and not my manner. Etienne takes care of tables 7, 8, 9, and 10. Agace and Doriane seem to share tables 1, 2, 3, 4, 5, and 6. There are many more tables inside, but I'm not sure who does what.

When I write, my pen drive is inserted in the side of the machine. I am afraid of losing everything. The world should know the story of Norman and Freddy as well as it should know about the kings and queens of England. Dare I say more so? Let me assure you, dearest readers, our lives are as worthy and true: as true as unicorns and oak trees. I have tried in these pages to set down what I can but I really don't know what made Norman the bitter young man I first met all those years ago. His humour could be cruel, and it most certainly had more than a hint of schadenfreude, which seemed to fly in the face of the humour of his gentle hero Ken Dodd. There is no doubt that we are shaped by our past and by our present, but there was nothing I could see that accounted for Norman's anger. His poverty? Many are poor. I wish I had asked him, although he would no doubt have parried with some sick joke about bestiality. It is too late now, of course. Everything seems too late.

His voice returned to me strong and clear as I sat at the table. The words were clear but the images in my head were fragmented. He had been on at me for a few days, unrelenting, and I confess I was exhausted. It was a terrible London early evening and I had put him to bed. Although it was warm, clouds had appeared, and the sky was, for a few hours, dark before the rain broke. The tiredness of the day I put in one part down to that unique capital humidity: the other part was my age, where ennui characterises every evening. The city rain came down and I turned my head to stare at it through the window.

'It's not just the disease...'

I was fixing his ventilator, placing it on his bedside table. It was a fantastic piece of kit that blew air into his nostrils and down into the lungs. At this stage, he only needed it at night time but we were told that it would likely become a permanent fixture. This was the machine that would do the breathing for him when his body could no longer.

I was about to slip the mask over his face but he turned his head.

'I just can't do it without Janice.'

'What are you talking about? You fucking betrayed her all of your time together.' I was in no mood to let him away with anything. His breathing was short and weak.

'I don't understand any of it. I just can't do this life without her.'

I clamped my fingers around his chin and turned his face towards me.

'I don't know what to say. You were the one who said you were a player. You were the one who left her alone all those times. You were the one who broke her.'

'I was never anything without her.'

The kettle that I'd put on for a cuppa was starting to boil over next door. I was always one for filling it up to the top. As I stood up to deal with it I was confused by what he was saying. Maybe it was just the days of needling me or...

'You hear? Nothing without her.'

'Well let's get on the fucking Ouija board! I'm sure she'd love to hear that now! Why didn't you tell her that years ago?'

'I did.'

I stopped at the bedroom door.

'What? You told her all that? Fuck off. I know you. You never spoke to her.'

'We had our talks. We had our time on the pillow. We had moments that we shared.'

I had to get the kettle. Before it spilled over. The mess. And me to clean up.

'I'm not listening to your shit. Your feeling sorry for yourself.' I wouldn't have it. I wouldn't have it anymore.

'Feel sorry for you.'

'For me? Me? Don't feel sorry for me, boy! Don't you dare! You old slap! Don't you dare!' I was saying *kettle* but moving back towards the bed. I remember my voice getting louder and a rage building up inside.

'You never knew anything. Nothing,' he said.

Accusing me of knowing nothing a man with O level metalwork and an A Level in bitterness and anger. He was goading me, that's what it was. I told him:

'I won't rise to it, Norman. I won't, you know.' But this time he'd got me. This time I was being provoked. And he knew. I see that now.

'You understand nothing. You read but understand nothing. You see but miss everything. That's been your problem. Freddy "Fuckwit" Foster.'

'What don't I understand? I understand you all right! I understand you all right!' But I was shouting. The neighbours would hear. I was trying to get above the kettle. The sound of the boiling kettle with the water spurting out. It was boiling water on the kitchen top. And it would have to be me to clean up the mess. And his voice, low, soft, between short breaths.

'She never wanted you.'

I asked him who he was talking about. I told him that he didn't know what he was talking about. *Who?* I asked, but I knew he was speaking of Janice. *Who?* I repeated. And he just looked because he knew he almost had me.

'She told me on the ship.'

'We've done with that. That's past.' The band was tightening around my head. I didn't want arguments any more. I was too old for arguments. I was tired of them. I backed towards the door again.

'She got rid of the baby.'

The thing about an electric kettle is you don't want water getting in the switch. Apart from health and safety you could ruin the appliance. That was on my mind. I tried to focus on the water, foaming down the sides and into the switch, but once again I replied.

'Norman, Janice lost the baby. It was the drugs, and the stress. The stress caused by you.' I'd gone over the top and tried to clamber back. 'It's in the past. I'm sure you loved –'

'She killed your baby. Not mine. Yours. She killed your baby for the simple reason it was yours.'

I remember nothing of what happened immediately after he

spoke those words. When I left the flat Norman's still body was on the bed; the kettle was on the floor in the kitchen; the lead from the laptop was dangling loosely down the front of the desk, and the laptop was on Norman's motionless chest.

'Vous êtes pale.'

'What…?' Etienne was leaning over me. I sometimes feel that one day I shall be trapped in the past and never able to return. The laptop was in front of me and I had been tapping away. Perhaps it was the wine and the heat that made me weak. I hadn't passed out but I did lose myself somewhat.[273] Perhaps I had lost control of the past. Wouldn't that be a fine thing?

'Maybe you go home, Frederique?'

Where did he mean? Home was gone and would never be again.

'I'll have some water. Water would be fine. Thank you.' Yes, Etienne, home has gone. It is in the past, a place I know all too well.

I am nearly at a close, or a beginning. I have, I am aware, updated my memory and saved today's version. If I sit down to write this story in ten years I'll tell another tale. What will I leave out next time? What will I have to add? The past is always here, always contemporary. I understand that I am constantly moving towards root and not leaf, trying to get a sense of myself, nothing more. My growing up, the Brittle Bone Charity Dance, those days had already dimmed. The shape of our time had already done its best or worst. The ashes of those days had already cooled. Imagination is needed to present past truth.

Norman would have certainly told a different story. Maybe

---

[273] Things were getting worse with my sorry arse of a body. Every day I awoke again to a little more decay, a little more rotten, a little more the stinking putrefaction of the years; the breath like a moistened corpse signifying everything that is not life.

that's what he did that night. And what of Janice? What did she think of Norman? What did she think of me? What did she think of herself and the times that she lived through? Our past – Norman, Freddy, Janice – isn't fixed; it isn't just so. So, this can only be my story between this moment and the next, from where I am.

I have an envelope before me on the table. I borrowed the pen Etienne uses to scribble down orders from people he will never know. I write the name and address of a London publisher in a very fine and old-fashioned hand. The written word: another sign of age. Etienne keeps looking over at me, as though he might have to rush over and stop me from falling over. There is another sip of the wine left in the glass. Afterwards, I shall walk, however slowly, and with quiet steps, up to the post-box at the top of the hill, passing whomsoever, perhaps nodding in recognition towards a fellow who shares the universe and nothing more for however long.

So let us go now, you and I …

Behind me, tables and cafés and houses and the pebble beach and blue sea and yachts and ships and a sky so enormous and clear with a sun that has shone on me from my first yawling meconium and amniotic fluid screams beyond the great betrayer memory to this morning's room separated by more than years and miles. And I shall carry a package that purports to contain some sense and points to lives that carried neither. Can I say yes, yes, here it is, the true story of nothing and for nothing? Yes, yes, here it is: the true story…

End

Freddy Foster
Nice, South of France

Appendix 1

I should probably elaborate here, like Arthur Askey, although this is not intended as a workshop in comedy. The theatre comedians did indeed repeat lines and some of that did indeed carry on into radio. Some of the performers spat their gags out like they were firing a BESA machine gun. Tommy Handley had people's ears glued to the wireless, and Ted Ray also, with their often funny rapid delivery. Radio gave them a microphone and this allowed a new kind of intimacy with the audience. So, what killed the old guard off? Naturalism, dear reader. The kitchen sink boys of the mid-fifties influenced the comedians of the future. The great Hancock didn't race through his Galton and Simpson scripts. The moments were to be savoured. Osborne might have kick started the movement but comedy reached new heights when Hancock performed *Look Back In Hunger* and made the transition to TV. It was like comedy had always been waiting for that small screen in the corner of everyone's living room. Norman and Freddy were television comedians. We were influenced by it and wrote mostly with it in mind. Here is an early sketch that needed the subtlety that only the box could capture.

FREDDY (PIGEON 1) *and* NORMAN (PIGEON 2) *dressed as pigeons.*

PIGEON 1

How you doing, Harry? Yesterday was a fine day. The city never looked so good. The sun coming out is good news for us pigeons. Oh yes. What about old Trafalgar Square and that party of schoolkids throwing their rolls and sausages on the ground? A feast it was. A feast, Harry, I tell you. And then when the old dears got off the tour bus and started scattering crumbs. Yanks they were. Yank women with their big glasses and their crumbs. You know you never spoke a truer word when you said that we were a part of the tourist industry. That we are, Harry, me old son. We bring wealth to this great city, that we do. Never a truer word…But as we saw, it has its dangers. What about that hawk? The hawk that swooped down from the sky? Like a *Doodlebug* coming down…Nearly two hundred miles an hour, Harry, I tell you. I kid you not, old pal. I kid you not. And then that cute little sparrow was taken. Snatched away from its home…its family…Its life, actually, Harry. Its life snatched away in a moment. Fluff and feather everywhere. And the look in her eyes? She didn't see that coming. Well, not at two hundred miles an hour. You wouldn't, would you? Still, it would have been over quickly, Harry. Over very quickly. You know you were right, Harry, when you said we didn't know we were living. We don't. We don't know we're living, Harry.

PAUSE

PIGEON 2:
I'm not Harry.

Now. Let's have a good look at that. The first thing that might strike you – it does me – is that it's dated. The mention of doodlebugs would have some kind of resonance with the Britisher even in the early 1960s when it was performed. Before that decade was out? No. And what of the repetition? Is Freddy contradicting himself? Well, no again. The kind of repetition used gives a natural voice to the speaker. It doesn't sound like it's being repeated so people can hear. And what of the subtlety? The camera could catch the beautiful facial expressions below and above the beaks. Imagine you were in a theatre up in the gods? You'd want projection and big movements. We drew it out, walking slowly up and down, pecking away. And do you know how long it took to get into those costumes? Half hour. What would a theatre audience have been doing? Twiddling their thumbs and digging into their ice cream tubs. No, telly was a godsend to the new comedy.

Here's one I wrote much later. This sketch was very detailed in the movements, much more than I am presenting here, and couldn't have borne the loud gestures and voices of the theatre comedians.

FREDDY
I have to get over there.
NORMAN
Why?
FREDDY
It's where I want to be.
NORMAN
Where are you just now?
FREDDY
I'm here.
NORMAN
You don't want that?
FREDDY
No.
NORMAN
You want to be there?
FREDDY
Yes, I want to be there.
NORMAN
What's there?
FREDDY
Well, it's not here.
NORMAN
Here's bad?
FREDDY
There's better. I'll go over.

He walks a few paces from NORMAN.

That's strange.

NORMAN

What?

FREDDY

I walked over here.

NORMAN

What's strange about that?

FREDDY

I wanted to walk over there.

NORMAN

You were over there.

FREDDY

No, I was here. I said so.

NORMAN

There?

FREDDY

No, here.

NORMAN

But there was here.

FREDDY

Now there is here. Where are you?

NORMAN

Me? I'm here. I've always been here.

FREDDY

I could come over there.

NORMAN

You mean here. Well, you can, but…

FREDDY

But what?

NORMAN

You'll be here, not there.

FREDDY

Can you ever be there?

NORMAN
Never.
FREDDY
Even when you get there it's here.
NORMAN
That's it.
FREDDY *points at camera/audience.*
FREDDY
Where are they?
NORMAN
Don't even go there.

This sketch had a lot of movement and scratching of head reaction etc. But I feel its existential qualities were lost on the mob.

Appendix 2

Journal entry Sunday, 1st August 1965

Did *Blackpool Night Out* tonight at the ABC Theatre. The show was compered by Mike and Bernie. Was complimented afterwards by Pearl Carr. She told me we were favourites of her and Teddy (Johnson). The Beatles performed and – I thought strangely – Paul was left alone on the stage to perform *Yesterday*.[274] John might have burst his egotistical bubble by returning and saying *Thank-you, Ringo!* I had a chat with Lennon backstage which I think went something like this:

LENNON

Have you bought my book, Freddy?

ME

What's it called?

LENNON

A Spaniard In The Works. It's a pun.

ME

No, John, it really isn't.

LENNON

It sounds like one: Spanner, Spaniard.

ME

That's all, John. It just sounds like another word.
That's not a pun. It doesn't mean anything.

At that LENNON opened up the small book he was cradling and wrote something inside.

LENNON

Here, you tell it like it is, Freddy.

He handed me the book and followed the rest of the group through the exit door and a wave of screaming. I opened up the book and read the inscription: *To Freddy, love from Ken Dodd!*

---

[274] There was always a lot of darkness to the mop tops songs. This is probably no surprise when you consider the post war Britain we were all born into.

He's a funny bloke, Lennon. It is a.m. and I am sitting up in bed in a boarding house in Hornby Road. I left Norman with some floozie at the Shovels Inn. That was some hours ago. I'm going to sleep.

And that is the entry that I wrote in my journal a few hours after our meeting. I'd met him several times before. I have no bad memories of him.

Appendix 3

I found this in my papers. It's not dated but it has to be late 80s or very early 90s. (I have found another script from this time folded in an album of Janice's. I scanned it and it sits in my pen drive. I have become quite the expert.) I had been doing solo stand up and was getting tired of being laughed at. It's interesting in that it is very anecdotal and more conversational. I would improvise my pauses etc, unlike Frankie Howard who wanted everything, including ad libs, scripted. I had a table, a bottle of red and a glass centre stage. Later, I would go over the thing and note where the laughs, if any, came. The sheets that I'm taking this from are covered with curses, and doodles of students with blood pouring from head and body wounds.

Good evening all. Here, fek like old George Dixon there. Evening all. It was a quite night

in the town when a couple of youths came out of the Christian Fellowship bagged up

with Irn Bru and Tunnock's Caramel wafers. That night they had one middle name:

trouble. Yes, ladies and gentleman this is my nostalgic tour. Last resort of the dying

entertainer. What is it you call it? Retro? Yes, Retro. When you get to my age it's all you

have. Looking back. Should write a play, call it Look Back In Minor Annoyance. Used

to be I'd go for the laughs but these days what's the point? What is the fucking point?

The sharp one line has given way to the laboratory school of comedy. Don't worry, I'm

not annoying them. I'm not important enough. You may laugh. No, please, you may

laugh. They say all good things come to an end. That must be why I'm still here. Things

have changed, though. I walked through your bar earlier. The Peter Pan. Some of

you don't look old enough to eat solids. It's strange, when I was your age universities

developed posh accents so as they could fit in with the cloth of the dreaming spires. I'm

talking another language, aren't I? What's this old prat doing up there? What's it all

about? No, yes, they aspired to talk posh. Cos posh was all about. Not Posh Spice. She's

not posh. Heard her speak? Nah, neither have I. And do you know why Cozzhe's not

posh? Sorry, that wasn't such a clever joke. Not much of a joke of any kind. You know

the secret of great comedy? Nah, you don't, do you? That's why you're down there and

I'm up here. To be honest I wanted to go to university but they wouldn't let me in. I was

told that it was open to all, but not really. That was a great lie. You had to be clever

at school. That was a problem saying, I didn't go. I grew up in Glasgow just after the

war. What? You didn't know that old Freddy Foster was from Glasgow? I left there a

long time ago. Headed for London because the streets were paved with showbiz gold.

School was old school. Like how I did that? Old school. I heard it on the TV. I like to

There was more of that, but you get the idea. It was pretty
bitter really. A lot of those spots at the time were filled with
bile. I often stood, the children screaming at a spotlit

antidilivian old duffer. I know that I wanted to say, *I lived, you little fuckers! I was that contender! Most of you are going to end up accountants or selling house insurance over the phone. Enjoy it now because there's a bitch of a cold wind whipping around the corner.* I didn't say that though. Who does? I just hated going out on stage by that time. Just couldn't be bothered dragging my sorry arse in front of them. And once that's gone. Well, what have you got left? I had a few good years.

Appendix 4

A Couple of Guys

We're a couple of guys
Just swinging by
Trying to bring laughter to your world
So if you open your eyes
Your heart will follow
Yesterday's gone, forget about tomorrow
We're just a couple of guys,
With stars in our eyes
                        So let's have fun

You have the time
It's no trouble
Kick off your shoes
                We'll burst that bubble
                Of despair
                We don't care
                Life's a funny thing
                Coz…
We're just a couple of guys
                With stars in our eyes
                                So let's have fun.

Appendix 5

Letters

i

My dearest Freddy,
It seems like ages since we have met. I miss my shiny faced boy. I saw you on telly last night and felt so proud. You looked so grown up in that suit. The right wee man. Did the television people provide you with it? Although I did not laugh I am sure there are those that like it. Is your partner from London? He sounds English. Mrs Mackenzie downstairs has gassed herself. This was a shock as I was only yesterday talking to her about bananas. It must have been just after our chat that she put her head in the oven. Well, that's the news. I know that you're busy but try and write a wee line.
Oblige,
Mammy

ii

My dearest Freddy,
I had a very quiet birthday. I went to the shops as usual but bought myself a snowball from MacLean's Bakers. You know my favourite is coconut. Thank you for the card. I read it several times while eating the snowball. A new family moved downstairs in Mrs Mackenzie's place. They are a bit rowdy and the man is a bit of a drunk. I'm thinking that only my Freddy doesn't drink to collapse. What is it with men? Sometimes I'm glad you never had a daddy. Talk of the devil,

I'd better go now as there's a lot of screaming in the close.

Oblige,
Mammy

iii

My dearest Freddy,
I went to the doctor with my head. He told me to get more sleep. I told him I can't sleep, that I'm always tired, and I have headaches all the next day as a result. I was quite tearful so he gave me a cigarette to calm me. There's a picture of him and another man on his desk. I think it'll be his brother. I got a prescription for pills. I have a drawer full of pills. Now I'm not an expert but I think that last batch have done something to my bladder as there's definitely some leakage now that wasn't there before. Thank you for telling me of your time in Blackpool. I'm sure it was very nice. If you like that sort of thing. Have you noticed that Dec Cluskey of The Bachelors has a manly smile much like Frank Ifield? If Mrs Mackenzie was alive to hear the filth that the new family come out with she'd be black affronted. And in her old house at that. She'd gas herself all over again. And I'm not one given to gossip but I think he has some bit of stuff and the wife is none too pleased. Well, who would be? Although how any woman with an ounce of God fearing decency would go near that bogger I don't know. It's enough to give you the dry boak so it is. I'm going to go now and get three of the seven pills a day I have to take. If you can a visit would make me in my glory. But I understand if you're too busy.
Oblige,
Mammy

iv

Dearest Freddy,

Just a wee line to tell you that the arthritis in my fingers is getting worse. My left hand will not open fully and the fingers are permanently shut. The pills the doctor gave me for it might be all well and good, but I can't always get the lid off. The headaches seem to be a bit better as I've only had two this week. When it's particularly bad it's like a band around my head. I could scream. You were mentioned by some skinnymalink on television last night. I didn't get his name but he had a big nose. The sleepy pills seem to be working as that's the back of six and I'm jeeked. Thank you for that postcard of The Scott Monument. It's not a place I've been to but sure I would like it. Thanks as well for the few pounds in the envelope you sent. I bought the weeks food so that was a help. You're still my wee Freddy.

Oblige,

Mammy

v

Dearest Freddy,

Well, looks like we'll all have to do a shift as the council has told us the building will have to come down. It is a bit of an eye sore, I'll agree, but it's the memories that seem to come down with the buildings. Down the road they have some of those high flats, but they don't seem right. I've never been in one but I've been told they don't have stairs. They use lifts. I'm a bit funny about that if I am moved in there. I've not seen you on the telly for a while so I'll imagine you're doing the theatre. I know that was one of your passions – although God only knows where you got it from. I can only hope the years ahead will be a bit better to people around here. Maybe

you don't see it on your London telly but life can be pretty tough for people just now.
I miss you, Freddy.
Oblige,
Mammy

Appendix 6
Liverpool University 20th October 1997

My mate, Brian, is a keen cyclist. Well, by that I mean that he can't afford a car. When Mr Tebbitt told us to get on our bikes he did. It was at 6 o'clock on a Monday night when he left his wife and four kids. Skedaddled. Brighton, here I come! Bit of a party goer is Brian. Bit of a raver. Likes a bit of the John Travolta. Likes a bit of the how's your father as well. Listen to this. He went to a party once and this young lady was searching through her handbag. Her car keys spilled out onto the table. Quick as a flash, Brian whips of his bicycle clips and tosses them down. Didn't realise it was that sort of party, he quips. Don't laugh, ladies and gentlemen. Oh, you're not... It's not easy getting old. Last time I got fucked was when I bought shares in British Steel. Hey, Black Monday? Isn't that when that essay is due and you've got a bitch of a hangover? You're a great audience, you really are. I've got to say that. I've got to say it because I haven't been paid yet. You know that some people say that students are lazy, shiftless, drunken, shag monkeys. And they're right. And we're jealous. It's over-rated all this working for a living. Not that I would know much about that. Here, you might have noticed that I'm not part of a double act tonight. Oh, you thought I was! Leave off the vodka and wacky baccy. If you want to lose your eyesight have another ten minutes in bed in the morning. No, my partner of many a year is laid up with a bad attitude. He hates me. No, I'm only kidding lads and lassies. We're solid, regardless of what you might read. And it's been a long time. When the papers talk about us the word antediluvian always comes up. I'm just saying this to quash any rumours of our demise. Let me tell you here and now: Norman and Freddy are here to stay. We never argue, unlike some I could mention. We don't have – what's it called? Creative differences? Norman always does as he's told. You know when The

Beatles broke up? You remember them? Scouse moptops? I
see tonight that the haircut is still a winner with some. When
the Fab Four broke up it was said it was musical differences.
That would be a euphemism for I fucking hate you! I met
them, you know. They were crossing the floor of a club while
Tom Jones was doing a sound check. John Lennon shouted
over that Jonesy was a poof. Tom Jones gay? If Tom Jones is
a poof then I'm Arthur fucking Scargill. And if Jones had got
hold of Lennon that day you'd be saying 'Who's Mark
Chapman?' I'm only kidding, my friends. John Lennon was a
very talented individual and sorely missed, I'm sure. He once
asked me to tell him a joke. I said, What's the difference
between margarine and butter, John? I don't know, he replied.
You fucking pleb, I said. He couldn't stop laughing. Liked the
acerbic stuff. No, Norman and Freddy are here to stay. Here,
it's dark in here, isn't it? I've got the spotlight and I've got the
microphone, so hecklers don't win with this old boy. You
think what? You think this is desperate? You don't know
desperate. Try showbiz. Go on, I dare you. Try showbiz…

EDITORS NOTE:

The illustrations were found in Mr. Foster's papers.
Interestingly, the writing did not match known handwriting of
Mr. Foster.

Robert O'Neil
Gangway Publishing

R D McGregor

R D McGregor

Next novel, *Bad Things*, will be published 2021.